Letter Writer

A novel inspired by a true story.

Sandra Bobek

To B –
You are a doll!
Thank you for your
support.

ISBN: 1463609272

ISBN-13: 9781463609276

Library of Congress Control Number: 2011910590

For my mom, my brother, and my best friend, Bear—
with my love

Many thanks for your love and support, and lots of love to—
Terri, Bill, Madeline, Lynn, Camielle, Michelle, Justin, and of course
Betty

Thanks CE—in spite of yourself

Chapter One

Tess is cleaning up the kitchen from the mess she made fixing herself dinner. Yes, she is always messy in the kitchen. That always bugs Greg. She thinks being messy in the kitchen means she is being creative. That's probably not true, but it is how she likes to look at it.

This is close to the same routine she goes through almost every night while talking to Bear—either planning some part of the next day or hashing out what happened today. You wouldn't know she is married, the way she spends so much time just with Bear, her dog. Her life up to this point has not been easy by most people's standards.

She married the first time when she was nineteen. Cisco would drink with his buddies when he got off work, and then come home and use Tess's head as a punching bag. After hearing too many times the following morning, "It will never happen again," she left. She had only been married for eight months, so it was easy to get the marriage annulled. Besides she didn't like her married name anyway, so she changed it back to McQuarry, her maiden name.

A decade or so ago, her father disowned her because she stood up for her brother in a disagreement between them. When she married Greg, she thought she would finally have some security, a real home, and the real family she had always wanted but had yet to find.

Tess has short, spiky light-brown hair, gray eyes, and is five six without her ever-present cowboy boots on. She has always been a tomboy because she roughhoused with her brother and his friends when she was a little girl. Her mother made her take ballet to try and smooth out her rough edges, but it didn't work. Sometimes she seemed shy to people who did not know her, but her close friends knew she was funny, spontaneous, and fiercely loyal. She was someone they could always trust. So it threw her when she was trying so hard to make her marriage work, and she found out that she was the only one working on it.

It's hard for her to understand why it all seems so lopsided. They both made a commitment and said their vows. Now she realizes, she's been lonely in the marriage for far too long, and it is time she knows for sure if he really loves her. Maybe he has been staying just because it is convenient for him.

She looks at Bear and says, "Maybe if we take a trip somewhere…just you and me, boy, for a couple of weeks. Maybe, just maybe, he will miss us and realize what he would lose if he didn't work on this." She wonders as well how many other women have asked that same question when they felt this way.

Talking to Bear, she realizes she loves the way Bear tilts his head, like he is listening and understanding every word.

She looks at the kitchen clock. It's nine fifteen and, with the kitchen finally straightened up, it is about time for her to get cleaned up for bed. Getting up at five every morning makes staying up late really difficult. She has gotten into a habit of watching TV until she falls asleep, so the silence of being alone is not so deafening.

For the past eight years, she has worked for a computer company and is at her desk by seven thirty every morning. There's only one good thing about working for such a large corporation. There is no dress code, and with so many people around wearing jeans every day, her cowboy boots don't get noticed. And she's been there long enough, with enough seniority, the way she dresses doesn't faze anyone anymore. And going to work early means she can get a jump on the day, without someone needing something, because she has at least an hour or so before other people show up. There is also the added bonus of getting to leave at four thirty, if there is nothing to keep her there.

It's boring work, but she tries to find something interesting in it. If the salary, stock, and benefits weren't so good, she would have quit some time ago. But Greg insists she must work. She likes to be busy, but at this point she is starting to feel like he just doesn't want to support her doing something she loves, like her photography. In a perfect world, she thinks, "I would be out every day taking pictures of landscapes or in the darkroom processing the black-and-white prints."

Her love of photography goes back to her childhood. She wasn't very close to her grandmother, but there was one thing they shared, and that was her Granny's Brownie box camera. Sometimes her Granny would keep her, her brother, and her sister, and if Tess were very good, Granny would let her take a picture with that camera. Granny would stand behind Tess, talking her through the motions of holding her breath, and very slowly lower the lever on the camera so that the shutter would trigger open. The camera had to be held at her waist, because the viewfinder was on top, and you had to look down into it. Granny was a cold woman. She was raised that way, but she showed love and patience to Tess when they took a picture together. To Tess, that was something very special.

It has been a long time since she tried waiting, so she could have dinner with Greg—or even tried to find out when he would be home. She no longer waits to hear from him either. Every time she called to try and get some information, Greg would either blow up at her or talk in generalities. Since Tess is committed to her marriage, she tries so hard to please him and to make everything so easy for him. She is a pretty good cook, keeps up the house, and usually has the laundry done. She could have been an interior decorator, because everyone who sees their house asks Tess if she will help them with their house. Her marriage is now at the eight-year mark. They did not have any kids, and he spends all his waking hours working in a self-owned business of restoring vintage motorcycles. She remembers when she first met his mother. She said he didn't have blood in his veins but had motor oil instead. Tess is starting to realize how right she was.

Thinking back, she remembers seeing him more when they were dating than she has in the entire eight years they have been married. When they were dating, he would drive almost one hundred miles on Wednesdays just to have dinner with her. He would take off the entire weekend just so they could be together and have fun. Now he won't take a Saturday or Sunday off unless there is a car or motorcycle show to go to. Tess has tried everything to get him to pay more attention or just spend time together. She really wants him to take Saturday off so they can just be a couple and do "couple things," like wake up late, get breakfast at some small café, and then take a long walk—together. But the "togethers" never happen. Most of the time she is by herself and, fortunately, she is independent enough that she can make the most of her time.

Tess talked Greg into a couple of vacations and did her best to reclaim his attention. But her efforts have been in vain, because she has tried to get the attention of a man whose only focus is on hunks of metal, called Indians and Harleys. He doesn't know how to "not work." He is not a bad person but totally misguided. Greg has no idea how to relax. He has a couple of friends who feed into the macho attitude—"Your woman waits for you at home"—which is prevalent in small towns where not much is going on. The good ole boys stick together, and if any of them looks even slightly like they might "break free," the rest quietly reel them back in. Tess thinks it is odd that every time she has brought up something to do together, Greg has suggested that she go out with her girlfriends. Then, when she has made those plans and told Greg about them, he calls while she is out and asks where she is, because he is at home. Coincidence? Not very likely.

She decides to take a vacation without him and just be with Bear, so maybe he will figure out how much he needs her. She feels that, since they have put so much time in the relationship, it must be worth saving. She does not want to be a mere statistic—another marriage that just could not make it. Her choice is to drive to northern Arizona and northern New Mexico to takes pictures and just enjoys her time in the Four Corners.

Tess loads up the Jeep with everything from a sleeping bag to a cooler with food and water and takes off for her adventure. She has to drive north from Austin to get going in the right direction—but decides to take a couple of extra days to stop off and see her aunt and uncle who live out in the country just north of Waco.

Her uncle has been very ill with cancer. His prognosis is not real good, but he assures her that he is not going anytime soon. Uncle C has always been very close to her, and they have had a very special bond. He has been a constant in her life, and she is grateful. Ever since Tess got her driver's license, she has driven over to see them because she feels appreciated there. It has always felt like she belonged there more than her own home. He parents never knew what made her tick, nor did it seem like they tried to understand her, and Aunt Barbara and Uncle C always seem to understand. They give her love unconditionally, especially when she felt like there was a big lack of it. She also feels like Billy, their son and only child, is another brother for her.

Her aunt and uncle were married when she was sixteen and he was seventeen. He joined the Marines after talking his parents into signing a release for him to join when he was so young. Because they never wanted to be apart, they got married before he left for San Diego and the Marines. They started their lives together and became inseparable. Even these days, close to their fiftieth wedding anniversary, they still hold hands in the car. She waits on him hand and foot, and he dotes on her. When she speaks, he listens, and when he speaks, she listens, really listens. They listen not just with their ears, but with their hearts and their understanding. They appreciate each other, every day—every moment. They know it's precious, and they do not take it for granted. They honor each other with the promise. There is always so much love in their house. There is always the promise, *the* promise. The unspoken, unbreakable promise of unconditional love and support, of always being there for the other person—no matter what. That's the promise.

Aunt Barbara told Tess one day, when they were sitting at the dining room table, that her mother always said: when you meet the man you're going to marry, there is a promise in his eyes. It's an unspoken promise, a pact that's made when you realize that this is *the* person for you. The one person with a connection between your soul and his soul, and when you finally connect, there is a promise. Tess would ask them at least once a month if they wanted to adopt a girl to go along with their only son. They would smile and say, "Tess you know that's not possible, but we will always be here for you." And Tess would know that was plenty.

Tess always secretly hoped that she was one of those babies switched at birth. She never felt like she was part of her family and, quite frankly, didn't want to fit in. Her childhood seemed to lack the kind of love that most parents and children take for granted. Tess did not remember her mother ever saying to her, "I love you." It seemed that was the normal thing, the everyday way the world lived, so she didn't think that much about it. She saw people act differently in movies, but it was not part of her world, so she thought it was just something made up. Then, as she spent more time around her aunt and uncle and was exposed to a really normal relationship, she realized how warped her life at home actually was.

Growing up, Tess felt like she did not fit in at home. Communication was pretty much non-existent, and she vowed to make a change as soon as possible. So as soon as she was eighteen, she moved out of her parents' house. She graduated from high school, and two days later, she moved out. Her urgency was like that phrase: This is not a dress rehearsal. This is it…now or never! And she had to be on her own, so that the heavy cloud she felt hanging over her would go away. Little did she realize how unprepared for the real world her parents had left her. She didn't know how to balance a checkbook or do a lot of other things an independent person should know how to do. But it didn't matter. It was the school of hard knocks.

Tess loves going to visit her aunt and uncle, except when she is trying to watch what she eats. Aunt Barbara could be anybody's grandmother because she always wants to feed the world. If she can feed you, she gets to show you her love. And she is a pretty good cook. A lot of southern food and Mexican food are usually on the menu. This is typical of central Texas. If you are a native, you grow up on chicken-fried steak with cream gravy and biscuits one night—and tamales and enchiladas the next. So sitting around the kitchen table with Aunt Barbara and Uncle C is a very familiar thing. There is always lots of "cussin' and discussin'," as they call it. The world and everything in it is discussed at kitchen tables. Tess treasures all the time spent with them. Uncle C asks her everything that is going on with her world, and she tells him everything, gets his advice, and beams with his praise. He tells her, "Tess girl, you got the world by the tail on a downhill pull, don't ya?" It's a question that needs no answer.

After a couple of days with Uncle C and Aunt Barbara, she and Bear hit the road west. She looks at a map long enough to get a couple of main highway numbers to follow, so she can get in the general area. They get into her truck and drive away. The weather is perfect for travel, with nothing but blue skies, white puffy clouds, and miles and miles of open road. They could drive for two or three hours, then take a break so Bear could walk around and get a little relief. He seems to like traveling, especially when he has the entire back seat to himself.

They stop overnight in El Paso, because that is the halfway point, and she just can't drive any longer. Things are starting to blur a little, so it is time to find a hotel for the night. Tomorrow they would get to Flagstaff and kind of base out of there. She is really looking forward to not having to wonder if and when Greg would get home from work—or if he would even call to tell her what to expect. It is all miles away right now.

The next morning there is no need for an alarm clock, because Bear wakes her up at 6:30 a.m.—just as the sun comes up. Tess gets up and gets dressed and takes Bear for the walk he is begging for. Once they step outside, cold air hits them in the face, and they see their breath. It's one way to wake up quickly. Tess tells Bear, "Hey boy, if there is any way you could make this quick, I'd be really grateful!" Bear looks at her like he understands, and maybe he feels the same way. Regardless, they walk up one side of the block and back, and Bear is ready to go in. "Geesh, I was not ready for it to be such a chilly morning, Bud. Let's go to the room, and I can get some coffee, get cleaned up and packed, and then we can be on our way." Tess feeds Bear when they get back in the room, and she gets busy. There is still a good day's drive ahead of them, and the earlier they get on with it, the better off they'll be.

I can't help it, she thinks. Don't you just love drive-through breakfast. It's so easy and cheap. And it makes it too easy to eat on the road. So with the early start, they should make Flagstaff by evening and not have to drive much in the dark. The drive itself doesn't get interesting until after El Paso, anyway. Up until then, the road looks so long and deserted and is really boring. But today they are traveling to an area that promises to be interesting—and filled with new things to take photos of. It's such a beautiful day that Tess is forgetting, if only just for a while, the longing in her heart and the marriage she is questioning. The blue sky, with sporadic clouds, gorgeous scenery, and open road makes her ask Bear, "Could it be a more perfect day?"

She puts a new CD in the stereo and keeps cruising. The hours just fly by. They are making really good time on the highway, and she sees a sign that says Winslow. Tess starts laughing to herself and says, "Bear, we are going to take a very short side trip." She starts digging in the CDs and finds the Eagles Greatest Hits and puts it on. She smiles to herself, takes the exit, and starts looking for someplace to pick up something to eat.

Skipping the songs on the CD until she gets to "Take It Easy," she laughs and sings along to a song she's heard for years and just couldn't resist. The part of the song comes up that she is looking for, which is "standing on a corner in Winslow, Arizona, and it's such a fine sight to see…" She giggles that she is actually taking this exit for an old rock-and-roll song. Oh, well. It was funny to her.

She picks up some fried chicken and hits the highway again. Bear, of course, wants some chicken too, so they share while driving down the road. They get into Flagstaff not much past eight and find a place to sleep for the night. It feels really good to her to just lie down and be quiet for a while. Bear just lies on the floor, then rolls over on his back like he is finally home. What a funny dog. Why does it look so odd when dogs do that? Lying on their back all spread-eagled? Just happy, I guess.

Before she knows it, she is waking up, and it is morning. She just lay down to watch a little TV, and the next thing she knew it was morning. She didn't even get a chance to get out of the clothes she wore all day or wash her face or anything. But she slept well, and she isn't going to worry about it. They are in Flagstaff and now need to get a game plan for the day. Guess they should go ahead and go to Canyon de Chelly in Navajo Nation and check that out first.

She has read so much about that area and really wants to see it firsthand. So she gets out the map and finds the best way to get there. Since she isn't familiar with the area, she wants to make sure the cooler has ice, food, and water. That way if anything happens, like a problem with the Jeep, or if she gets lost, she and Bear will be OK until they get help or get back to town. Set for the road, they head out. Tess has read that Spider Rock in Canyon de Chelly is a spiritual place it, and she decides she wants to see it first.

The weather is great again today, a little chiller than yesterday but a day to definitely appreciate. The drive is not that long, and there are some nice shops along the way in Navajo Nation. She stops to see whether they are selling "locally made" wares or something that is imported from some other part of the world.

The shops have all locally made things, including really beautiful T-shirts designed by some local natives. It is a treasure trove to her. All this beautiful art, pottery, jewelry, sand paintings—made by hand, not imported from Japan. She wishes she had a lot of money, so she could buy everything to furnish her house. They are even a couple of buffaloes outside in a large corral that Bear is very interested in. She lets Bear out of the Jeep to take a whiz, and the next thing she knows, he is trying to get in the pen with them. Now what would he do if he did get in there? They would probably use him as a footstool. Goofy dog. But it is still interesting to see him wanting to play with them. They are really big. If it didn't promise to have a tragic outcome, Tess might let him get in the pen, but Bear is too important to let him get close to trouble. Bear may have good intentions, but with animals that big, there is no guarantee of his safety.

So off they go to Spider Rock. The morning was very chilly, but the afternoon is quite warm. The canyon was truly beautiful in the morning sun, and there was a very distinct smell to that area of the country. Spider Rock can be seen from a rim of the canyon, and the sight of it's amazing: two tall columns of rock that have been carved out of the wind and dust. It's nature at its best. In the Navajo legend, Spider woman lives in Spider rock, and Spider woman taught the Navajos how to weave. Weaving is a very important part of their culture. Tess stands there looking at this beautiful scene and watches the activity on the floor of the canyon. This vista a good example of why she wishes she had fixed her camera, and kept up with photography.

There are information signs posted at the entrance of the canyon saying that the Navajos still own the entire canyon, and the only way to go on the canyon floor is with a native. Tess would like to see the adobe ruins on the other side of the canyon, which are built into the canyon wall. But she has found out that the hike down the canyon and across the canyon floor and back would take about three hours. With Bear in the Jeep, that would be too long and get too hot for him. So she has to save that trip for another day. In the meantime, the two of them will hike around the canyon rim, enjoying the amazing smell that is the Southwest, a combination of juniper, cedar, and pinion. There is nothing like it.

It is dusty and getting really warm. Tess takes lots of shots of Spider Rock and the canyon itself, which is a major source of beauty. She has gotten into a habit of keeping black-and-white film in her 35 mm camera and color film in a great little snapshot camera. That way, she can have the same view in color or black-and-white. She prefers black-and-white in an artistic sense. But some of the scenes she sees are nice to have in color, like the reds of the clay dirt that make up these canyons.

Bear gives a little whine and looks at Tess. "Are you hungry and thirsty boy? Let's go back to the Jeep and get some lunch." They lower the tailgate, and Tess reaches into the cooler and gets some cold water, along with something to eat. She puts a bowl of cool water out for Bear, and he is not stopping until it's gone. Then he decides he is interested in what she has in her hands for lunch. Tess ignores this and just keeps eating and looking around at the beauty surrounding them.

Being outside, surrounded by nothing but nature, with her best buddy—her dog—makes everything in the world seem right. She is able to let go of all the aggravation, from her marriage, her basically thankless job, and a life she hasn't chosen but, instead, has fallen into—or unfortunately settled on. The beauty of the day could make anyone forget her worries.

After lunch, they get back in the Jeep and decide to check out the rest of the canyon. They find a thickly wooded area and park in the shade for a while. Tess gets out and lets Bear wander around and smell every bush and tree in the area, where he always leaves his own "mark." After their shady break, they load back up. She notices that the sun is starting to hang a little lower and decides to head back to the hotel, so she can easily find it in the light. Tomorrow is another day and another adventure.

She picks up some dinner on the way back to the hotel, and they get in and settle down. Another walk before bed for Bear, and then they can relax and get ready for the next day. Tess checks out a couple of maps and decides that tomorrow will be a good day to go on down to Sedona. The maps show a very small road off the main highway, and it looks like it could be interesting—and might provide places to take pictures. It also looks like it should be a shorter way to get to Sedona. With a direction decided and her game plan in place, she decides to get to bed early and get an early start in the morning.

She and Bear go for one last walk, and the evening air is very cool but smells like the mountains. The weather in April is cool in the morning and evening and warm in the middle of the day. That makes it so nice and different from the weather in central Texas, where it doesn't vary much from morning to night. Any change from everyday weather routine seems to heighten her awareness. As the sun starts to set, it's her favorite time of day—twilight. In the time between daylight and dark, when shadows hint at magic, the hard-edged lines of reality soften, making it possible to believe that fairies just might exist. Maybe they are just hiding under the leaves of the shrubs.

You can see them if you just believe hard enough—and open yourself up enough. Oh, if it were only that easy or true. There is even something magical in the word itself, twilight, as well as serendipity, rainbow, and melody. Like saying these words gives her a certain power or insight.

They walk back to the hotel, and it's dark. Once they get to the room, Bear settles down quickly, and seems to have his own routine. Looking over at him as she starts to get in bed, she realizes that he is snoring. As long as she has this big fur ball in her life, Tess thinks she can handle just about anything. He is a never-ending source of the unconditional love that she's never really had. She goes over to him, gives him a quick kiss on the forehead, and gets in bed. He squints one eye open, then goes back to sleep. She sighs, smiles, and snuggles into the pillow, then pulls the covers under her chin and closes her eyes.

Hearing a whimpering sound inches from her face, she opens her eyes halfway. It's morning, almost, and Bear is sitting there smiling, panting, and whimpering. "OK boy, I'll get up. I guess you want a walk right this very minute, don't you?" She stretches, gets out of bed, pulls on her baggy jeans and sweatshirt, puts on her tennis shoes, and grabs the leash. Bear is at the door waiting. Hooking the leash on his collar, she grabs her keys and opens the door. Glancing at the clock on the way out, she makes a mental note that it's 6:15 a.m., and he is just a little early. Outside, it's chillier than she thought it would be. She shivers a bit and decides to jog a bit, so they can get the blood pumping. Then maybe it won't seem so cold. She soon discovers that jogging won't work because Bear needs to stop to take care of "business." Oh well, as soon as that's done, they can go back inside, then get on with the day's adventure. Every day is an adventure if you look at it that way.

With the Jeep loaded up and Bear in the back seat, Tess checks out of the room and climbs in. They head down the freeway. Tess knows it will take about fifteen to twenty minutes to get to the turn off for the road to Sedona. It's a beautiful bright sunny day, and they even manage to get some drive-through breakfast before they hit the highway. They drive up on some road construction, and there are no signs of where to go, according to the map she checked last night. In fact, it's downright confusing. She can't go twenty miles per hour on the freeway! So she heads where she thinks the right turn will be—and ends up going opposite the right direction. She winds up in a park with picnic tables, where she can look at the compass on the Jeep. It's not showing the direction that she needs to see. She pulls over and lets Bear out of the backseat for a minute while she checks the map, looking for where she went wrong. Seeing a different turn than the one she noticed last night, she says, "OK that's what we will do."

Bear wanders around for a little while longer and then runs over to her, like "OK I'm finished." She opens up the back door. He jumps back in, and they get on their way.

Back at the construction area, she makes the turn and gets on the side road. A wooden sign shows the word "Sedona" burned into it, above an arrow pointing to the entrance on the wooden fence. She takes the dirt road, which seems really flat and peaceful.

The trees are so tall and beautiful, and the Jeep creates a dust storm behind them on the dirt road. They pass a beautiful serene lake, and she wonders if this is the right road to the red rocks and cliffs that she believes are part of Sedona.

After a while, the road starts winding and isn't just straight and flat. The turns become sharper. They go downhill slightly. Then, following a really big turn, she sees a red rock valley that exceeds her expectations of "scenic."

At a widening in the road, she pulls over and just looks at the valley below. They have been driving for a couple of hours, so Bear is very ready to walk around and check it out too.

Standing in the bright sunlight, Tess admires the beautiful scene below. She looks up in a tree, and a black crow is almost close enough to touch. It just watches her and Bear and talks, or it could be called squawking. She looks at him and remembers an old Indian legend about crows and shape shifters. Shape shifters are Indian shamans that can change their outward body into different animals to perform special deeds or to gather special knowledge. This crow just sits there, which seems kind of odd, kind of surreal. She begins to feel that this is no ordinary crow. Tess thinks, "Maybe it is Uncle C checking on her and Bear." Then she laughs to herself and takes some photos, then stares again at the valley below, smiling. If this was a wrong turn, it was definitely worth it. What a beautiful view. She looks over at the tree, and the crow is still there. Bear quits wandering and comes back to Tess and sits down. She looks down at him and says, "Ready to go, Bud?" And they climb back in the Jeep.

The road is definitely going downhill now, with nothing but sharp turns and red dust. The views from every turn are breathtaking. So the trip down to the canyon floor is very slow because she stops so often to take pictures. It is so easy being the only person on this road, which is kind of weird. With every turn a different view, she almost can't believe her good fortune. She has always believed in "wrong turns" that actually are the right turns. This only proves it to her.

The music playing in the Jeep is only adding to the wonderful morning. At one stop to take more pictures, the Jeep looks almost burgundy because of all the red dust on its black paint.

At the bottom of the road, she sees a sign saying that this is a national park, and they hit pavement. They drive up to a stoplight, and her cell phone rings.

"Hello?" Tess answers.

"I have been trying to reach you all morning. Where are you?" says Greg.

"We were out of range I guess. We just got into Sedona," Tess replies. "What's going on?"

Tess pulls out on the main road of Sedona and drives down the street, while Greg talks. "I got a call this morning from Carol, Billy's wife, and she wanted you to know that your Uncle C died this morning." Tess is stunned. She just keeps driving, not knowing exactly where she is going. She doesn't say anything. She just tries to process what she heard.

"Tess? Are you there?" Still silence. Greg continues, "Are you OK, Tess?"

"Yeah, I'm here. Just give me a minute."

Tess sees a parking lot in front of a small store with wind chimes out front and tie-dyed banners. She parks the Jeep, turns off the motor, and says, "When did he die?"

"He was put in the hospital a couple of days ago and passed around eight this morning. Aunt Barbara wanted you to know that there will be a service for him Saturday afternoon and a graveside service after that. Are you OK?"

Tess's voice cracks. "Yeah, I'm OK."

"Tess they know you're out of town. They said to make sure you know that, if you can't make it, they'll understand."

Not make it? Not make it to say goodbye to one of the most important people in her life? "How can I not be there?" says Tess. "It's Thursday, and if leave right now, I can be there tomorrow. So I'll be heading back today."

"Just make sure you take it easy and don't push it. Stop when you need to, OK?"

"Yeah, sure..." Tess's voice trails off. "I'll talk to you later. Right now, I just don't want to talk."

"OK, then I'll let you go. Call me if you need anything."

"Yeah, OK." Tess hangs up the phone.

Uncle C is gone.

It's very hard to believe that he is not here anymore. Tess pours more water into Bear's cup in the back seat cupholder. Giving him a quick kiss on the head, she tells him she will be back in a minute. The windows are cracked, and it's only around about fifty degrees, so he won't get hot. She peers in the back seat before shutting the door and says, "I love you."

She needs to walk around for a while and soak in the news. The shop she is parked in front of looks friendly enough. She goes in and finds a small shop of wind chimes, incense, candles, jewelry, and lots of other colorful things. This is just what she needs—a place where she can wander and stare and not seem like she is out of place.

So she picks up something from the shelves, from time to time, and looks at it—and puts it back. She is stunned, forgetting to breathe. Nothing makes any sense. She absent-mindedly picks up some incense and a medallion necklace and carries them around. She looks at other things too, just to act like she is engaged. Maybe an hour or so goes by, and she thinks: I need to drive back. I need to leave. I have to get on the road. What am I doing here?

She goes to the counter, pays for what's in her hands, and walks out. Tears start streaming down her face. She slides behind the wheel and sobs. Bear nudges her arm and whimpers. She turns around, and he licks her face. She hugs him, turns around, puts on her seatbelt, and turns over the engine of the Jeep. She sits there for a second and thinks, "OK, what's my game plan here?" She starts talking out loud to Bear. "I guess we need to get something to eat for the trip back, and I should go ahead and fill up the gas tank and give you a short walk."

On the map, she finds the shortest route from Sedona to Austin. She folds the map so she can check it easily while driving, then puts the Jeep in drive and leaves the parking lot. A few blocks away, she pulls in to a fried chicken place and orders a box of fried chicken for the road. She also gets a Diet Coke and asks for a handful of napkins. At an empty lot across the street, she pulls over so she can give Bear a short walk, and then drives to the highway.

She is taking the state highway north to the interstate, then going west. She looks at her cell phone. It's not picking up service again. Tears keep coming down her face. Her thoughts are all jumbled, and the only thing she keeps thinking is that she needs to talk to Aunt Barbara to make sure she is OK. How must she be feeling to lose her "other half"?

The state highway goes through a national park, but Tess feels numb to its beauty. She thinks: I need to come back here someday. Maybe then I can appreciate it as it should be appreciated.

In the late afternoon sun, light filters through leaves, creating patterns on the road. She suddenly remembers the crow that sat in the tree watching her and Bear. Could it really have been Uncle C's spirit,? He did tell her, before she left, that this is his favorite part of the entire world. And that he was jealous she was going to be here, and he wasn't. He also told her to take lots pictures so he could see them when she got back.

Oh God! She could feel her heart breaking. It is hard to breathe. She just wants to scream. She keeps driving down the road. There is only the noise of the road and the Jeep. She opens the window, hoping it will make the pain less somehow. How can anything make this hurt less? She tries to concentrate on keeping the Jeep between the broken white line and the solid yellow one. Just keep it between those lines, she thinks.

She sets the cruise control at the speed limit and tries to digest what is going on. Maybe she really shouldn't be driving. But then how would she make it back in time? She can't afford to take a flight and leave the Jeep, and what would she do with Bear? Too many questions and absolutely no answers. She just keeps driving.

Finally she hears the cell phone beep that she has service. She picks it up and tries to call Aunt Barbara. She gets Carol on the phone, and Carol sounds as bad as she feels.

"Carol, are you OK? It's Tess."

Carol says, "I'm OK. The thing right now is, how you are?"

"I'm driving back right now, just outside of Sedona. I should be back there sometime tomorrow. How is Aunt Barbara?"

"She is as well as can be expected at this point. I know she and Billy would want to talk to you, but they're at the funeral home taking care of arrangements. You know everyone would understand if you don't make it."

"Not being there is no choice for me, Carol, you know that. There is no other place on this earth I need to be except there."

"I know that."

Tess sighs and says, "Well, I'm on my way now. Tell Aunt Barbara and Billy, if they need me, my cell is working now, and I intend on driving straight back."

"I'll let them know," Carol says, "but I don't expect them back for a while. You be very careful on the road. Are you OK to drive? You can call me back if you need to, you know."

Tess thanks Carol, who has to be one of the sweetest women she's ever met. She is so very glad that she and Billy found each other. Since Billy was always so sweet to her, it was nice that she could talk easily to Carol. And it was hard to believe they had four daughters.

She would see them all tomorrow. She now has to concentrate on driving because it seems so difficult right now. She wants the miles to fly by. Maybe some music would soften the feelings she has right now. She pulls out a CD randomly from the case stuffed between the seat and the console. It doesn't matter what it is. She just wants something to drown out her thoughts. The windows are still open, and the wind feels good.

Uncle C is dead. What was the last thing she said to him, and what was the last thing he said to her? She has always told him she loves him, so that is not the problem. So what is the problem? The problem is no longer being able to see him and talk to him and laugh with him and feel the love he had for everyone, including me, thought Tess.

It didn't hurt this much when she got the call from her mother that her father had died. Or did it? She starts thinking about that morning, when she was living in Los Angeles, and her mother called as she was getting ready for work. Her mother rarely called her anyway, but that Wednesday morning it seemed really odd. Tess said, "Mom are you OK?" Her mother said she was reading the paper and noticed in the obituaries that her father had died.

This stunned Tess. Ever since he disowned her, she had tried to forget about that pain. But her mother's call slammed the door shut on ever being able to talk to her father again. It was like the pain of losing her father would never go away. Now tears are coming down her face again. Like the wound of her father's death has become new again, and there is nothing she can do.

Her mind switches again. Just keep driving. Just keep the Jeep on the road and between the lines. Concentrate on what you're trying to do. Just hold on.

At least she moved back to Texas when her mom got the report that she has terminal cancer. So she's living closer if she needs her. Tess has never needed her mom before, and they have never been close and have barely understood each other as human beings. But she knows it was the right thing to do, just in case. And just this minute, she understands that her future, as she knows it, is completely changed. Little does she realize by how much.

The driving gets a little easier as the miles go by, but the pain does not. All she can do is try and concentrate on the road and drive. It is starting to get dark and she is in New Mexico. She would be in Texas in the morning. She is trying to think of anything but her profound sadness and great loss. Nothing else matters.

Bear has to nudge her or make a noise in the back seat to get her to remember to stop and walk him. She doesn't mind and even feels a little guilty at not thinking of it herself. But somehow he understands, and they are a great team. As the miles go by, it is sinking in. Her anchor or buoy, or however you want to look at it, is gone. How do you measure that kind of loss? It's only after time has gone by that you can really measure it.

Daylight turns to dark, and the road keeps going on. Thank goodness she has to stop for Bear and gas occasionally, so she can get out of the Jeep and walk around for a bit. She notices her hands are shaking. Is it from driving or from her insides crumbling? Maybe it's a combination of the two.

She still feels numb and guesses she will for a while. All she knows at this moment is that she wants to be with Aunt Barbara, Billy, Carol, and their girls. So she can be as close to his spirit as possible. She finally talked to Aunt Barbara on the phone earlier, and it was pretty nondescript. One of those conversations—each asking the other, are you OK? And replying yes, but knowing you're not. But she heard her aunt's voice, and that was a comfort. She wishes she could hug her. And she would, tomorrow.

It is dark, and she is really close to Texas now. She can tell because the road is getting flatter, and the roads are better. She would be going through the most boring part of the drive in the middle of the night. Guess that has its good points. Bear has been jumping in the passenger's seat again from time to time. Wonder if he knows that his movements sometimes make her shake off the monotonous mile-after-mile, when she drifts almost to sleep. On goes the radio, and she gets some gum out of her console while she rolls the window down. The road can be so very boring sometimes. Tess can't afford to get comfortable, because it only leads to sleep. She's been driving for about nine hours now and has at least that much longer to drive before it's over. She is feeling so exhausted.

It's now around two in the morning, and the red flashing lights in her rearview mirror have definitely woken her up. "Oh no! Now what?" she sighs. She pulls over and thinks to herself a checklist of what could possibly be wrong. She has had the cruise control set on the speed limit, and her lights are working. What's wrong?

The Texas Highway Patrol officer gets out of his car and strolls up to her window. He wears cowboy boots and a cowboy hat with his brown trooper uniform. She's already gotten her driver's license and insurance in hand and rolls down the window. "What's wrong officer?"

He says, "Ma'am you were going sixty in a fifty-five limit."

Tess starts telling him that she's been driving since late yesterday, because she just got a call that her uncle—who was closer to her than her father—just died. She is driving back to Austin to go to his service today. And as she starts on this story, the tears come, pouring down her face. Her face is red, mascara streaked down from her eyes. Her nose is red, and she has the sniffles. Not a pretty picture, but one that he has pity for evidently. He looks at her, takes out his ticket pad, and looks down at the ground while she recounts all the torment she is feeling, rambling on and on, and if she didn't know better, he is kicking the dirt slightly from discomfort.

She finally stops, takes a quick breath in, and says she is sorry.

The officer starts writing and says, "Ma'am, the nighttime speed is fifty-five, but I'm going to just write you out a warning, on the condition that you take it really easy getting to Austin. I would really hate it if you had an accident on the way back home."

Tess assures him that she will be very careful. And she grovels a bit, with lots of mumbled thanks, takes the warning, and waits until he gets to his car and starts to drive away.

Tess looks up at the sky and says, "Thanks Uncle C! You gonna be my angel on my shoulder from now on or something?" Though the question is rhetorical, somehow she feels a little better. She is definitely wide-awake right now. Police have that effect on her, probably on most everyone. But there is still so far to drive.

She starts noticing signs in west Texas warning of deer. At this time of year, they are a really big concern, because they can do major damage—not only to a vehicle but also to the passengers. She would really have to stay awake now. If a deer jumps out while she is snoozing, she could be really hurt or worse. Bear seems to sense this too, because he has been jumping back and forth from the backseat to the passenger's seat more often now—even leaning over and licking Tess in the face. Sloppy wet kisses from a hyper dog will get your attention when you feel yourself drifting asleep. She even opens all the windows, because temperatures in the low fifties will shiver you awake.

Finally, she notices a roadside convenience store that's open in the middle of the night. One Mountain Dew, coming up. She didn't like the taste much, but the caffeine would be a big help. Usually, the coffee in these places is not very good in the middle of the night. Since Bear is being so helpful, keeping her awake, she will grab him some of the red licorice that he loves so much.

She starts seeing deer on the side of the road, and it's eerie how their eyes look when the headlights hit them. They don't dash out in front of her but scatter away. The road is winding more, so she knows she is in the Hill Country, and some of the town names are starting to sound familiar. She just might make it. She looks at the clock and, to keep her mind working, she starts reciting the names of the states in alphabetical order. Anything to keep her alert. Maybe she could do state capitals next, in alphabetical order. She counts up how long she's been driving, and it's sixteen and a half hours straight. She is about a hundred miles or so from Austin. "Just hang in there," she thinks.

She pulls over to give Bear a break and stretch her legs a little. It's really cold now, and oh no! She smells a skunk. She rallies Bear to hurry back in the Jeep, so they don't get hit with the scent. That would not be fun. So they escape the skunk smell except for what's still in their nose. Tess pulls on the road and feels like she can now make it home.

The last hundred miles seem to go a lot more quickly. Maybe it's because she knows the drive is almost over or because it's getting light. Everything is looking very familiar, and for that she is grateful. She even manages to get into Austin before rush hour. That in itself is a blessing.

Now that she's so close to home, she even hopes that Greg has already left for work. She hasn't seen him for almost a week and is dreading going home with him there. Guess there's not a whole lot that can be done about that now. Except to remember the feeling of not wanting to be there—and try and come up with what she needs to do to remedy her situation. It's more evident, now that Uncle C is gone, that there's no reason to remain in a loveless marriage.

She pulls up to her house, and Greg's car is still there. She braces herself, parks the Jeep, then opens the back door for Bear to get out. He seems really grateful to be on familiar turf. The dog next door, Sasha, comes running over to greet him, and they take off running in the yard. Tess is starting to gather up stuff to take inside. She gets up to the front door and puts enough down so that she can unlock the door. It swings open wide, and she starts taking things into the living room. Greg is nowhere to be seen—yet.

Bear and Sasha are chasing each other in the yard and run in front of Tess into the house. They almost knock her down, as they brush up against the bags she is lugging in the front door. With the noise and the dogs barking at each other, Greg sleepily walks out of the bedroom and into the living room.

"Hey you made it. Welcome home," he says as he walks over to Tess and kisses her on the cheek. Tess thinks, "Don't strain yourself." Greg turns around and goes through the bedroom, into the bathroom, and shuts the door.

Tess keeps unloading the car. She just wants to get it done, so she can lie down for a good long while. Hopefully, Greg will leave for work pretty quick, and she can be by herself. With every trip inside the house with more stuff, she wonders how she packed all this in the Jeep and still had room to move, but she did. Now she needs to put everything where it belongs. With the Jeep unpacked, it's all piled up in the living room, but she doesn't care. She just wants to sit down.

Just as she gets a little comfortable, Greg walks back in the living room and asks if she needs any help unloading the car. She tells him no, it's done, and she is going to put everything away after a nice little nap. He has to get on to work, of course, but will try and be home at dinner-time. He asks when she is going to China Spring to see Aunt Barbara. Tess says she is going early in the morning, because the family is going to the funeral home to receive visitors, and then there is a graveside service the next morning.

So she will be there, probably, the whole time. "Did you plan on going?" Tess asks, almost hoping he would say no.

"Yes, I plan on being there if you're OK with that." What could she say but "Yes, OK, fine? She has not seen him for almost a week, and maybe it's because she's tired or hurting from the loss, but she almost couldn't care less. Then she thinks that it's nice that he wants to try and be there for her, even though she questions his motives. Time will tell.

Greg leaves for work, and Tess takes off her clothes as she walks toward the bedroom. Bear is already asleep on the floor. Sasha got called home a few minutes ago, and Bear has wasted no time curling up on his spot on the floor, off to dreamland. She joins him there in dreamland in less than five minutes. The next thing she knows, it's around four in the afternoon, as she wakes up. Bear is getting restless and comes over to lick her hand. That means he wants her up so he can get outside. She sits up, slowly gets out of bed, walks over to the patio door, and lets him out. Turning around and seeing the living room piled with all the stuff that was in the Jeep makes her want to turn around and go back to bed. But if she is going to leave town in the morning for another couple of days, she has to get some of this put away. So she spends the next two hours trying to straighten it up. The next thing she knows, the news is on the TV that's playing in the background. She manages to skip dinner. Of course, Greg is not home yet, and he hasn't called to say he is going to be late either. Nothing new there.

She decides to take a nice long hot shower and get to bed. The whole idea gives her a big smile. There is nothing like your own bed.

As sunlight wakes her up, she remembers that today she has to say goodbye to someone who has been a cornerstone of her life. She keeps thinking, "I have to remember to breathe. I can only imagine how Aunt Barbara feels losing her life partner, someone she basically grew up with, someone she can never talk to again, much less hold and be held by. I have to see her and make sure she is OK.

How do you go on when your world is crumbling in front of your eyes?" With that she gets up and gets going.

The funeral home parking lot is packed. She parks the Jeep, walks in, and immediately sees Billy. He beelines for her and grabs her in a bear hug. She feels a little better. But when she looks at him, all she can think is how much he looks like his dad, and she starts to cry. He gives her one of those knowing looks and says, "Yeah, I know." And she completely understands what he means. He nods toward Aunt Barbara who is talking to a few people and being her ever-charming warm self.

Tess stands dumbfounded, watching Aunt Barbara. She can be so gracious to everyone, even when she just lost the true love of her life. Tess stands there watching her, feeling her throat catch and making it really hard for her to breathe. Aunt Barbara sees her and walks over and gives her a long warm hug, saying, "I know what you went through to be here with me, and you know I love you for it. Did you have any trouble on the road?"

Tess admits to getting pulled over by the Texas Highway Patrol and to letting her story just gush out to the officer. She says that Uncle C must have been her angel at that moment, because she only got a warning. Billy laughs out loud at that and says, "That sound just like something he would do!"

Aunt Barbara just smiles, takes her hand, and leads her over to the casket. She says, in a voice only Tess can hear, "You know we both love you like a daughter, and he was so proud of the person you're becoming. I'm just sad that he won't get to see more of your story unfold." With that Tess knows that no matter what, she has his love with her. And no matter what, she will always love Aunt Barbara.

The room has a lot of people coming and going, giving Aunt Barbara, Billy, Carol, and the girls lots of love. Almost without exception, every person has a funny story with Uncle C in it or a sweet memory of something kind he did for them. It's all those memories that Aunt Barbara will have to live on for a long time.

Finally it's time to go, and Aunt Barbara reminds Tess that they are having a get-together at her house, and she really wants her to come out. Tess says she will follow them. Even though Greg was supposed to come to the funeral home, she hasn't seen him yet. She turns on her cell, and he has left a message that he is on his way. So Tess calls him back and tells him to meet them at Aunt Barbara's.

The road out to Aunt Barbara and Uncle C's house is very familiar, and Tess lets her mind wander, just trying to enjoy the scenery. April in Texas is time for the bluebonnets, Indian paintbrush, lazy Susans, and every other wildflower known to this part of the country. Sometimes the bluebonnets are so thick that you can stand in the middle of a field and feel intoxicated by the smell. It's unlike any other. So Tess just rolls the windows down and tries to enjoy it.

Greg is already at Aunt Barbara's when they get there, and he walks over to Tess, kisses her on the cheek, and asks if she is OK. All she can do is look at him, and he doesn't push any further. He tells her they will get a room at one of the hotels on the highway for the night, whenever she needs a break. She tells him she appreciates it, and they go inside.

The people from Uncle C and Aunt Barbara's church have brought over so much food that you'd think they were feeding an army. But that's so typical of small towns and the people in them. Because everybody knows everybody, it's not unusual for everyone to give until it almost hurts. And speaking of hurts, Aunt Barbara is filling everyone's plates with almost every kind of casserole known to man. So if they all eat everything on those plates, there is going to be some hurt and some belts loosened. She just loves to feed people, and it's true that you can't feel anything else if you're in pain from hunger.

The evening is winding down, and people are starting to leave. Tess gives Greg a glance like it's time to go. They both get up, make their goodbyes, and get the time and place for tomorrow morning. Aunt Barbara says to meet them at the house, and they will go from there.

The next morning, Tess walks in, and Aunt Barbara is still getting ready. She asks Tess if she slept well. Tess gives her a shrug of the shoulders and a partial smile. Aunt Barbara says that they are all going to go to the cemetery, then come back to the house, and she is welcome to stay as long as she likes. Billy and Carol walk in the room and both give her a big hug. They all ask each other if they are doing OK. The girls are running in and out of the house, and their laughter is like a breeze in the air.

Graveside, Aunt Barbara has a tight hold on Tess's hand. If it weren't so reassuring, Tess would realize that she is losing feeling because her circulation is cut off. Aunt Barbara is saying hello to everyone there and introducing Tess every time. She is not letting go of Tess's hand. They take their places, and Tess wants to be strong for Aunt Barbara, and just wants to hold on for dear life!

The pastor reads from the Bible and tells some funny stories about Uncle C—and they sing a song that's in the program that was printed up. The pastor says some more from the Bible, and they lower Uncle C into the ground. Tess is trying hard to breathe. Aunt Barbara is holding her hand even tighter and sniffing back tears. Aunt Barbara leans forward and throws in the red rose that's in her hand, and then everyone else adds the yellow ones they were given.

Aunt Barbara turns to Tess and says, "Let's go back to the house now." They load up in the cars and drive away. Aunt Barbara rides back with Tess and Greg, and they don't talk much. They just ride the short distance in silence.

Once back at the house, everyone hangs around in the kitchen. All the ladies from the church have put out more food. And they are urging everyone to get a plate and eat. Tess looks over at Greg, and he walks toward her. He gives her a hug and says, "Are you OK?" Tess just nods her head and stands there trying to absorb all that has happened. She tells Greg to go ahead and eat, and she is going to check on Aunt Barbara. He heads toward the food, and she walks to the back of the house looking for Aunt Barbara.

Tess finds her staring out her bedroom window into her backyard, motionless. She walks over and asks her if she is OK. Aunt Barbara reaches for her hand while still looking out the window and says, "I'm glad you were here today. It just goes to show you, Tess, you never know what life will bring you. I thought he would be with me forever."

They both stare out the window together in silence.

Chapter Two

The cell phone on the worn-looking table next to the bed starts vibrating across the tabletop, knocking into an empty glass, then into a small clock. Nico, half awake, reaches out to stop the movement. He flops his hand on top of the phone and picks it up. He taps "answer" and groggily says, "Yeah…?" The voice on the other end of the call makes him sit up and drop his legs over the side of the bed. His bare feet hit the concrete floor, making a dull smacking noise. He keeps listening as he rests his elbow on his thigh. While running his other hand through the top of his hair, he keeps mumbling "Yeah, I know…I'm sorry."

He purposely ignores Alexandra, who is becoming more and more indignant still lying in bed. Rolling over to face the other side of the bed, she lets out a loud sigh and yanks the sheet around her as she gets up. Throwing the sheet together in front, she stomps into the bathroom and shuts the door so loudly that Nico jumps while continuing to listen on the phone.

He stands up and starts pacing with the phone to his ear. His hand gestures as if he is trying to make a comment, but he can't get a word in.

He just keeps nodding in agreement to what he is hearing. He stands still and finally says, in a monotone sing-song way, "Yes Mama, I'll be there within the hour. Is that OK? And yes, I'm sorry for not remembering, and I will make it up to you. So let me get off the phone, and I'll get cleaned up and will get there as soon as I can. Will that make it alright?"

He hangs up with a sigh and drops his arms to his sides. Looking at the closed bathroom door, he scratches the back of his head muttering, "I guess I'm about to see why she woke up with an attitude."

He walks over to the door and lightly raps on it while leaning in, almost humming, "Alex…Oh Alex? Are you OK?"

The door abruptly opens, leaving Nico a little off balance, as a fully dressed irritated woman almost stomps through the doorway and into the bedroom. Nico fumbles, pulling on some boxer shorts while trying to follow her into the room. While he stumbles, Alex stands with her hand on her hip, giving him a hard look, reminding him of his promise. They have planned to spend the day together having a long breakfast and taking a walk by the pier. "And I know, as soon as you answer the phone, someone else is going to remind you that you promised them something before you promised me. Isn't that right?"

Nico mocks her stance and halfway laughs, trying to make light of the situation. He says, "Do you always get so upset over nothing?"

Nico lives in old storefront that has been converted to an office, then converted again to a small apartment that is also his studio. It has a concrete floor and bare wood beams overhead. And most sound is amplified because the furniture is sparse, with hardly any rugs and a big openness of space. When it was made it over into living quarters, they discovered the first bonus—skylights that allow the perfect light for painting.

Alex makes a huffing noise and stuffs her scarf and a couple of other items into her big handbag. She stands up and throws the bag on her shoulder, then stomps to the door where she turns around and says

"This is not 'nothing'! Did you have any intention of spending the day together, or was that just a ploy for me to spend the night, Nico?"

"Of course I was going to spend the day, but when my mama needs me, I must go. You understand don't you, sweetie? And we can see each other later. Wouldn't that be OK?"

"Don't sweetie me! You just like to make promises that you don't have any intention of keeping. What I don't understand is, why make them? But then a lot of what you do, I don't get either. So, thanks but no thanks, Nico. See ya."

With that, she goes out the door and shuts it soundly behind her. Nico turns around and starts looking for his jeans. He finds them under the chair, grabs the T-shirt on the back of the chair, and finishes getting ready. Then he rushes out the door.

On the way to his mama's house, he turns on his stereo and lets his mind wander. The song's lyrics are about feeling something he has never really considered much before. And he has a gut reaction but doesn't know why. It also makes him wonder why ,when Alex said she doesn't want to hear from him, it didn't affect him. They both understood that it was for fun, but her reaction makes him think she was reading more into it. But still—shouldn't it bother him more? Then he gets distracted by a new sign along the way and starts thinking about something else.

When he gets to his mama's house, she is in the kitchen cooking lunch. He strolls in and plops down in a chair at the counter, facing her as she stands in the kitchen. She takes something out of the oven and looks at him, giving him a look that this dutiful son definitely recognizes. He starts in with his excuses for why he is late, gets up, walks into the kitchen, and leans against the cabinet—then looks at her.

She takes his hand and gives it a little smack with her hand. "Should I even ask you—when are you going to settle down and see some nice girl, my baby boy? Because, if I know you, when I called a while ago you were with someone from the night before. Am I right? And lord knows, you're not going to ask her to come with you. Did you even tell her that you were coming here for lunch, or did you say it was something more important?"

"I did have someone with me, Mama, and I just didn't want to spend anymore time with her, if I could be with you instead. And besides, Mama, she knows what I'm about. She doesn't have any false expectations. The more I know about her, I know it would not even be possible to be in a relationship with her, mainly because she is tiring."

"What do you mean *she's tiring*? Is that all you can say about her? That sounds ungrateful and a bit callous, my dear son. Since when are you so bored with life and living it that you take for granted the way other people feel? The more I talk to you, the more upset you're making me, Nico. I just don't understand you sometimes. And as for your sister, she called and said she was going to be late. So we need to save a plate for her, and we will give her a 'go' plate for Roger."

"So what's to understand? I feel pretty content with my life, except that things don't seem as vivid as they used to. I mean, it seems like my feelings and energy levels are kinda dulled. Does that make sense? I'm content living by myself. When I get up every day, I look for excuses instead of painting. Everything is the same, but it's different."

With that comment, she places the last dish on the table for lunch. She motions her hand for Nico to come to the table and sit down. Once they are seated, she grabs Nico's hand, bows her head, closes her eyes, and says a short Catholic blessing over their lunch. They start dishing spoonfuls of food on their plates, and they sit quietly for a few minutes concentrating on lunch.

Mama finally breaks the silence and says, "I can't believe I'm saying this, but maybe you need to take a step back and remember that it won't always be this way. It could be something as simple as being more grateful. I know you so well, but I don't know what you're thinking, and your actions lately are a sign to me that you're not really happy. Sometimes I don't know if you're so oblivious to your own charm that you just instinctively use it. You seem to be able to talk your way into or out of anything. And even if you don't remember much about your father, I swear you got that from him!"

"He gets what from papa? Sorry I'm late, Mama, but you know how the restaurant can be, and you always told me to make sure to take care of the customer. So that's why I'm late. What did I miss? Is there a plate left for me? What are you two talking about? Did you hear the latest, Mama, about your fair-haired son? It's pretty juicy. What do you say, Nico, been 'laying low,' big bruddah? Ha-ha! You should hear the things I've been told."

Sera breezes in the room and goes directly to one of the chairs at the table. She doesn't let anyone else say anything. And once she finishes, Nico rolls his eyes at her last comment. He turns to look at his mama and shakes his head no.

"Well little Sera, I really don't know who you have been talking to or what you're talking about. You know you shouldn't listen to gossip; it's not good for you. People that talk about me obviously don't have enough of a life to keep them busy, so they think they can talk about my life instead of living their own. You know what they say, sweet sister, things are always greener on the other side of the fence."

Becoming calmly quiet, the three concentrate on lunch. The conversation starts up again when Sera decides that she is not going to get anywhere, and Nico is not going to admit anything or do anything to upset Mama.

They talk about the new store being built across the street from their mama's small restaurant, about the new priest's assistant at the parish, and about where Roger is and what he is doing. Then they settle in to talk about the weather. It was right about that time that Nico could make his exit and go home.

As Nico is driving back home, he absentmindedly turns on the radio, and his only thoughts are "What should I do about dinner?" He walks in his front door and looks around as if trying to remember something, slightly shrugs his shoulders. Then he plops down in the old love seat in front of the window. He sits there a while, looking at the easel in the corner, the paint tubes stacked up, and the brushes standing up in glass jars he has collected. He then picks up the TV remote and starts surfing the guide to see what is on. Conveniently forgetting all about his painting, he settles on watching Cash Cab. He dozes off to sleep and wakes up with someone power-selling a set of knives. After turning off the TV, he gets up and walks to the bed, taking his clothes off as he approaches the bed. He plops down on the bed naked and falls asleep.

Next morning, he opens one eye at a time, after being woken up by the sun streaming in the window. He yawns and sits up. Slowing walking over to the kitchen area, he sets up the espresso maker for a double cappuccino. He is mumbling to himself that today will be different, and he'll get to work. His thoughts go to his manager, Maxwell, and he wonders how long it will take him to start calling again, asking when Nico will have progress to show him.

He digs around and finds something to wear. The espresso maker is steaming, and the cappuccino will get him going. He moves around the room to the music he has turned on and starts setting up what he needs. His easel, the rolling cart full of paints and brushes, and one really large white canvas stretched over a sturdy wooden frame—all put into place and ready for some imagination and some elbow grease. All the pieces are there, ready, except for one thing, a new vision.

Nico has tried different approaches for weeks, like getting a cup of tea, sitting in front of the blank space, sipping a glass of wine, listening to different music—working different times of day, different times of night, after a long walk through the park, after having sex, and every other kind of "after" you can possibly think of. It all comes out to the same thing. He can't bring himself to put anything on canvas. Sometimes he almost feels like he has been over-thinking the situation so much that it freezes him up.

So he tries to deal with it. And when that doesn't work, he tries to ignore it and turns all the blank canvases in the room to face the wall, like they are all in time out. He knows there is something to say, but it's not happening.

It has gone on for days, and then weeks and then months, so that his savings are starting to run out. The very few paintings that are on loan to galleries don't look like they are going to sell anytime soon. So he is starting to check out other options, because it's also getting boring to not be creative. And he doesn't know how to fix it or where to start.

Maxwell is not going to be patient forever, and he is going to wonder when his client will start being productive and give him something to work with. Managers don't like their favorite clients to sit on their butts and not put out any work. Nico has not exactly been sitting on his butt, but he hasn't been doing any work either, and that is so very frustrating.

Then one Wednesday morning, his cell buzzes, and it's Maxwell—and the obvious question from him is "When can I see some new work?"

"I know you need more from me, Maxwell, but I'm all dried up. I haven't been able to create anything for months now, and I don't know why. I appreciate your hanging in there with me, but I think I'm gonna have to take up Roger's offer until things change. I just don't know what will break this block I've got. I can't seem to get rid of. And you know me. I can't just sit around here and wait for it to happen. It's starting to drive me crazy that I can't shake this feeling. It's like I know it's in me—I just can't tap it."

Maxwell says he understands. He will check in, in a week or so, and see if anything has progressed. Maxwell asks him not to be so hard on himself. It will happen; he knows it will. He tells Nico that he has faith in him and is there for him if he needs him.

Nico's father was not around while he was growing up, so he has always felt responsible for his family—his mom and his little sister. He has hated to put himself in a position that might put his lifestyle in jeopardy, or leave him unable to support himself, much less help his family if they needed it.

They have been protective of each other. Though Nico has wanted to take care of his mom and sister, in turn, they have felt the same way about him. The love of the family has been so strong because of the way they were all raised and their sense of tradition.

Annamaria Moratelli has always been proud of her two kids, Nico and Seraphina. They are her life. She lives for them. Wednesday night dinner at Mama's house is always a great break in the week, and of course, her cooking is so wonderful. They also have family meetings, and the meetings are usually serious stuff—but always centered around a good meal that Mama has cooked. It's no wonder that Mama Moratelli is known for her wonderful cooking. It was, in fact, what had saved them.

Nico could never imagine his life without his mother and sister. His father was gone too early in his life, and he has never really gotten to know what it would feel like to have a family with a father. So it's understandable why Nico is very protective of his family, and they of him.

Sera naturally asked his permission when she wanted to get married to Roger. And because they had gotten to know each other so well, Roger understands Nico's protectiveness, and he is now quite close to Nico as well.

But it wasn't always this way.

Nico was only eight when his father died in a horrible accident at the factory where he worked. Nico shrugs off this loss, like it's a small thing, but he still feels it at times, sometimes very strongly. His father now seems like a legend, because of all the stories he told about his childhood, all his dreams when he was a boy, and what his life was like in a tiny village in Italy.

His father, Antonio Giuseppe Moratelli, was born in Manarola, Cinque Terre, Linguria, Italy. Tonio, as he was known all his life, was the fourth generation to live there. The Cinque Terre are five small villages on the Costa Ligure of Levante. Those villages, from north to south along the coastline, include Monterosso al Mare, Vernazza, Corniglia, Manarola, and Riomaggiore. Since 1926, the Cinque Terre towns have been part of the province of La Spezia. They have remained the same for many generations. And in this isolated territory, the characteristic Ligurian culture has also remained unchanged. The five villages were only reached by the outside world about one hundred years ago, when the railway line was built.

This region is characterized by typical steep slopes, cultivated with vines thanks to terraces that have transformed the territory through man's hard work. The coast falls straight to the sea, with cliffs that are often vertical. Small creeks and enchanting beaches are found among rocks, and the sea has depths rich in fish. The climate is mild, making for an easier life, day to day. The area is now a destination for tourists because of its amazing beauty.

Like several other villages, Manarola is surrounded by vines and is situated along a stream. The wine of Manarola is very famous, and the Via dell'Amore starts here. It's an easy-to-walk, paved path, two kilometers long, connecting Manarola to Riomaggiore.

Located in the upper side of the village, the church of San Lorenzo is part of the area's romance. It was built in 1338, with a beautiful rose window dating back to the fourteenth century. Nico has heard about it all his life from stories his mama tells. She reinforces these dream stories with her take on her childhood, before she met their papa, and how she saw her world.

The legends of the "five lands," as they are called, were the basis of all his father's bedtime stories, told to Nico and Sera when they were very small. To hear their father talk about it, you would think that God had truly put heaven on earth. It was a naturally beautiful place, and the flowers and plants that are native to the region are beyond compare. These villages have a slower pace and a gentleness to them that the villagers almost take for granted.

Looking like pastel jewels adorning the rocky coast, the towns seem to defy gravity, the way they cling to the rugged cliffs. The sea below them is always sparkling blue, and even if you only read about them, you may dream about them forever.

Tonio met Nico's mother in a village festival in Riomaggiore in the spring. Annamaria and Tonio fell in love almost at first sight. Almost, because Tonio's best friend, Angelo, had seen her first and was trying to get to know her. But when he introduced Tonio to Annamaria, after he just met her, he knew he was not the one for her. Tonio was the one. So Angelo laughed it off and has always been a special friend to them. He was the best man at their wedding.

They fell in love and married when they were young, and by the time they were in their twenties, they moved to America. They became U.S. citizens after they settled down in Brooklyn, and Tonio worked at the textile mill almost as soon as they arrived. The hours were long, and the work was hard, but Tonio thought it was all worth it. He was getting his chance to make a difference and start his family. It was what he had dreamed about when he was a boy. He and Annamaria were madly in love with each other—and also in love with America. Every day was like an amazing adventure for them.

But as they say, all good things must come to an end, and so did their luck as a family. When a freak accident happened in the textile mill one Tuesday, they came and knocked on the door. Annamaria was home with her two children, who were eight and six at the time. Nico was home from school with a cold, and Sera only went half days for kindergarten. Nico would tell his aunt, later, that the world never looked the same after that visit from men he didn't know who made his mama cry.

Annamaria could not bring herself to speak until two days later. She was in such shock, and her sisters took turns staying with her until after the funeral. It's the news that no family ever wants to get, "We are sorry to inform you that…" And then everything changes. All life changes, and there is nothing you can do about it. But Annamaria was strong. After she buried her husband, she sat her two young children down in front of her and told them she would be there for them and not to worry, because she would figure it all out.

Annamaria had not worked since they moved to America, but she was not afraid of it. She thought she would ask around at local shops to see if they needed help. She had lived in the same area since she and Tonio moved there from Italy. She knew most of the owners by name and considered some to be friends.

Tonio was seventeen, and she was sixteen in Cinque Terre, when it all began, and it was acceptable for people to get married and start their lives really early. At only thirty-five, she was a widow with two young children, and she was only going to receive minimum widow benefits from the factory. She knew she must do something.

The bakery down the street from their apartment said they could use her help in the mornings three days a week. She was thankful for it, but she knew she couldn't go to work full time, because who would watch her children.

Mrs. Walsh across the hall in her apartment building said she would watch them a couple days a week. That really helped, but she needed more than that. She hardly had any money and finally called her sister for advice. Her sister, Isabella, moved to Santa Monica, California, just a year after Annamaria moved to Brooklyn. Issy got very lucky and met an amazing man—and got married. She kept telling Annamaria that she had two extra bedrooms that she could live in until she got her feet on the ground.

Things got to a breaking point, and Annamaria agreed to move in with her sister, all the way across the country in a place she had never even visited.

She packed up and moved her children to Santa Monica, and she was there for only two days before she started begging Issy to let her do some cooking. Finally, Issy relented and told her she could make that Friday's dinner for the whole family.

Annamaria not only cooked an amazing dinner that night, it got to be a habit. Issy's husband did really well for himself and knew lots of people that liked to fund new solid business ventures. Rick knew any venture that had Annamaria's cooking and her personality would work—and work really well. So after dinner one night, Rick told Annamaria he would like to set her up in a small Italian café to cook for a few people each night, if she was interested. He didn't want to intimidate her and throw the whole thing on her at once, so he thought he could get her interested with a few days each week and go from there.

Annamaria was ecstatic about the idea. It would bring an answer to her prayers that, hopefully, through her hard work, she would be able to make ends meet and take care of her family independently.

Rick arranged for her to meet with a couple of his associates, and they talked about strategies for opening a new café. Annamaria said she knew exactly what she wanted to call it. Before the even asked, she said, "Cinque Terre Café." She quickly added that it translates to "five lands."

She asked what she had to do to make this possible, and they handed her the contract, which required her recipes and her execution of those recipes. She would also have to be present at least five days of the week, and she would make a salary for the first year. Then she could start ownership, making repayments to them. They all knew it was a win-win situation.

Twenty years later, it's one of the most successful restaurants in Santa Monica, with Annamaria still present, as well as her children from time to time. She's had the same waitstaff for most of that time, and they know most of their customers by name.

Annamaria was especially pleased that the restaurant had introduced Sera to her husband, Roger Featherstone.

Roger had never been to Cinque Terre before, but his friend had and wanted to go. Jerry had been seeing a girl, who had a friend, and they wanted to introduce her to Roger. Since Roger was hard to get out of his house, they finally twisted his arm for a blind date. And the café was the chosen destination.

Roger was ten minutes late, and he started apologizing as soon as he walked up to the table. Jerry's girlfriend, Gina, was thin with long dark hair and a constant smile. Her sister Brenda, on the other hand, was blonde, with hair about shoulder length,= and an elusive smile. With Brenda, it was difficult to know if she was flirting or being sarcastic or if she meant some of the odd things she blurted out.

Roger sat down and was introduced to everyone, and Brenda looked at him coldly. "Are you always late or is it just for me?" she asked, then flashed a smile that did not feel warm.

Roger apologized again, then Jerry popped up and said, "I hear the food is really great here. What do we want to order?" With Jerry's comment, they all started checking out the menus. The two girls sitting next to each other glanced at each other and started giggling, making faces like schoolgirls. They pointed at the menu and whispered about the restaurant, because it's wasn't the high-profile kind of place that they expected to go on dates. It wasn't one that had fancy airs, just good home cooking.

As luck would have it, they were seated in Sera's section that Friday night. Sera wasn't about to take any attitude from two "wannabes," and the other staff had noticed the women's attitude pretty quickly. First they wanted imported "flat" water, not that bubbly kind, and it had to be at room temperature. Then they wanted every item explained to them while making faces at what Sera was describing. They wanted everything substituted and nothing cooked normally.

Every time Sera went to the back of the restaurant, Josephine, her mama's dear friend and constant employee since they opened twenty-odd years ago, teased Sera about the Princesses at her table. Josephine was like everybody's mama at the restaurant, always looking after everyone. This was great entertainment. And they got a good laugh. Sera mentioned to the group in the kitchen that it had been a long time since she'd waited on such inflated egos. She said the guys weren't so bad, but their girlfriends were the worst! In fact, one of the guys really seemed sweet and was very good looking, but with a girlfriend like that it made her wonder.

On every trip back to the kitchen, Sera revealed a new line that one of the women had said that was absolutely self centered. She not only didn't let it get to her but was also able to laugh at it with the group waiting to hear the next remark. Sera really could hold her own with anyone. She had worked in her mama's restaurant from the time she was in her teens, and she had seen just about everything—until now.

But every time she returned to the table, there were more demands—and never a thank you, except from Roger and Jerry. She was starting to think that Gina might be OK, but it was hard to tell with Brenda's influence. Brenda was not only demanding, and unnecessarily so, but also seemed to take her cues from the early Paris Hilton/Lindsay Lohan brat handbook. But as the night wore on, Roger's nerves wore on too. As his main course was served, Roger was giving Jerry looks like "I gotta get out of here!" But Jerry was not picking up on the lead.

Then their dates headed to the ladies room, together of course. Roger took that opportunity to let Jerry know he was leaving and would have to make it up to his buddy. He explained that he would be getting a call, and he would leave right after that call.

About three long minutes after the girls returned, Roger's phone rang, and he did the "un-hun, ah-ha," and "You don't say" into the phone—until about thirty seconds later, he said to the caller, "I certainly understand that. And I know that you need me to handle that immediately. I'm sorry too, and I'll see you within the hour."

Roger hung up his cell and turned to the group to say, "I'm so sorry but I have to leave now. There is an emergency that I have to deal with. I had a great time, and let's do it again soon. By the way, dinner is all on me."

With that he went to the front desk and handed them his credit card. After a brief wait for the bill, he signed it, added a large tip, and walked out of the restaurant to his car. While Roger waited for the valet to bring his car, Jerry walked outside and apologized for the set up, saying that he'd never met Brenda before. But he thought that, since she was a good friend of Gina's, she would be OK and at least fun for Roger. At least he got out of his house for a night and wasn't stuck there watching old movies or playing video games.

Roger said, "Dude! A night watching old movies and playing video games is better than listening to those two cackle." And with that, Jerry laughed and agreed and went back inside.

Roger got in his car and drove into the night. He turned on the radio, and a funny thing popped into his head. That waitress. She kind of stuck in his mind. She was gentle, quiet, and had a true grace about her. He didn't remember her name, even though she had told them all. The quacking dates were so wrapped up in their own chatter that they missed that information, and unfortunately so did he. But he wouldn't the next time.

Weeks passed and he could not forget her. So on a Wednesday night, about three weeks later, he went back by himself. He was seated in Josephine's section and soon discovered that Josephine knew almost everything about everybody. When he started asking inconspicuous questions about staff—and then about the one waitress that he couldn't forget—it got kind of interesting.

Josie learned what a charmer Roger could be, and she found herself smiling broadly every time she went back into the kitchen. The kitchen staff started asking her questions about the smiles and wondering who was putting the sparkle in Josie's eyes. By the time she began clearing the main course, Roger got his nerve up and finally approached Josephine about one of the waitresses who worked there. He described how she looked and said that he had been in a few weeks ago with some friends, and she had been so professional with his difficult friends.

Josephine's eyes lit up because she knew that he must have been talking about Seraphina. She didn't recognize him at first, but it was all coming together, and she started to smile broadly. She let him go on and on describing the girl, and with each phrase he spoke, it was obvious that it was little Sera. When he was finished, she looked at him and put her hand to her chin, as if thinking about it, pondering who it might have been, making him wait to see how anxious he got.

She said, finally, I think I know who you mean. She asked if he could remember anything else, and he said "Yes, it was her giggle that got me." Josephine could wait no longer. She said, "You must be talking about Seraphina."

"Seraphina?" Saying her name made Roger look like he had just struck gold. "Seraphina."

Roger shook his head to get his mind out of the clouds and asked, "Where is she? Is she working tonight?"

Josie told him that tonight was Sera's night off, but she would be back. She had Wednesdays and Sundays off. Josie believed she could trust this man with this precious information. She said, "Her name again is Seraphina Moratelli."

Roger mumbled it to himself, over and over again like a mantra, very softly and very reverently. He skipped dessert again, and when Josie handed him the bill, he overtipped her, which really made her night.

The next day, when Josie saw Sera, she didn't mention a word, because she wanted to wait and see what would happen.

Not three days later, Roger came in again, by himself and asked to be seated in Sera's section. While he was waiting to be seated, Josie walked over to Cindy the hostess and whispered to her to seat him in Sera's section. The hostess immediately smiled, got a bounce in her step, and acted like there was a private joke going on. She seated Roger at Sera's best table, making sure he was facing the best way, and went to the kitchen to let Josie know what she had just done.

Josie walked over to Sera and fluffed her hair and straightened up her apron. Sera gave her a funny look and went out of the kitchen.

Sera walked up to Roger's table and gave her usual greeting, "Welcome to Moratelli's. My name is Sera, and I'll be serving you tonight. Have you been here before?"

Roger responded, "Yes, Sera, a few weeks ago, but it was with some people that I don't know very well."

"Have you had a chance to look over the menu or check out the specials? I would be happy to give you any details about them if you like."

Roger replied, "I have heard so many good things about this place, and this is my second time. So if I may, I would like you to serve me one your favorite dishes, so I can really get something different. Would that be possible?"

Sera looked at him, kind of confused. When he smiled at her, she just said, "Sure. Just tell me how hungry you are, and we can go from there."

"I'm starving!" he said.

She laughed., "OK, I'll handle it then. Shall I bring you some wine?"

"Only if it's what you would suggest with what you're serving me."

Sera's smile started to grow. She thought this could be interesting.

At the bar, she got a bottle of white wine made in Cinque Terre, her favorite year. It went beautifully with the Buridda, a traditional Ligurian fish stew that was her mama's family recipe. She brought him lots of toasted Italian garlic bread, still warm from the oven. This was definitely not his customary order, but he felt like he was on an adventure, and she was his guide. He was fascinated.

He asked lots of questions about the dish, about the wine, and about Sera but tried to make it feel like it was not direct questioning. By the time he finished the main course, Roger had decided to have desert, because he didn't want the dinner to end. He and Sera chatted whenever she brought things to the table or just checked on him, and whenever she returned to the kitchen, Josie was there, looking at her—smiling.

Sera finally said, "What? Why are you being so goofy, Josie?"

Josie responded, "Oh, no reason." And she walked away.

But she kept peeking at table eleven and knew something special was happening. Josie looked like someone seeing an everyday miracle unfold right in front of her. She looked at heaven briefly, made the sign of the cross, kissed her thumbnail, and whispered, "Thank you, God. That is a reminder of hope at its essence. If it turns out to be true love, so much the better."

For the rest of the evening, Josie almost danced around, feeling light-hearted from the hope that's all around. And it seemed to ripple to the rest of the staff, so that everyone had goofy smiles on their faces. They had no idea why, but something was in the air.

Sera cleared the large soup bowl, emptied bread baskets, and put various other things away. She scraped the white table cloth with the back of a butter knife, getting most of the bread crumbs cleaned away, while asking if Roger would like anything else.

With a satisfied grin on his face, he rambled about how he would never have thought a fish stew could be so great. The wine was wonderful with it. And did they always serve it on top of that amazing fresh bread? He was so delighted that he'd let her order for him.

He paused for a minute and looked at Sera smiling at him. Ssuddenly he looked in her eyes, and he just knew. He just knew he was home simply being around her.

She then said, "I guess you're up for dessert then? I'll bring you my favorite, which did not originate in the Cinque Terre area of my family's roots, but I think you will like it."

She walked away to get a glass of Sciacchetrà to go with the tiramisu that she asked the kitchen to make in a special way for him. She took the glass of dessert wine to the table and told him that this dessert wine was made by selecting the best grapes from the harvest and setting them to dry on mats.

She explained, "The drying concentrates the sugars in the grapes, which are pressed during October. The resulting must is fermented, and what emerges is amber-colored nectar, with a flowery bouquet and an intriguing taste. Though sweet, it can have a fairly dry finish and is an excellent dessert wine. Its complexity increases with age, and it can be a rare treat. I hope you enjoy it. It's from the same village my family is from."

He took a taste and looked up at her with a smile that was indefinable—and she understood.

She went to get the dessert, which was the house specialty. She placed it in front of him, twisting the plate slightly so his view was perfect. She said, "This tiramisu is from a very special recipe. Did you know that the literal translation for tiramisu is 'pick me up'?" Surprising herself, she turned faintly pink and began stumbling over her words. She tried to back away slightly.

Roger was taken off guard but was completely flattered that she was flustered. She didn't seem like the kind of person who would let anything get to her.

As he started eating the dessert, Sera walked back into the kitchen. When she saw Josie, she started mumbling to herself about what a screwup she was. How stupid could she be to say something so unlike her? She usually was a little less crass and a little more dignified.

Josie asked what happened, but all she could get was snippets of what was said, along with the topper—the translation of tiramisu being pick me up. After about thirty seconds of silence, they both started laughing so loudly that everyone in the kitchen turned to look at them.

Sera took Josie's hands in hers, kissed her on the cheek, and shrugged her shoulders. Then she went back to table eleven.

By this time, Roger had almost finished the dessert and the wine. He was savoring every bite and every sip, smiling. Sera walked up and asked if he needed anything else.

He said, "Yes. Would it be against the house rules for you to sit with me for a few minutes? My name is Roger. And I remember seeing you when I was here before."

Sera looked coyly around and noticed it was later than she realized. There were only a few tables of diners left in the restaurant, and all her other customers had gone. She realized that he had spent the entire evening eating dinner very slowly and seemed to be enjoying every minute of it.

Before she completely realized it, she was sitting in the chair across from him, asking if he always spent his Friday nights going to restaurants by himself.

He smiled broadly and said that's not what he usually did on a Friday night. But this one was special, and he would probably think about it for a long time. He tried to explain that he had been working two jobs to help his mother out, and he had only lately gone back to working one. He asked about her schedule and what she liked to do. What were her favorites? Does she go to other restaurants, or does she just like Italian?

This made her smile and she said, "I like all kinds of food, but I just happen to think that Italian is the best." And this made him laugh.

Before they knew it, another hour had gone by, and the restaurant was closing. He took out his pen and a business card and wrote his cell phone number on the back. Putting it on the table, he slid it over to Sera saying, "Sera, I think you're quite lovely, and I would really like to see you again. Because I do not believe in pressuring anyone, I'm giving you my number. If you decide that you would like to spend some time together, you can call me, and we can make it happen. Soon I hope."

Almost a year later, Nico walked his baby sister down the aisle at their family church, where she married the most amazing man—Roger. It turned out that everyone loved him, and the reception of course was at the restaurant. Mama wouldn't have had it any other way. It was joyous and passionate, and the ripple of happiness and love throughout the room was remarkable. There was lots of laughter, of course, along with a few tears. It was really lovely.

Sera absolutely glowed during the wedding. She was excited because she got to invite all the people she loved to help them celebrate. As it turned out, she loved a lot more people than she realized. The church was packed. And everyone was invited to the reception at Mama Moratelli's cafe.

During the reception Nico found his mama out on the patio by herself. Walking over to her, he took her hand and asked if she was OK.

She said, "There are not a lot of days that I wish your father was still here, but today—especially today—I really wish he was here. He would be so proud. I could not have asked for a better match for her."

Nico smiled and pulled her into a hug and said, "Mama, I *know* he is here today, and you're right, he is very proud."

With that, Mama sighed, buried her head in Nico's chest, and sniffled a little. She hugged him back, then pushed him away and said, "Let's go celebrate. Sera and Roger deserve nothing less. Maybe I'll have grand-kids soon with some luck!"

Chapter Three

Mile after mile goes by with nothing said. If it weren't for the radio, the car would be completely void of sound except for road noises and the occasional squeak. Tess wonders why Greg asked her to come to this car and motorcycle meet if he was going to act like she wasn't even there. "Why should I waste time off just to be ignored? Asking for days off should be used for something more fun," she thought. "I'd be better off working, then going home to an empty house, than being blatantly ignored. Bear is much better company, and besides I hate having someone else take care of him—he grew up so fast."

With that thought, she gets a peculiar smile watching the scenery roll buy. She thinks about when Bear was born and how hard it had been to get Greg to let her have him. It's funny how things happen. Greg's father's dog, Nikki, had escaped their back yard while in heat for the first time and found that big black mutt and then had puppies. Nikki was so pretty, and she created really pretty puppies. She was a solid white husky with ice blue eyes. Just beautiful, and she had a great temperament.

Nikki had seven puppies, and as they grew, they took over the backyard. They were such fun, rolling around, chasing after each other. Three were white like her; three were shades of brown like a squirrel; only one was black and white. All of them were adorable. Tess used to take a break from Greg's family gatherings and go play with them. One of the brown puppies, with a white star on his chest, constantly followed her.

She would pick them up, one by one, cradle them like a baby, and rub their bellies. Each one would go all drooly-wobbly, except the one with the star on his chest. Every time Tess scratched his stomach, he would cross his front paws around her wrist as if trying to hold on to her hand. After this happened three or four times in a row, Tess started paying more attention to him. She talked to him and started to feel like he was listening. She laughed at the thought, but then it would happen again the next time. And then again, and she started to get the idea that maybe she was ready for a dog—this dog in particular.

She had a beautiful dog a long time ago, before she really knew how to care for one. She had not been in a good place for a dog. He had needed more space to run and more time than she had to give him. So when she reached a point when she felt like it was not fair to the beautiful pup, she found a good home for him with a family in the country. They could do the things she was not able to do. So she felt, with the new puppy, that she was getting a second chance.

But this puppy, as big around as he was long—looking kind of like a barrel—was another story. They had a big backyard that Greg's dog Turbo had never really used. It was fenced in and really nice. Greg took Turbo to his shop with him every day, and the little time that Tess saw Greg was the same little time that she saw Turbo. So Turbo wasn't really her dog. Turbo was part schnauzer and was much more like an old man in a dog suit—nothing but attitude. He could be really funny, but you always knew who had the upper hand. He was a great dog, but not her dog.

Why couldn't Tess have a puppy to keep her company? Tess and her sister-in-law, Anna, talked about the puppies, and Anna helped her decide that she really should take this little roly-poly home. But Greg had fought her all the way, and Tess could not understand why. It wasn't until Greg's whole family told him he was being unreasonable, and a family friend wrote a letter to Greg, that he finally gave in.

She named the puppy Bear for a bunch of reasons that seemed reasonable to her and took him home. He was her constant companion and her shadow. And all the lonely evenings weren't so bad because she had him to talk to or to take for a walk or just be with. He had become her best friend. Now she misses him when she can't take him with her. With that thought, she sighs.

They pull up in front of the hotel, where trucks and trailers are filled with amazing-looking and amazingly expensive motorcycles and vintage cars. Large groups of people are standing around inside and outside the hotel, with lots of glad-handing going on.

Tess is reminded of how few of these people she knows—and how uncomfortable Greg makes her feel around them. It's like she is watching some secret society of which she's not a member.

Greg goes inside to check them in and Tess tries to get things together in the Jeep, so she does not have to make as many trips in with their things. She is hoping that, since it's so late, they could spend some time together in their room, because it's going to be an early start in the morning. But once they get to their room. Greg wants to go back downstairs to see what he's missing.

Tess wonders what he thinks he's missing that's so important? And on this they collide. She wants some time with him and all he wants to do, it seems, is to run the opposite direction.

Tess cannot remember such a horrible argument ever before—with anyone. She sits on the floor in the dark, when it's over, looking out on Dallas through the floor-to-ceiling window in the middle of the night, crying her heart out. Greg has gone to sleep hours ago, exhausted from the fight, and Tess is still too hurt to shut her eyes.

She goes through all her pleas, over and over. "Please stay here and give me some time with you." "Please stop running away every time we get around each other." "Please realize what you're doing." "You have to participate in a relationship to have one." They all fell on deaf ears.

Why should it be so difficult to get someone to see that he's not paying attention to what's going on? Tess does not understand. It's not right for her to almost have to beg him to be with her. She doesn't get it.

She sits on the floor and watches the few cars drive down the street. The lights are off in the room, so the only light comes from outside streetlights and traffic lights. She watches the traffic lights change… green, yellow, red…green, yellow, red…green…

She watches a freight train travel in the distance, and one lone walker going down the street in the dark. All she can do is cry. "What the hell am I going to do?" now keeps running through her mind, and she struggles to breathe through her stopped-up nose. She has wiped her eyes and nose on the T-shirt she's wearing and hasn't realized how much or how hard she has been crying. "I just don't understand this," she keeps thinking.

Sitting on the floor is becoming increasingly uncomfortable, and she feels so emotionally exhausted that she walks over to the bed and lies down with all her clothes on. Curled up in a ball, she faces the wall, wanting everything to go away.

The next thing she knows, it's daylight and she's by herself. She rolls over on her back and stares at the ceiling. She can't imagine staying all weekend under these conditions. She gets up, sits in the chair, and finds a note on the table, from Greg.

> Gone to help Gary and RJ set up at the show—will be back later to get cleaned up for the banquet tonight.
>
> Greg

Well that doesn't really tell me anything, she thinks.

Tess drags herself into the shower, thinking that might make her feel better.

Drying her hair, halfway listening to the TV, she decides it's a nice day for January. The sun is out and it's not too cold. She could take a walk, and maybe that would help her get in a better frame of mind.

She spends all afternoon wandering around in a park not far from the hotel, and almost wishes she had a book so she has a good excuse for sitting under a tree. Then she sits down anyway, feeling emotionally drained. She doesn't realize she has dozed off until she wakes up later, after a lovely nap. It was a welcome break from all the tension. She walks back to the hotel and starts getting ready for the banquet, and Greg comes into the room.

He's almost the same as he was yesterday. As if the fight hasn't affected him at all. Tess isn't surprised, because it's like he has no heart anymore.

They get through the banquet with fake smiles and return home the next day with no bloodshed. As soon as they get back, he jumps in his car and goes to the shop. The long weekend is over, and they are back at the house. She's alone with Bear and the empty house on Sunday night. You'd think that anything at the shop could wait until Monday, but then again, nothing about this seems the way it should. And with every passing day, she's realizing that things would never be the same.

She doesn't think he's being unfaithful to their marriage. But with all the time he spends working, with the late hours, so far away in another city, she couldn't swear it isn't happening. She's even asked Greg's father to talk to him, and he backed down from it! What? Maybe he knows something she doesn't know. But you might think that his family would be a little more supportive. The only one that seems to hear her is Annie, her sister-in-law.

Tess's thoughts spiral through this chaos. Is this it? Is their marriage over? Are nine years suddenly amounting to nothing? With her mother's health declining, it seems like her world is collapsing. She keeps Bear close, as the one constant in her life that won't abandon her—and loves her without fail.

Greg starts sleeping in the guest room, and Tess knows for sure—it's done. All the damage has been done, and it's an empty cause.

Every day she spends as much time as possible with Bear, and she really understands the love. It's the only thing that makes her happy. Unconditional love, companionship, and a ready ear to listen to her talk about anything. She has a very best friend.

On every trip she makes to see her ailing mother a hundred miles away, Bear keeps her company. She talks to him while she drives, and he roams around the Jeep when he gets restless. He jumps from the front seat to the back, putting his butt on the seat, while his front paws are on the floorboard and his head rests on the armrest. She loves Bear more than life itself. They're inseparable.

Tess's mom was diagnosed with lung cancer, emphysema, and congestive heart failure over three years ago. She has been given a year to live. And obviously she's still fighting it. Her mom and her dad both chain-smoked Pall Mall cigarettes for over fifty years, and it took its toll. Tess's dad died eight years earlier from cancer, and now her mom is really sick.

Her health started declining so much that she has been put on oxygen and has health workers coming by the house. She takes off the oxygen mask and goes on her front porch to smoke two or three cigarettes. Then she comes back inside, puts the mask on, and continues watching TV.

She loves her Cowboys football and loves watching bowling. She also has a favorite show that's only surgeries that are very graphic. She loves it.

A year ago, Tess's sister Carrey came to live with their mom to take care of her, and her mom sold her car. It all seemed like a good idea, because Carrey had no real direction in her life and nowhere to live, and their mom needed the help.

For the first year, Carrey was pretty good about grocery shopping, paying bills, and taking their mom to the doctor. Then she started disappearing for weekends that worked themselves into weeks. She had access to all of their mother's bank accounts, which kind of worried Tess because she did not seem very responsible.

Tess checked on her mom every other weekend to see if she needed anything. She would go by Aunt Barbara's house while she was in town, and they would talk about her mom's situation. Aunt Barbara and Tess decided that her mom was decling in health and needed more help than she was getting.

With Tess no longer feeling that she has a marriage, and her mom really needing help, she winds up visiting her every weekend. She goes to the grocery store for her, cleans her house, helps with laundry, cooks, and freezes some meals for her. Her mom also seems to enjoy and need her company. They talk about soap operas that her mom loves, and Tess starts watching too, so they have something to dish about. It's fun, and it's harmless.

Spending time together, they get to know each other again. But every time Tess asks about her sister, her mom gives some kind of generic answer. It looks like Carrey has not been around at all for their mother like she'd promised. It bothers Tess that Carrey has control over her mother's bank account. But Tess knows her mom well enough to know that she cannot bring that up unless her mom does so first. So it is not a subject for discussion. After all these years, she's basically paying for a little peace. She just lets it go.

On one visit to her mom, Tess recalls their most recent Thanksgiving, with Aunt Elaine, her mom, Carrey, and Greg. Tess and Greg spent Thanksgiving morning with Tess's mom and the afternoon with Greg's big family.

Tess's mom brought up Christmas. It was also her birthday, and she said that, this year, she didn't have the money or the way to get Christmas presents, so they should not buy any for each other.

Feeling bad for her mom, Tess suggested she just write them each letters expressing what she would always want them to know. Tess said she would buy her some beautiful stationery to use, and that could be their Christmas present. Her mom loved that idea.

She also reminded Tess and Carrey that, when the time came, she wanted to die in her house. She absolutely did not ever want to be put in assisted living. Her mother also reminded them that she did have a living will, because she wanted to make sure that, just as she lived by her own rules, she wanted to die by her own rules. Mom asked them every time, "Am I clear on this?" And the girls always replied, "Yes, ma'am."

That Christmas her three-foot-high artificial tree has the really worn old ornaments, lights that halfway work, and three envelopes. Her tree is the same every year, because she has an old dish barrel that moving companies use to move dishes and breakables, and she always drops the fake tree down in that and stores it until the next year. There is never a change in the tree unless a light burns out.

There's an envelope for Carrey, one for David, and one for Tess, with their names in their mother's handwriting. Since David is still in prison, her mom leaves his in the tree. She didn't know then that the tree would stay up until almost Valentine's Day, hoping that David can find a way to come home. But he never does. Her health gets worse and worse that spring. When Tess drives to see her every weekend with Bear in tow, she can see changes in her that she doesn't want to mention, because Tess and her mom know things are getting worse.

Greg is staying in Taylor, near his shop, most of the time, and she rarely sees him any longer. She knows it's not going to be long, and they will finally talk, and it will be about a divorce.

Her mom has been eating less and moving around less. And one weekend, she starts talking to Tess about her life and some of the things she has gone through. She starts confiding in her about things that Tess had only imagined. At that point, every weekend when she visits, the TV stays off, and she and her mom just talk.

They talk about her growing up with eight brothers and sisters—and all but two girls and one boy dying of different childhood diseases. Things that are unheard of today, except in Third World countries. Growing up with an outhouse, and how rough her life has been. She talks about what she did as a young woman and how the world was then. She even talks about how she met Tess's father and how much they loved each other. She felt her early life with Tess's father was exciting, because he was in the Navy and they moved around the world. She also told Tess what her hopes had been. After hesitating, Tess finally asks, "Mom did your life turn out like you thought it would?" Her mom just smiles and says that nothing ever turns out as you plan.

And after every visit, Tess feels closer to her mom.

Tess is gaining a new found respect for some of the things her mom has gone through, and she cherishes this time with her. All these discussions remain just between Tess and her mom, and on her way home, she wonders where Carrey has been each weekend while she was there.

Tess has also wondered where her brother is and misses him terribly. She knows he's still in prison but has not been able to contact him. He could always make Carrey behave a little, and Carrey was never belligerent to him like she was to Tess. Maybe being nine years apart made Tess and Carrey such opposites. But no matter what the reason, there is a gaping divide in their relationship. And Tess is tired of always being the one who gives in, who has to forgive, and who has to always go the "additional mile" to try and get along with her.

David is only two years younger than Tess, so they grew up closer. Because they moved every year when their father got transferred, they have been each other's best friend. When Carrey came along, things changed, not only with David and Tess but also with her mom and dad. Carrey was eight years younger, and she had overheard a long time ago, before she knew what it meant, that Carrey was an "oops baby."

She has always thought that Carrey took some kind of drugs that make her behavior so erratic. She disappears for days or weeks at a time, and their mom has never seemed to question it. If Tess didn't know better, she might think she welcomes the break.

Tess gets a call from her mom's friend across the street, saying that her mom had to be admitted to the hospital. She's a little upset that her sister didn't call to tell her.

Driving to see her mom in the hospital, she remembers that Uncle C passed away the previous April. It's now March, and obviously it will be April again soon. Just the thought of it gives her an uneasy feeling.

When Tess walks into the hospital room, her mom is asleep. Her stomach drops. She definitely looks worse than before. Tess sits down and waits for her mom to wake up and says a private prayer. She's just getting to know this woman and understand her more, and she doesn't want it to stop just yet. But she doesn't want her to be in pain and completely uncomfortable, because that's no way to live.

Then her mom wakes up, seeming a little groggy. She's on some pain medication, and Tess learns that she had gotten really short of breath, and they thought she was having a heart attack. They were able to get her through it with minimal damage. But obviously, things are not the same. Her mom says it's getting late, and Tess should go home so she can rest. Tess ignores her request and sits quietly for a while.

A couple of hours later, Carrey shows up and seems startled to see Tess sitting there. They exchange pleasantries, and then it digresses. Carrey does not want Tess to come by their mother's house. So Tess doesn't push it, but she thinks, "As soon as I leave here, maybe I should go by there." But because it was late, and she had to drive home almost a hundred miles, she didn't.

Tess drives back to Austin and goes to work the next day wondering what really is going on at her mother's house—and how much longer she will have with her mother. She feels an uneasiness creeping in. When she talks to Aunt Barbara about it, she has the same impression. Barbara says that when she's in town, she will drive by Tess's mom's house to see if she can tell what's going on.

Tess goes to see her mom at the hospital that Saturday, and she can tell she is fading. It has only been four days, and she is definitely fading. Tess takes a break and drives by her mom's house, herself, to see if she can tell what's going on. She doesn't see any cars in front of the house, so she stops and goes up to the door. There is definitely no one home. She walks around back and the back door is open. She goes in, and her mouth drops open. All the furniture has been pushed away from every wall and bunched up in the middle of every room. The house is really small, only about eight hundred square feet, with two bedrooms and one bathroom. That was all Mom wanted.

But she would be horrified to see what's going on. Every bit of floor is covered with trash—empty soda and beer bottles, cans, fast-food wrappers of every kind, big plastic bags half full of garbage, ashtrays filled with ugly cigarettes butts and candy wrappers, and tossed and torn magazines. Tess tries to walk through each room to see if, maybe, one room escaped this gluttony. But every room has been completely trashed.

She also notices that mom's strongbox, which contains her will and important papers, is beside the couch with the box open, and all the papers are disheveled. It's obvious that Carrey has been looking to see what she could take and trying to figure what she can get away with.

Tess sees her mother's beloved carved teak boxes that nest inside each other against the bedroom wall, halfway under trash. She picks them up and decides to leave with them.

Tess hurries out the back door, before anyone appears. Once she gets far enough away, she stops the Jeep and sits dumbfounded. How in the world could someone let her living space get so filthy? What would make someone do that to someone else's home—especially her own mother's? She was in shock.

When Tess gets back to the hospital, her mom is awake, and Carrey is there. Carrey's behavior seems aggressive to her, but Tess does not want to make a scene in front of her mom. But she did manage to ask if Carrey is staying at the house. She said yes, and her childhood friend Andrea has been staying with her for a few days. They plan on painting the house while their mom is in the hospital.

Tess says, "How long do you think that will take?" Carrey says only a day or two, because they are halfway through it now. Tess, amazed at how she could lie so straight-faced, only nods her head. She knew

Carrey could be devious, but it is almost frightening how bad this is. They keep up all the obvious pleasantries in front of their mother, but Tess starts to wonder how far Carrey will go.

Tess has been coming down once during the week, and then on the weekend. And after three weeks of this, her mother starts getting worse and worse, so Tess starts coming down every other day.

She's told that Hospice is now involved, and they set up a meeting with her. Laurie the hospice nurse tells her everything that's going on, where her mother stands, and that her health is now steadily declining. They want to honor her wishes to die at home and are trying to meet with Carrey to arrange delivery of a hospital bed to her mother's house. But they can never get Carrey to agree on a delivery day or time.

Tess does not have a good feeling about this.

While she's sitting in her cubicle at work, her good friend Shelley stops by. Tess tells Shelley about the phone call she got from her mom from the hospital yesterday. She was pleading with her not to let them take her to a nursing home. Tess didn't understand what was going on. Her car was in the shop, and she couldn't get there until the next day, Tess told her. Her mom was practically crying, asking her to tell them not to take her out of the hospital. Tess tried her best to calm her down and find out more details—or learn where Carrey was. But she could not get anyone to make sense of the situation. Her mother hung up in midsentence, and when Tess called back, there was no answer.

Her mother is fading out of her life. She has a brother she could not get ahold of, a sister who is spiraling out of control, and a divorce on the horizon. Shelley does not know what to do to help, so she just tells Tess that she will be there for her. She's her mentor and her friend.

It seems like any other Tuesday until the phone rings. It's Laurie the hospice rep, saying over and over how sorry she is. Tess says, "What?" And then Laurie realizes that she has not been told. Laurie says, "I'm sorry Tess, but your mom died last night. The nurses found her early this morning, and we cannot find your sister. We thought she'd let you know what was going on."

Tess drops the phone and slumps into her chair. "No, no, no, no, no, this cannot be happening like this…," she mumbles. Shelley looks at her and knows what's happening. She looks at Tess, grabs her arms, and says, "You need to listen to me right now, Tess." Tess nods. Shelley goes on, "What did the lady just say on the phone?"

Tess mumbles, "That she was sorry that my mom died." Thank God for Shelley. She takes control of the situation and asks Tess what she needs to do, then asks if she needs to go to Waco.

Shelley says, "OK. Are you alright to drive?" Tess nods again. Shelley has her sit back down and then goes to find her manager. Tess puts her elbows on her desk, head in her hands, and stares into space. She wants so badly for things to makes sense, but they don't. Why wouldn't Carrey have at least called to tell her? Instead she hears the news from a stranger.

Shelley comes back and says, "You're going to grab your purse and come with me. You're going to follow me to your house, and we're going to pack a bag for you, and you're going to drive to Waco. Is that understood?" Tess just nods. She does as she is told. She is totally numb.

They get to Tess's house, where she wanders around, not really packing and not knowing what to pack. She tells Shelley that she feels like she's in neutral. Shelley packs for her and tries to get her to talk, making sure she can function for the hundred-and-one-mile drive.

Tess starts coming around, then asks Shelley if she will call Greg and tell him. Even though they are not together, she thinks he might want to know.

The drive to Waco is filled with crying bursts and then quiet. Bear is very subdued in the backseat. It seems so much longer than an hour and a half. She drives straight to her friend Lucy's house, and she and her roommate, Laura, go with her. They drive Tess to the funeral home to see her mother. The attendants take her to a room, and then they go and get her mother. They wheel her in on a gurney covered in a sheet, so that she can say her goodbyes.

Tess just stands and looks at her. She is cold and stiff, but they have put some makeup on her, so she doesn't look so pale. Tess tries to talk to her. She winds up circling the gurney, without a word, for the first five minutes or so, then breaks down and cries. She is all by herself, with no one to tell her to be strong. She doesn't have to be anything other than what she needs to be at that moment, and she sobs.

About fifteen minutes later, the attendant returns and asks her if she needs anything. Tess asks what's going to happen now.

She's told that her mother arranged for her funeral in advance and that she wanted to be cremated. Everything is completely arranged, except they need a nightgown for her to be cremated in. Tess decides to go see Carrey and see if she can get one from the house. The three of them drive over to see what they can find.

When they walk up to the door, it's open. So Tess knocks on the screen, opens the door, and goes in like she always does. From the back of the house, Carrey starts screaming at her to get out of her house. Yelling obscenities at her and screaming at her to get out of *her* house, so loudly that she is red in the face. The other two girls look at each other and at Tess.

Tess tells her is it not *her* house but their mother's. And Carrey screams, "Get out, or I'm calling 9-1-1!" Tess replies that she just wants to get a few things, like her baby book and the VCR that she gave her mother last Christmas. Carrey yells at them to do it and leave, but she is still calling 9-1-1. Lucy and the other girl are dumbfounded at all the trash on the floor and the way the house looks, and Carrey keeps yelling at the top of her lungs to get out.

Tess says she also wants the rings she gave their mom. Carrey storms off to get them and practically throws them in her face, with another scream to get out. Tess and the other two girls take the items and put them in Laura's truck. Just as they drive away, a police car arrives at the house. The three of them can't even think of anything to say until they get around the corner. Then they keep repeating that they don't know what to say.

They go shopping for a nightgown for her mother, still in awe of the ridiculous situation. All three are muttering under their breath, "What the hell is going on?" and "Carrey must be high on something!" Tess gets a call on her cell phone from Greg, asking if she needs anything and asks when the service will be. Tess tells him the service is tomorrow, and Greg asks if she would like him to be there. She tells him if he wants to that would be fine.

After she hangs up the phone, Lucy says that he probably feels a little guilty. Tess halfway smiles, thinking that, at this point, it doesn't even matter. Her friends take her out for dinner and try to get her to eat, but she doesn't. She just feels numb. She calls Aunt Barbara and tells her everything that has happened, and her aunt is appalled. She tells Tess to come and spend the night at her house.

Aunt Barbara's mother is dying too, and there is nothing anyone can do to make the situation better. So she and Aunt Barbara sit at her dining room table over a cup of coffee, trying to get to the next day, hoping it will be better.

Next day is the service. Tess gets ready and arrives at the funeral home an hour before the service will begin. She notices all the plants and flowers, then starts to notice that most of them are addressed to her attention. Reading the cards, she realizes that her friends will be her family now.

She waits around, then she suddenly turns to see David. Thank God, David is here. He practically runs to greet her, and they hug. They both start crying, then let go and start walking toward a small meditation garden. David apologizes for not getting in touch and for not letting her know how to find him. She tells him all her letters came back as "undeliverable." It's like they have never been apart.

Tess says, "I spoke with the funeral director yesterday, and he said since she is being cremated, they can split up the ashes three ways for us each to have our own goodbyes if we want.

Overhearing this, Carrey almost runs up to David and Tess. Without hesitation, Carrey almost yells, "Not with my mother you won't! I will not have her sitting on someone's shelf. I'll never agree to it." David and Tess look at each other with an understanding that they do not want a scene, and they drop the subject.

People are starting to come in to pay their respects. Carrey tries to act saintlike, saying things like, "Yes, it was hard taking care of Mother at times, but I was always there for her." After hearing her lie like that two or three times, Tess has to get out of earshot, because she just could not stand to hear it anymore.

Tess's friends start coming into the funeral home. They include her friends from Austin and from Waco, including Aunt Barbara and Greg. She sits with all of them at the service with David by her side. Then she and David have a short chat in the hall away from everyone.

He tells her that he has to go back to prison, because he's only out for the funeral, and she needs to listen to him. He says that she needs to go to the bank and get their mother's account frozen as soon as possible. He says that he knows Carrey will try and withdraw every cent she can as fast as she can. He says he will try and get to the house to get the will and the other papers, because he's the executor. But he doesn't know if he can get there quick enough.

She agrees to handle it as soon as possible. And David reminds her that they cannot trust Carrey. He knows for sure that she was systematically drawing money out of their mother's checking account this entire time.

David says, "It may look like I'm her best friend but, Tess, you shouldn't be fooled, because I'm not. I don't trust her, because I know that, as soon as she can, she'll cash in Mom's bonds and her savings account and her checking account. I don't know if we can stop it, but I need you to try. But I'm your friend and, of course, always your brother. So don't worry. We'll get through this somehow."

And with that, he was taken back into custody to go back to prison in Houston. Tess watched as all hope of things being fair went out the door with him. She knew in her heart that Carrey would pull whatever was necessary to get all the money she possibly could from the situation.

Later that day, Tess goes to her mom's bank and speaks with the manager. She explains that her mother has died and shows him the obituary. She also tries to explain that her brother, who is executor of the will, is out of town on an emergency—and that he has asked Tess to have all the accounts frozen until he gets back.

The manager is kind and polite and says he will do what he can, but he cannot promise anything. So Tess let it go. She turns around and just lets go of the fear that Carrey would get off with everything but the house, which is legally in David's name. She drops her shoulder as she walks toward the door and just lets it all go. She lifts her head up and pushes open the door and just says "fine" to herself under her breath.

Tess drives over to the Seven Seas restaurant to meet up with everyone who has been at her mother's funeral to support her. Even Greg shows up, when she has hardly seen him in the last couple of months. He quit participating in their marriage. She does not know what is going to happen or when, but she just knows all she can do is coast until he makes a move. He is living in a room at his shop and only rarely comes by the house where she's living.

She walks up to the small group, standing in twos and threes. One by one, they all manage to give her a hug and a warm word or two of condolence. She feels numb but goes through the motions and tries to be responsive. But she knows she's falling short.

As the evening wears on, Greg comes over and asks if she is driving back to Austin after dinner. When she says yes, he offers to follow her to their house to make sure she makes it OK, and she nonchalantly accepts. When she walks away, it dawns on her what has just happened.

Greg has been ignoring her for months, and now suddenly he's being kind, and she doesn't know exactly how to take it.

When it's time to leave, they drive off with Greg following in his car, which they affectionately call "the turtle." It's a fifteen-year-old Mercedes diesel station wagon. So not only is it old, it's also noisy.

When they get to the house, Greg helps her carry in plants and cards that have been sent to her mom by her friends. Once they have everything inside, Greg says "Do you want some company? Would you like me to stay for a while or for the night? I know you must be hurting, but I don't want to make you uncomfortable."

Tess replies that some company would be nice. So they turn on the TV and sit on the couch in silence until Tess says, "I'm really tired, and I think I want to go to bed." As she gets up, Greg asks her if she wants him to stay. She says, "Sure."

Tess washes her face and brushes her teeth, puts on an old, very big T-shirt, and crawls under the covers where Greg is already. She turns off the light and lies back. "Thank you for coming to Mom's funeral today. I know it wasn't easy for you to be there for me, but I appreciate it." And with that, she rolls over and closes her eyes.

The next thing she knows, Greg is stroking her arm, then he gets more and more amorous. Tess's eyes are closed, and she's half asleep, and then it dawns on her that he's making a pass at her! He has ignored her for months, and now on the night after her mother's funeral, he's trying to get laid! How dare he, she thinks. How ridiculous. She rolls over and turns on the light and asks him "What *are* you thinking? Do you really think I would be in any kind of shape for sex?"

Greg sheepishly replies, "Well, I thought you might need a release...Do you want me to leave?"

Tess says, "No you can stay, if you mind your manners." She turns the light back out, and they both snuggle under the covers, and Tess falls into a deep sleep from sheer exhaustion.

The next morning, Greg is nice but leaves as soon as he can. So this morning is like every other morning when they were living under the same roof and getting along. But it seems surreal. Tess makes some coffee, opens the patio door, and sits on the patio. Bear comes out and lies down at her feet. They both just sit, with Tess staring into space. When she hears the beeper saying the coffee is ready, she gets up.

She winds up wandering around the house, as if she has never been there before. One day runs into two and then three, and then it's a week later. She doesn't feel any better or clearer, if there was lesson she was supposed to learn. All she knows is that she's missing her mom terribly. She takes Bear for long walks and tries to find something to make her alive again. She doesn't know what to do. She feels so empty, and it seems like nothing makes sense.

Her friends call her off and on, and a few come by to check on her, but she never bothers to answer the phone, because she doesn't want to talk to anybody. Time goes on, and things don't seem any better or any clearer. She has long talks with Bear, one-sided of course, but he's an excellent listener.

One day, while driving home from running errands, she notices bluebonnets starting to bloom on the side of the road and thinks of her mom. She walks into the house and picks up the phone, out of instinct, starts to call her mom to tell her about them, and realizes she's not there anymore.

She holds the phone in both hands and collapses to her knees in tears, realizing that she could no longer talk to her. She could not call to ask questions, or share something that happened, or just tell her she loves her.

She's gone.

Tess sits on the floor for such a long time. Then Bear comes over and starts licking her in the face. She hugs his neck, and he doesn't shy away like he sometimes does. He seems to know that she needs him. And then he just lies down beside her, putting his head in her lap, looking up at her.

She looks at the phone, then nervously laughs at herself and gets up. She grabs the leash, and Bear beats her to the door. She feels that, if she walks for a while, maybe she could get her head clear. So they start exploring the neighborhood again. It's a lovely April morning, and Bear is loving being outside. As they walk, she lets her mind drift.

Some of the cobwebs in her mind start clearing away, and she starts making some decisions. She decides she must get a divorce, and she no longer wants to work for the big corporation. And she no longer wants to be reminded of everything that's really no longer part of her life. She decides she wants to move back to Los Angeles and start over. She has lived in L.A. before and only moved back to Texas because of her mom's ill health.

She's glad she moved back, because she finally connected with her mom. But with her gone now, all the reasons to stay there seem empty. She calls Courtney, one of her best friends in L.A., and tells her of her decision. She is thrilled that they will be living in the same city again. Courtney tells her it has been too long since they were living close to each other, and she's been worried about Tess since her mom's death.

Tess says she just has to do something, because everything reminds her of Greg or her mom, and she just needs to get away from it all. After losing her Uncle C, her nine-year marriage breaking up, and then losing her mother, she figures it can't get much worse—so she is going to try and begin again. She makes plans and starts working on it.

Tess tries to sell everything but her basic things, cashes in her 401(k), and loads up a truck with her house stuff. She packs up her Jeep with her immediate needs and Bear, and moved. All of this happens in three weeks. She finds a friend who will drive the truck to California a week after she leaves. So she has one week to find an apartment for her and Bear before the truck gets there.

She keeps thinking about her mom. When she calls Aunt Barbara, she gets an update of what's going on in Waco. She hears that Carrey has been having garage sales with everything that her mother owned. There never seems to be a good report when her sister is involved.

But she lets it go and tries to concentrate on the future for her and Bear. She gets on with her day. Then without thinking, she picks up the phone to call her mom—before she remembers she can't. She keeps repeating the same action, trying to call her mom and realizing that she isn't there anymore. Until one day, it dawns on Tess that she could write to her. She could write her mom all the stuff that she wants to tell her. And so she does. She writes pages and pages. And it all comes pouring out of her.

All the hurt and anger and pain that she has been feeling goes on the paper. She cries as she writes and tells her mom all that she is feeling. She puts it in an envelope and seals it and puts in the back of the book she's been reading—and tries to move on.

She finds an apartment in the valley. It's cute and small but just enough for her and Bear. There is a patio with an iron railing. And because it's on the second floor, she can leave the door open for Bear to lie on the patio and watch everything going on down on the street.

They take long walks and make trips to the beach. They just spend time enjoying looking at new things everywhere they look. It's all so healing for her, and of course Bear is just happy to "be."

While Tess is reading at the beach, glancing at Bear while he naps in the shade of the umbrella, one of the letters to her mom falls out of her book. She decides she will address it to "Mom in Heaven" and then drop it in the mail on her way home. This makes her feel stronger and more alive and she decides to find all the letters she's written to her mom and mail them. Maybe it's silly, but it feels right to her. She spends her days just finding things for her and Bear to do—and tries to be happy.

But she still feels her heart is broken. She looks for a job, after a while, and tries to make a life for her and Bear. Every day gets a little easier, but now and then, she finds herself reaching for the phone, wanting to talk to her mom.

Chapter Four

Nico, Roger, and Sera are sitting at the kitchen table in Roger and Sera's house, having just finished dinner. They are talking about Roger and Sera's attempt at starting a family, while drinking the remaining wine from the dinner that Sera prepared.

"Nico, when we first started dating, Roger made it very clear to me that he had serious intentions. We talked about how important our families were to us and how we both wanted a family of our own someday. And it was his passion for what he thought was important that made me really admire and respect him."

"That's wonderful, Baby Sister. I'm happy you have found your knight in shining armor, but I don't know what you're getting at."

Sera continues, "Because of your past and the situation you now find yourself in, it makes me wonder where your priorities lie. I think that's affecting your creativity. You don't seem happy, and you say you're not being creative. So it makes me wonder if you're going about things the right way. And possibly the larger question is: do you *want* to be happy?"

She pauses and watches Nico's face change. His eyebrows scrunch together in a puzzled look. He takes another sip of wine, and it looks like he is seriously considering what his sister has just said. He then laughs and sits back in his chair saying, "Why do you want to analyze me, Baby Sis? I'm perfectly fine, except for not being very productive lately. It's just a *small interlude* away from genius."

The room is quiet for a very long minute, and then Sera gets up and starts stacking their dinner plates. She clears the table of all the used dishes and silverware while Roger and Nico sit speechless, sipping their wine.

Music plays softly in the background, and they let their thoughts drift for a few moments. After Sera makes several trips to the kitchen counter, the table is fairly clean, and Roger tops off Nico's glass with the last of the wine.

"Nico, you know the funniest thing about me and Roger is that Italian food is not Roger's favorite. After all this time, dating and then being married, it's not his favorite!"

"Now wait a minute, Sera, I admit that it's not my favorite. But anything you cook for me *is* my favorite because you made it for me." There is no way Roger would ever want Sera to think he wasn't appreciative.

Nico says, "You know I was trying to kid around a little while ago about not being productive. But you're right. I do worry."

"Nico, you can't beat yourself up about this," says Sera. "You know you'll be painting again really soon. I can just feel it. It's not like my big brother to be so skeptical of his talent. When was your last showing?"

"It was almost two years ago, and they sold the last painting about six months ago. So Roger wants to know when he can start planning for the next collection. But I face the canvas, and I see and feel nothing, and I don't know what I can do to change that. The fact that I'm not creating anything is just as much of a problem as not having money coming in. It's getting to the point to where I'm going to have to do something, even if it's manual labor, to pay my bills."

Roger takes another sip of wine and says, "If you're serious about taking any kind of job just to make some money, we need people. I could get you on where I work. It's not that interesting, but it would be a way to pay your bills. Just let me know, and I'll set something up."

Sera chimes in, "Roger tells me all the time that they hire temps because they get backlogged. And if you took the job, you could ride down with Roger and even save on gas."

Nico tells Roger how much he appreciates his offer, but he wants to try and work this out. Otherwise, it might stifle him for good. He pauses and drifts away in thought. Is it something more than a creative freeze? Could Sera be right that his life is missing something important? Has he missed something crucial that he should have recognized?

"Nico? Nico! Are you with us?" Sera waves her hands in front of him to get his attention and bring him back to the table. He has obviously missed some of the conversation.

"Sorry, Sera, I drifted away for a minute."

"I know! Where did you go?"

"Just kinda spaced, I think."

"OK. No more wine for you. And I bet you think you're driving home."

Roger chimes in. "I know your sister's face when she gets like this. You know she's made up her mind. You get two choices, Nico. You can spend the night in the guest room, or I can call you a cab. You know I would drive you home, but I've had just as much wine as you. So that's not an option. What do you say?"

"Guess I'll stay in the guest room, unless it looks like a nursery already. Ha-ha. And since I'm staying, you wanna open another bottle?"

Roger looks at his watch, then at Sera's face, and says, "Well, since it *is* Friday night, and Sera looks like she's fine with it, I know just the bottle."

Sera adds, "Besides I haven't served the dessert I made for you guys. Roger, would you please get that bottle you're talking about? I'll get dessert, and we'll take our time."

So they stay up until a little after two in the morning, just talking and laughing and enjoying themselves. When Nico finally stumbles into bed, he ponders his life for less than thirty seconds, then passes out.

The sun shines in the window very brightly, and Nico is awakened with the sunrise. He squints up at the window, feeling his head throb a bit, hoping he'll see a shade or blinds, so the brightness won't be so unforgiving. He fumbles a bit with a pull-down shade then, once it's closed, plops back on the bed.

He stares at the ceiling and sighs, realizing that he really is awake now and won't be able to go back to sleep. He thinks, "OK, I can just lie here staring at the ceiling, or I can get up and go home and take a nap at my place later. OK, that wasn't a tough choice."

He gets up, dresses, and walks down the hall to the kitchen. It's now 7:15 a.m. and his sister is puttering around her kitchen in her flannel pajama bottoms and a T-shirt. Turning, she's a little shocked that Nico is standing in front of her.

"Well, this is not what I expected this early. Oh, *good morning*! How are you feeling?"

"Not bad. I've got a small headache but nothing that a good cup of coffee can't take care of. Know where I can get one?"

Reaching for the cabinet behind her, she pulls out a nice dark-blue mug. She hands it to Nico and says, "The coffee pot is behind you, and you know where everything else is, so help yourself, please."

"Wonderful! It smells really good. This will give me a perfect start to my day. So what are you doing? Why are you up so early?"

Leaning back on the cabinet, Sera holds out two aspirin for Nico and says, "Well, first of all, I can never seem to sleep past seven, unless I'm sick. Second, I love Saturday mornings in my house with my husband sleeping contently. It makes me happy to make coffee, then make something really nice for Saturday morning breakfast."

"You know, once you start a family, this leisure time will be non-existent. So appreciate it while you can." Nico pours a little milk in his coffee mug and walks to the stool on the other side of the kitchen bar. He leans on the counter and rubs his face in his hands. Picking up the mug, he smells it and takes a big swig. "Hmmmm, you really know how to make a good cup of coffee, Sera. Tell me what's for breakfast, and I'll tell you whether I have to get home early or not."

"Are you trying to be funny, because if you are—you're not funny. I'm making fresh blueberry pancakes. Are you interested?"

"I think I'd like to stay. Are you including bacon with that? That sounds like just the thing for Saturday morning. By the way, have you seen the weather reports lately? I thought they said we're going to have more June gloom, but the sun woke me up this morning."

"Yeah, I thought the same thing. But if you look outside now, the sky is kind of hazy, so maybe that coastal fog is coming in…" Sera starts pulling things out of her cupboards to make pancakes and walks to the refrigerator to gets eggs, milk, butter, and blueberries. Back at the counter, she works across from Nico.

"This is perfect. Now I can get you to talk to me. I want you to tell me if you have started seeing anyone. The last time I talked to you, you were seeing Alex, I think her name was. So what happened?"

"She's been out of the picture for a while. There really isn't anyone. I just haven't connected with anyone lately. I'm not really interested. I did the club scene, and that got old. I hung out at galleries and had a couple of favorite haunts, but it seems, like everything else, I burned out on it."

"Could my big brother be growing up? I told you a long time ago that people who hang out at those places are fine for a while. But at some point, you have to go home, and your reality is something only you can decide."

"Sera, I would have argued with you on that. But lately, it hasn't been making me happy, and I'm spending money I don't need to spend. And if I don't start producing soon, I'm going to have to do something like Roger suggested last night. I just keep hoping…"

As his voice trails off, Nico rests his chin on his hands and watches his sister make breakfast. He starts smiling, watching her buzz around in her kitchen. He realizes that she is so happy. He sits there contently, watching her, sipping his coffee, and smiles. He daydreams about being in his own kitchen and watching someone special cook for him. Then is brought back by Sera's voice asking him how hungry he is.

"Nico, you might not realize it, but you seem to be getting superficial. You pay more attention to the way things look rather than the way they feel. I think because you have seen so many girls, you don't let anyone get beyond your walls, because you don't get to know them first. You're seeing only with your eyes and not with your heart. So your heart isn't getting the connection. Does that make any sense to you?"

Nico takes another sip of coffee and just nods. Sera puts her hands on her hips and shakes her head at him. She leans forward, grabs a spatula she has on the counter, and swipes it at Nico's head.

He ducks and laughs at her.

Roger comes shuffling into the room in pajama bottoms and a T-shirt and asks, "Did you save any pancakes for me?" He grabs a mug from the cabinet and pours himself some coffee. Nico and Sera laugh, and Sera says, "Of course! They're coming right up!"

Nico drives home after breakfast, listening to a CD that he just can't seem to remember to take out of his car. So he hits "play," wondering whether he should take it inside when he gets home. Then he promptly forgets the whole idea as he gets out of the car. He finds himself humming a song from the CD without realizing it.

He tosses his keys on the table next to the front door, slams the door behind him, and stands still for a moment. He looks around the room, picks up his keys, and walks right back out.

"It's Saturday morning," he thinks. He should go out for a walk—and he knows just the place to go! He drives down to Venice and finds a parking place only a couple of blocks from the beach. He takes a long walk on the beach, finding a place to stop and sit for a while and just listen to the waves. The "people watching" is fascinating, and the time flies by.

It dawns on Nico that it's way past lunchtime, and he phones his mama's restaurant to order a pizza for pick up. When he gets the pizza home, he opens a beer, and takes the pizza box with a couple of paper towels, juggling them all into the living room. He uses the remote to turn on his TV and finds a good news channel. By the time the news is over, he has finished most of the pizza and is leaning back on the couch looking for something more entertaining on TV.

He sets the remote down, deep in thought about his current situation. He looks at the canvases against the wall and sighs. He starts thinking, "Am I really going to be able to paint myself out of this one? Have I started looking at life with such cynicism that I no longer see the beauty in it? Is my sister right that I have fallen into an apathy-filled existence?"

His doorbell rings, and it's his friend Simon. Simon lives a couple of blocks away, and when he takes his dog out for a walk, he stops by Nico's. Simon asks how he is doing, and what he is doing, and notices the pizza box on the table in the living room. "Aha! Still getting Mama to feed you, huh?"

"Well, if I'd known I was going to have company, I would have gotten a large pizza. There's some left if you want a slice. Want a beer or a glass of wine, Simon?"

"A beer would be great, thanks. What kind did you get this time?" Simon opens the lid of the box, and his eyes light up. "Great choice, Bud, I love your mama's pepperoni supreme. But then all her pizzas are winners."

"So what brings you by, Simon? The pizza?"

"No dude, believe it or not I can do that by myself. I was just thinking about you and was wondering what you were up to and how things were going. The fact that you feed me is beside the point. Just giving you a hard time, you know that. I was just taking Jethro for a walk and wanted to know if you want to join us."

"Nah, I want to see the Lakers game that's coming on. You're welcome to stay and watch it, if you want."

"You know, Nico, I never figured you for a sports kinda guy. Anyway, I think Jethro needs to get out. And I think I do too. Why don't I call you later and see what's going on?"

"Sounds great. I'll be here."

When Simon leaves, Nico knows he probably won't hear from him tonight, and that's OK. He's content just being home for the time being.

Finishing the pizza he looks around the room, and starts thinking about his situation. He sighs and falls back against the couch. He kept hoping if he ignored the direction his situation was taking him, it would just get better on its own. But it hasn't. His options are limited since he is going through such a unproductive time, he is going to have to bring some money in somehow-at least until he starts painting again.

Being a practical person, Nico agrees that it's the best thing, for now, to accept Roger's offer. He agrees to work at the post office as a temp.

Deep down, he hopes that making money a different way will let him relax and spark some creative ideas, because it will take some pressure off, since he'll be able to pay his bills.

Nico goes for an interview and takes a couple of basic tests. When he passes, the manager asks him if he can start right away. He mentions that it's not often that he gets temps who are really smart, so he is grateful for however long Nico decides to stay. He can definitely use him for a long while. They decide that he will start the next day. And Nico is relieved that he can take a break without becoming homeless.

As he heads home, he decides not to force it for a while and to just let the "spirits guide him." He's reminded of what his mom always says about the divine order of the universe and all.

His first day of work, Nico is led into a large room where everyone is buzzing around, sorting mail, moving boxes, and shoving large canvas tubs full of letters. They all look like they know what they're doing. Roger introduces Nico to a rather large man with glasses resting on the end of his nose. He's Larry Hodges, supervisor of the sorting room. Roger tells Nico that he'll find him around lunchtime, and they can go grab a bite then.

Nico thanks him, while walking with Larry to a large wall with pigeonholes that have mail stuck inside. He explains the process to Nico and the easiest way to handle it. He gives him a few more pointers and tells him that, if he runs into anything he doesn't know how to handle, just to find him, and he'll help. He points to his office, saying that Nico can usually find him in there, and walks away—leaving Nico with a mound of letters and a bunch of empty holes to fill. He starts working and, by lunchtime, he is somewhat comfortable with what he's doing , so he can let his mind wander a bit.

Feeling a tap on the shoulder, Nico realizes that Roger has walked up behind him. He smiles rather sheepishly and says, "It must be time for lunch." They walk out together and Roger asks him what he thinks so far. Nico says that it's not bad and he can definitely handle it. As they walk, Nico is thinking that he's blessed to have such a good family.

A couple of weeks later, Larry stops Nico on his way to the "pigeon holes" and says, "Nico, I have a new job for you. You did really well with the sorting, and I really need help in another department. I hope you don't mind changing."

Nico replies, "Wherever you need me, Larry, I'm fine with." Larry leads him to a basement area that's piled with tubs of letters and small boxes. He starts describing the department and what should go on. He says that, if there's any way to find where these mailed items are supposed to go, they need to try and get them there. But for the most part, they're dead. He says that he has tried other help here, and they didn't seem to have a clue. But he thinks that Nico is smart and will try to figure out ways to cut some of the bulk down. Larry says he'll be happy if Nico can cut at least 5 percent and get them processed correctly.

Nico says he will do his best and asks whether he has any suggestions on where to start.

Larry says, "Maybe start in one corner and just go from there. It's kind of like: how do you eat an elephant? One bite at a time! Let me know if you have any questions. You know, once the post office accepts a piece of mail, it's a federal offense if it's opened by anyone but to whom it's addressed."

Nico starts moving the tubs around so he can get to one side of the room and starts looking through the letters. He comes across bad handwriting, partial addresses, and mail addressed to people that don't exist. He starts making piles of addresses he thinks he can figure out, ones that don't make any sense, and letters that are addressed to Santa Claus or the Easter bunny.

He does this for days and is getting through some of the piles. He feels like he is making a dent in the mountain of mail. About two weeks into this sorting, he finds a letter addressed to Mom in Heaven. He starts to throw it in the bin with the Santa Claus and Easter bunny mail, and something makes him stop. Something about the handwriting, or maybe it's the feel of the envelope—which is not especially significant.

He puts it to the side and keeps sorting. He tries not to think about it anymore but glances at it from time to time. He glances around to see if anyone is watching him, and with the coast clear, he takes that letter and stuffs it in his pocket. The sorting of mounds and mounds of letters goes on, and before he knows it, Roger is standing in the doorway, smiling, asking if he is ready to go home.

Nico gets home and pours a glass of wine, then sits down on the floor, his favorite spot. He reaches in his pocket, remembering the letter he stashed there earlier. He looks at the handwriting again and debates whether or not he should open it. He gives in, gently tears the envelope, pulls out the one-page letter, and starts to read it.

The letter is to a mother from her daughter. As he starts to read it, he gets goose bumps. It describes how much she misses her mother and what has happened since she died. The more he reads, the more his eyes fill with tears, and before he realizes it, he has tears running down his face. He finishes the letter, drops his hands in his lap, and just cries. The letter is only one page, but he sits there with his head in his hands.

He wipes away the tears and looks up and sees his empty easel and white canvas over to the side. He stands up and puts a canvas on the easel and starts to paint, remembering what the letter has said. All night, he stands there painting with the emotion that he read in the letter—until about four a.m., when he walks over to his bed and collapses.

The alarm goes off at 7 a.m. and he rolls over, looking at the beautiful painting he did last night. He debates whether to go into work or not, then suddenly becomes obsessed with finding out if there are more letters like the one he brought home. So he gets up and goes to meet Roger—to go to work at the post office, hoping there will be more.

Driving to meet Roger, he wonders who this girl is and what her life must be like. He thinks it must be really difficult to lose your mother, then thinks again about how grateful he is to still have most of his family. Suddenly, he has a new way of looking at the world, and he doesn't want it to stop yet.

Digging through the mounds of letters, he finds two more. After checking to see if anyone is around, he stuffs them in his pocket. He tries not to act like he has found catnip in this mountain of paper. But inside, he feels almost giddy, because he has found fuel for his creativity.

Once he's home, Nico makes a pot of coffee and opens each letter with reverence and as if it is very delicate. Each letter leads to a new painting, each painting better than the one before. Without fail, every one makes him cry or laugh or feel raw emotion that he has never felt before. He finds new passion for this writer with every letter, and like a junkie needing a fix, he goes to the dead letter office every day hoping that he'll find another one—another fix. Another window into a world he can only read about, but then he paints almost all night, night after night. He's so tired but ignores it because of this passion. That's the only thing that matters.

There are days when he doesn't find any letters, but he keeps searching and hoping for more. On days when he finds nothing, he goes back over what was written in the letters he found earlier, trying to put them in the order they were sent. He wants to piece the puzzle together.

He now feels like he's getting a picture of this woman, who she is and what makes her fascinating to him. "I want to meet her. I need to look into her eyes to know where she finds the hope to deal with the pain and loss she has felt. Where does her strength come from?"

He feels like a voyeur, peering into her life and her feelings—her innermost thoughts—like he is reading her diary. He is putting it all on his canvas, with no one the wiser. He feels he may care too much that she has lost her mother and feels all alone. He doesn't understand why he cares that her pain is so obvious, but there's nothing he can do about it.

It makes him wonder about the world at large and how so many people can be so disconnected. Too many people carry around such pain and loneliness, yet no one seems to notice. Have we all become so hardened to each other that we don't see people that need some small crumb of humanity directed their way?

When he walks down the street, he tries to set aside the walls he has built around his feelings—to see if he has just been blind all this time. Have people who are truly emotionally in need been there all the time, while he has been blind to them? He passes by women on the street and wonders: is that her?

He starts to take long walks so he can test his theory. He wants to see if he can confirm his suspicions about being oblivious—and wonders whether he is just starting to open his eyes and, possibly, his heart.

Has he always been only partially aware?

His thoughts go beyond his immediate surroundings to the world at large, with his emotions becoming raw and overwhelming. But he realizes that it's easy to care in this situation, because he can't get involved, and it's safe. He doesn't have to put up walls to protect himself, because he doesn't know who she is. He questions whether he is merely a conduit—from raw feeling to color and shape. One by one, his canvases are being filled. Every night, he feels the need to create. And then he looks at his finished work with a bit of awe and wonders why he never could have felt this on his own.

He feels the connection with this woman. He doesn't understand it but doesn't feel like he can question it. He revels in it, and he now feels like she is somehow part of his life. He thinks he must know what she looks like, but he has no idea how to find out. And what would he do if he found her? What could he say?

For now, he is content to imagine her life and what she's like. What are her favorite colors, and what does her voice sound like? He daydreams about the missing pieces of this puzzle and tries to paint them in along with what's obvious. Maybe this is what it's like for a child to have an imaginary friend, he thinks, and sighs.

"Why did I need to observe someone else's view of the world before I could see? And why do I feel the need to question it? I need to let go of this obsessive behavior and just be more in the moment," he says to himself.

He looks over the work he has made in the last few months. It represents his feelings so well that he thinks he can let the world in on it.

He finally calls Maxwell and asks him to come over. Maxwell, at first, gives him a hard time for being out of touch. When he realizes that Nico is not kidding and has something to show him, Maxwell gets really excited.

Maxwell is usually so cool that, without knowing him well, it's hard to know when he's excited. His face shows emotion in a one-to-three range, while the average person goes to six or seven. One would almost think he doesn't have any emotional depth, by the look he has—or lack of look. He's tall and has an athletic build and wears suits extremely well. He has a thin, reddish-blond mustache that's barely visible. Strangers might think he's made of stone.

Maxwell asks, "When can I come?" His voice has an almost urgent, excited tone that makes Nico smile.

Nico tells him to come over on Saturday afternoon, and they will catch up. Maxwell sounds like he can barely believe it's true. He tells his old friend that he has missed him but didn't want him to feel pressured, so he refrained from calling. Nico says that he has understood and hoped they would both be relieved when they had something to share. And he now he does feel like he has something to share.

Nico knows and trusts Maxwell, especially his opinion. He wants to show him what he's been doing to see if he can feel all that went into each one. So Nico starts moving the paintings around and putting them in some kind of order. He tries to group them as he would for a gallery showing. Then he gently turns each one around, so that only the backs are showing. He decides he will show Maxwell his work one at a time, so he can get a better idea of what's there from someone who has not seen it gradually building up.

It's important to be productive again, and Nico appreciates it more than anyone else. It seems to be all that matters. He feels like he's breathing again, like he is once again living in his own body. He feels his perspective has been realized and that he's now in focus.

In fact Nico is starting to get excited, as it sinks in that he has created probably his best paintings ever. He looks at each piece and sees all the words that "she" wrote. "What she's made me be able to feel—and then create—she will never know," he tells himself.

Considering that he could, very possibly, get in real trouble legally, he must keep this to himself. No one must ever know where he got his inspiration, and her letter must remain his secret.

When Saturday arrives Nico wakes up early, on his own, and starts fumbling around. He makes a pot of coffee and stands against his front door looking in his apartment. He's trying to figure out how his work will look as someone arrives and how it must be presented.

He moves the paintings around, then has them facing the wall once again. He takes a shower and debates with himself the entire time. Is one way better than another? Is it best to have them revealed one at a time? Are they good enough on their own, or do they need to be grouped?

He questions himself over and over. As time goes on, getting closer to Maxwell's arrival, he quits fussing over them and just leaves them alone. They wind up being grouped, facing against the wall as originally planned.

Maxwell arrives with Chinese takeout and a large bottle of sake. They're both relieved that their meeting is finally happening. But its real purpose is just about to start, and they both have a knot in their stomachs and would never admit it.

Nico warms up the sake, and they sit down at the table. They skirt the issue and ignore the "elephant in the room."

They start lunch and talk about generalities. It's as if they are delaying, maybe postponing an awkward situation if Maxwell really doesn't like what Nico has created. There are no guarantees that Maxwell will like his current work or think it will be able to show well. Knowing this, they are both very hesitant.

They finish their lunch and clear off the table. Maxwell sits back down, and Nico walks over to the first painting.

Nico says that this work is different from his previous work, because it was truly inspired. He says to Maxwell, "I hope you like these, because they have become important to me, in that I feel they ring true. And I will not be offended if you do not get the emotion that I hope is there. We are too honest, and I respect you too much, for you to do anything but tell me what you really see in these."

And with that Nico turns the first painting around for Maxwell to see.

Maxwell is almost startled by the obvious change in his work and finds that he cannot breathe. He is stopped in his tracks—speechless.

Nico prods him, asking, "Well? What do you think?"

Maxwell stands up and walks over and looks at Nico and says, "My friend, what have you done?" He looks at the painting, sighs, and just stares for a couple of minutes. All the while, Nico's heart is dropping.

It flashes through his mind that he has perhaps been so wrong, so out of touch, but how? He has felt good with every brushstroke and with every color he has chosen. How?

Maxwell finally starts to find the words and says, "Good Lord, Nico, I didn't know you could do this. I mean I loved your work before, but this is so raw and overwhelming that I hardly know what to say. Can I see more?"

Nico laughs and says, "Of course." He starts turning them around one by one. Each one makes Maxwell's smile bigger and bigger. Each one reveals something else, another view of what he was trying to express.

After the last canvas is revealed, Maxwell sits down. He looks around and tries to take it all in. He looks at Nico.

Nico is looking at Maxwell, anxious to hear his final take on what he sees. He doesn't want to push him, in case it's not the response he is hoping for. Perhaps he can delay a negative response. He just doesn't know what to expect.

Finally Maxwell finds the words and says, "Unbelievable." He turns away from the canvases again and says to Nico, "I knew you were good, but I never dreamed you could evoke this raw passion and strong emotion before now." He stands up again, pausing in front of each one, shaking his head.

He walks over to Nico and shakes his hand and just looks around. Nico is relieved, and his smile starts creeping back as he realizes what he has shared. They *are* what he has thought, and they make other people feel the same thing. He is almost dumbfounded. Maxwell starts talking about a showing and asks whether Nico is still creating these. And what was his inspiration?

Nico sits back down and Maxwell follows. They toast with the last cup of sake, to a good reception of their venture. Maxwell starts rambling about how he wants to reveal the paintings to the public and the press. This might be a national event—and could make his work really well known. With every breath, Maxwell talks about his plan of action, while Nico drifts in thought.

He decides he cannot quit the post office just yet. There could be more letters, and if there are, he wants to have them. He's not ready to give up this inspiration—and wants know what the diary says next. He's hooked.

So Monday rolls around, and he gets up and meets Roger and goes back to work in the dead letter office. , One day at lunch, Roger finally asks him why he has been so happy lately, doing basically manual labor, sorting through mountainous bins of mail, and he just smiles.

He is still finding letters, but there are not as many, and they are starting to have a different tone. They are revealing a different side of her, and he feels he has joined her journey. In most of the letters, it's not what she writes, but the way she describes it, that makes him care about it.

And with each letter, there is another painting or two.

He has all the letters in a carved wooden box with a lock on the front. He guards them. He makes sure they are his secret. And he never mentions them to anyone. The box is on a cabinet behind his kitchen table, trying to look inconspicuous. He even takes the key with him to guard his secret, wearing it on a leather cord around his neck.

Maxwell now calls about twice a week with an update. He gives Nico the plans he is making for the showing. He has secured the Santa Monica Museum of Art, which is associated with the Basil Grey Gallery they have used before. The museum has agreed to a one-man showing and an opening reception.

Maxwell assures him that he will have the press there, and it will be an event that's worthy of his work.

Nico tells him that, when the time comes to pick what will be shown, he will have an even more to choose from.

Chapter Five

Tess puts another letter in the mail to her mother and continues with Bear's walk. She, loves to be out early in the morning and gets no argument from Bear. Every time there is a change in seasons she feels a small awakening. When winter turns to spring, she has a new appreciation of the way it gets a little warmer and a little more enjoyable, and the days get longer by just moments every day. She feels a new hope when spring comes around, and hope is always welcome. It seems, lately, like hope is not always in abundance.

She notices, in the early morning and early evening, that the orange blossoms that are starting to bloom leave an amazing fragrance in the air that's almost intoxicating. Bear, by contrast, just sneezes, but his pace is quicker because it's cooler, and he seems more playful. He always listens intently to all the birds during the walks, but Tess thinks he is actually hoping to hear a squirrel make itself known, so he can chase it. That's his favorite thing.

She starts thinking again that she should either get her camera fixed or try and find one secondhand that works. When she is looking through the lens it seems to make her more observant. And it always made her feel god when she processed the pictures and showed her friends her prints. She has a hard time explaining to herself why she is not following up on the initial interest in showing and selling her pictures.

She lets her mind wander as they spend this time outside, and she always winds up thinking about David, her brother. She wonders why she has not been able to find him. Could he think, because she's moved, that she doesn't want to know where he is? She wonders why every letter has come back unopened. She sighs and tries to let it go.

She has more important things to do, like trying to find a job. Her best friend, Courtney, has started a catering company and says she will get Tess on her crew—or get her hired as her assistant—whenever she has an event. So Tess has sporadic work with her, but she really needs a full-time job and a full-time income.

She does count her blessings, having Courtney and her family living so close. Courtney has been married to Brad for over ten years now. And Natalie, Courtney's daughter, is now twelve going on twenty-four. It just amazes Tess how grown-up Natalie always sounds and how lady-like she always acts. Courtney has always been a great mom. And it's so comforting, whenever Tess visits her, to know that there are some things in this world that are just right.

Brad and Courtney met when they worked together at a golf resort, and they were both married to the wrong people. As time went on, Courtney finally decided that her empty marriage with George was never going to work out, because he didn't want the same kind of life that Courtney did. George didn't want to work the same hours. He purposely took the evening shift, so he wouldn't have to spend time with Courtney, which really hurt her. While she worked during the day, he would be home with his buddies, partying in their living room, and when she was home at night, he was working. After all, you cannot have a marriage if only one person is participating. So about six months after Natalie was born, Courtney got a divorce from him.

At the same time, Brad was at the end of a bad marriage too. They became friends because they were going through the same kind of thing, except that Brad did not have kids. But he did know that he was unhappy and needed to get out of the relationship he was in. After his breakup, he started to rely on Courtney's friendship.

So an unsuspecting friendship was born from an unhappy situation. They both had more than that in common—and soon discovered how much they liked and respected each other. Then they discovered that they liked many of the same things and in the same ways.

What really dumfounded them was how much they enjoyed each other, so much so that, when they weren't at work, they were thinking about each other. At the big resort property where they worked, they would leave little signals on their desks, then meet by a certain fountain, so they could get a minute away from everyone else and have some stolen time together.

There were many opportunities during workdays to see each other, because doing conference sales at a resort requires constant checking on events to make sure everything is on schedule. Not only is there a lot of responsibility, but there's also a lot of time that's not accounted for. So there were moments that could be stolen to spend together. And of course, on a golf resort there's golf. And they did like to play.

Tess and Bear get back from their walk, and she sits at the kitchen table with her laptop, checking help wanted ads. One can only exist for so long on unemployment before you get tired of coasting and not being able to do what you want. Then you decide to try and make some money. Bear is lying on the floor at her feet, snoring and jumping as if he's chasing squirrels in his dreams.

She rubs his back with the sole of her bare foot, while reading and sipping a cup of coffee. She finds a few ads with fax numbers and jots them down. She sends off some e-mails to the ads—and prints off a copy of her letter and resume that she will fax to the ads that only include a fax number.

She hates looking for a job and remembers what her mother told her a long time ago, that it's easier to find a job when you have a job. But when you haven't had a job in over a year, you have to try and find what you can. Then you have to hang on to it until you find what you really want, so that at least you're working.

She replies to a bunch of ads and, when she has responded to every ad that she could possibly qualify for, she gets a glass of water and more paper and sits back down. She writes to her mother again, explaining her fears about her future and how bleak it looks. She tries to keep her spirits up, but it's so hard, and she doesn't know what to do to make it different.

> Mom, you always seemed to have an answer or at least a suggestion, and I really could use your help right now. If I didn't have any savings, I would be completely desperate. But thank God that you taught me well.
>
> But I wish I could hear your voice telling me it's going to be OK—or that I could come home to see you and get a big old hug hello. And the next thing would be what we could make for dinner. I never knew my heart could ache so much from missing you. I can't find David, and of course Carrey is absolutely no help and a complete waste of good air! I really wish I could find David, because at least he can help me make sense of things. But I think that's the main problem, Mom; nothing makes sense. It's like everything is just a bunch of loose ends, and nothing goes together. Kind of like "connect the dots," but they don't make a picture. It's all just a bunch of jumbled dots.
>
> Mom, there isn't a day that goes by that I don't miss you, and it doesn't seem to get any easier either. I love you so much, and I can't explain to anyone why I feel like I have this blanket of sorrow covering me. I get glimpses of how I used to be happy, but now I don't know if I can ever be really happy again.
>
> I'm tired of crying myself to sleep and being afraid of what will happen next. Why does everything have to seem so screwed up?
>
> I love you, Mom, and I miss you so badly.

She folds the letter, slides it in the plain white envelope, and turns it over. She addresses it to Mom in Heaven. She puts a stamp on it and places it by the front door. She walks back to the couch, puts the TV on, and sits down. Before you know it, she is lying down and then her eyes close.

She wakes up, and one of those late-late shows is yakking away at her. She finds the remote and turns the TV off, gets up, and walks into the bedroom. Bear follows her. She's so tired that she doesn't even wash her face, just takes her clothes off and crawls in bed. She is back asleep almost before her head hits the pillow.

The sun is starting to creep up, and the dim light brings Tess around. It also doesn't hurt that Bear is breathing in her face with his tail wagging. He sees her open her eyes, and he licks her face. He is so much better than an alarm clock. What amazes Tess is that he's like this every morning.

Her feet slowly reach for the floor, and she tells Bear, "OK, Buddy. Just give me a couple of minutes to put some clothes on, and we'll go for your walk."

She sets up the coffee pot so that it's brewed when she gets back. She reaches for the leash, her keys, and the letter she wrote last night. Bear sits in front of her, waiting for the leash to be attached so he can go on his regular "sniffathon" of the neighborhood.

They get out the front door of the apartment building, and the orange blossom fragrance hits her. Geesh, Tess wants to smell like that! That is heavenly. The morning twilight is kind of magical, the time when it's no longer dark but not really light either. It's the time between. The irony is not lost on her.

Since it's Wednesday, she needs to call Courtney when she gets back—to see whether she has any catering jobs that Tess can help with. She really hopes to hear back from at least one of the people she sent her resume to.

She mails the letter, and then they head home. The sun is up, and it's going to be another beautiful day in L.A. She opens the door and can smell the fresh-brewed coffee. She sits down at the computer and checks her e-mail.

Eight new e-mails, and she only sees one—from Lucy. Oh, my God. How did Lucy find her? And what in the world is she up to? Tess opens it. The subject is: David.

> Tess, David is in the hospital after having fallen or passed out in the yard. I went to see him today, and he didn't quite understand why he was in the hospital. I don't know what's going on, but he had his first radiation treatment today. I don't know if you have contacted him, but if you want to talk to him, he has his phone, and his hospital number is 254-555-2832. He made some comment about having a stroke, but I don't really know what happened. L.

Tess sits there, dumfounded. Oh, my God. What to do? She gets up and gets a cup of coffee.

She calls Courtney and reads her the e-mail. Then asks what should she do? Courtney says, "You know you don't even need to ask. Of course you go." Tess asks if Courtney can take Bear for the few days she'll be gone, and Courtney says that they love Bear and will definitely take good care of him.

Tess goes back to her computer and starts looking for a flight that she can afford. She calls Lucy and tells her that she's flying in, then asks if she has a couch she can crash on. Of course Lucy says yes, and she wishes it were happening under better circumstances.

Tess flies back to Austin, rents a car, and drives to Waco. The hundred-mile drive seems like forever, because she has no idea what to expect when she gets there. She gets to the hospital, finds David's room, and walks in. He looks up, and she says, "Remember me?" And his right arm flies open for a hug. They hug for a good two minutes. David can hardly talk, and when tries to get up, he can't.

He says, "I'm so glad you're here. I know everything will be OK now, because you're here. I love you, Tess." He pauses and gets a confused look on his face, "I don't know how I got here or what really happened, I only know what they tell me, and it's not a whole lot. Maybe it will make more sense to you."

Tess sits on the edge of the bed and looks at David. Her heart is starting to break, once again, because she sees a shadow of what she remembers as her brother, not a vital happy human being. She's trying to get the words together to say the obvious but in a way that won't seem as cruel as the truth.

He asks how she's doing and where she's living now, and Tess answers all his questions. She also gives details when it seems right. David grabs her hand and hangs on. After fifteen minutes of fast and furious conversation, she is running out of immediate things to say and there's a pause. With the quiet, Tess starts looking around the room.

There's a knock on the door, and in come Hayley and Buck, her ex-husband, along with Lucy. Tess stands up, and they all hug and then stand around. Then David says he wants a cigarette.

Tess thinks, with all that cigarettes have done to him, and he still wants one. She's dumbfounded. Tess has lost her dad, her beloved uncle, and her mom—and now she's losing her younger brother—all because of cigarettes. Lung cancer can be so cruel.

She has to leave the room. She asks Lucy if she wants to get something to drink with her. She's going to get David a root beer as well. Hayley says she doesn't want anything but wants to walk with them. They will all be back in a minute.

When they get outside in the hallway, Tess can't help but break down and cry. Lucy walks over and gives her a hug, and Tess cries. Hayley is sniffling too. They all pause a minute, and Hayley tells Tess, "You know, we have to get him out of here and into an assisted living center as soon as possible." They tell her that Jennifer could probably help them, because she's been involved in other retirement homes and assisted living homes for years now, and she knows a lot of people who could help.

Tess asks them to call her and see if she could do something. Tess is only going to be there until Monday and has to fly back to L.A. midday. Hayley says that she has David's keys, and they should go to the house while she's in town and see what she wants to do about it.

Then they get quiet, because they all know what needs to be said next. David is dying, and they all know it. Tess is first to say, "What exactly happened, do you guys know?" Hayley says that he had a stroke while talking to the guy that lives across the street. And he just collapsed on the ground. The guy called 9-1-1, and they brought him here.

Lucy adds that he told her last week that he'd been getting some kind of treatments because he had some X-rays done, and they showed that he had cancer of the lungs, and it was stage III. The report was positive enough to give him hope. But when he got here and got re-examined, it showed that, actually, it was stage IV and spreading to his throat. That's why his voice is getting so bad. He doesn't really realize that the left side of his body is nonfunctional now too. So he can never be on his own again, if he gets well enough to leave assisted living.

Tess has to lean against the wall a minute, because the floor is not enough to hold her up. She tries to take it all in. Hayley puts her hand on her shoulder and tells Tess that she's not by herself. They would be there to help as much as possible. She then asks her what she wants to do next.

Tess just leans there for a minute, then says, "I want to make him comfortable, but I think he needs to understand what's happening. Can we do that? I think that would almost be a favor."

"Do we know anything about Carrey? Is she here or coming here?" asked Hayley.

Hayley says she has heard that Carrey is trying to come but won't be here until late Sunday. Tess looks at Lucy and Hayley and says, "OK, then we need to go to Mom's house today, don't we?" They all look at each other and are definitely in agreement.

They don't have any drinks in their hands and decide to quickly run down and get something, so it's not so obvious when they walk back into David's room. They had also promised David that they would bring something back for him.

After getting the drinks, they head back up the elevator, and Tess starts crying softly again. In front of the door to the room, Tess looks at them and asks, "Are my eyes a giveaway to what's going on?" They assure her she looks fine.

When they walk back in, David is in mid-sentence, asking Buck why he can't get up and go smoke a cigarette. Giving him a look like she cannot believe what she's hearing, Tess hands David a drink with a straw, and he says thank you.

Tess sits at the end of the bed and tells him what happened and what is probably going to happen. With Hayley holding his hand and with Buck close by, they give him a few details and an outline of what he can probably expect. Lucy and Buck are obviously just there for support, and they need that.

I don't care how much you think you're prepared for something like this, you're not Tess thinks. How can anyone possibly be prepared for what winds up being a "death sentence." And once it's all out, David doesn't seem too bothered for some reason. Right after Tess and Hayley finished talking, they waited for David to act like he got it, but they knew from his reaction that he didn't.

His lunch rolls in on a cart, and they take that as a sign to leave. Tess says that she's going to go get some lunch, because she came straight from the airport. David says that he hopes she'll come back later, and she tells him, "Of course, I will." They all file out the door while the nurse is getting him set up.

Outside the door, Hayley tells Buck that they are going over to the house and asks whether he wants to come. He says he wouldn't mind going along for the ride.

They follow each other over to Tess's mom's house. David has held the title since their mother died. It's a really small house, only about eight hundred square feet. It has two bedrooms, one bathroom, a nice sized yard, and a front porch big enough for one chair. When they drive up, Tess gets the same feeling she used to get whenever she drove up to this house. It's a feeling of dread mixed with unhappiness and a dash of uneasiness. She has never liked coming back to this house, but she had to so many times.

They walk up to the front door, and Tess notices that not much has changed since she was last here. The flower beds are slightly grown over, and there's a new-ish carport over the car in the driveway.

Hayley unlocks the door, and they walk into a mess. It's not quite as bad as when Carrey was here, but almost. They help her go through what's left in the house. And it's really evident that a very unhappy person was living here. Every ashtray is filled, and it smells smoky and dusty and full of bad vibes.

They all start looking around for whatever can be salvaged. There are some pictures scattered around, and Hayley walks around trying to gather them all together. Lucy asks, "Is there anything that you want to keep? We can take it in Hayley's truck, and you can store any big things at my house."

The four of them start checking things out, and Tess puts a few things by the front door, like a Japanese-looking vase that her mom had for years, an oddly framed piece of silk with a Japanese landscape painted on it, and an old photo album. In the front bedroom, there's a three-drawer dresser. Tess remembers her mom painting it coral pink. Tess asked her, "Why that color?" and she replied that it was her favorite color.

The drawers are lying on the floor, and the dresser itself is stripped down to bare wood. Tess turns to Hayley and says, "Will that fit into your car?" Hayley looks it over and says, "Hmmm, I don't think so, but I have a friend who has a pickup. I can get him to come over now, so we can get it to Lucy's."

Tess asks Lucy, "Well, would you like it? It would be nice if it was salvaged somehow." Lucy tells her that she will keep it, in case she ever wants to get it back. Hayley walks into the other room to make a cell phone call. Buck asks if they want him to check the storage room in the back yard, and they both exclaim that they'd forgotten all about it.

In the backyard, they try to get into the small shed, but it's locked up, and they don't have time to get a locksmith. So they walk around the yard a little, then go back into the house. Tess asks, "Who's taking care of David's dogs?" Hayley says that they're with a friend of hers who handles rescue dogs. She says they can stay there until they find new homes.

Lucy says, "A couple of David's friends say they can each take on one dog, but I was hoping we can find someone who will take both of them. I'm thinking that, if we split them up, it might be harder on them."

"Do you remember George Weatherby, Tess? He's the one who's talking like he might take both of them back to Houston with him, depending on David's health," adds Hayley.

Tess asks, "Did you guys call Jennifer to see what she can do for him?" Lucy says that they have and that they should get an answer later today.

They gather a few things, place them by the front door, and take turns taking them out to Hayley's SUV. In the meantime, her friend with the pickup truck shows up. They load the dresser into it, and Lucy gives him directions to her house.

Tess takes one last look around the house. Her mother bought it when she divorced her dad, because she didn't want to try and keep up with the larger house where Tess grew up. This little house had quite a few Thanksgivings and Christmases and, unfortunately, they were all very smoky! Tess's mom would always have her sister Faye over to celebrate, with the two of them smoking. Then Carrey and David had been allowed to smoke, and they also had cousins there. They all seemed to smoke. So the house always had a cloud of cigarette smoke in it.

There was laughter, and there were tears, but there was still love—even as dysfunctional as it was. Tess is kind of glad she doesn't ever have to go back in that house again. They finish loading the SUV and Tess locks the house back up, and Tess turns her back on the house and walks away.

The next day, an ambulance takes David to an assisted living center where the nurses say he will finish out his life. Tess gets incredibly sad. She has known it was really bad, but the full reality hadn't dawned on her.

The assisted living center or "old folks home," as some people call it, is the place no one wants to be, because it means you have lost your independence. You can no longer take for granted getting up, taking a shower, getting dressed, making breakfast, and going about your day. Maybe you'd like to drive by the store to pick up groceries or something. You cannot do that anymore.

Your life as you know it is over. There's just a bed, whoever comes by to visit, and whatever the cafeteria is serving everyone. The big deal for the day is whether or not you can see out the window.

Once David arrives, they settle him in, and then Hospice comes to visit. They determine that he will be under Hospice care and that they will make sure, as his disease gets worse, that he will not be in any pain.

Tess hears their diagnosis of her brother, but it doesn't really sink in. It just kind of hangs there in midair. They told her that he had, at most, two or three months to live, and that it's going to get worse. Since his stroke left him with no feeling on his left side, he can't take care of himself in any way.

David asked Hospice for a DNR form, because he does not want to just endure life. He wants to enjoy it. He seems to understand what is going on and doesn't seem afraid of it.

Tess tells him that she has to go back to California, but she will be back as soon as she can. He holds her hands in his and says, "I love you, Tess, and I really appreciate you coming and helping me out. Will you promise to be back, because I want to see you again?" Tess starts to cry and can only nod her head while she tries to hold back her tears. She manages to tell him that she will be back in two weeks.

The flight home seems very long, and she's anxious to pick up Bear from her neighbor who's more than happy to "puppy sit" anytime. Once she gets home, walks Bear, and finally sits down on her own couch, where she can be still for a moment, it really sinks in that, soon, she would not have her brother around anymore.

The next day, she calls Courtney to see if she has new events and Courtney asks her how it went. All at once it comes pouring out, and Tess doesn't stop until she has told her everything that she could remember. Then there's a silence for about ten seconds, and Courtney finally says, "Breathe."

After another pause, Tess finally says, "I think I need to work to get this off my mind, because if I just sit here and think about nothing more than this, I'm going to go crazy! Plus, I need to make some money so I can afford to fly back to see him in two weeks. That's also on my mind."

When the two weeks fly by, Tess makes plans for another trip to see David. She's been in touch with Hospice and her friends Hayley and Lucy. And she's been calling the nurse's station at Carrollwood, where David has been staying. There's a lot of contact, but there is no new information, meaning that nothing has really changed.

Tess spends three days there and, on the first day, runs into Carrey. This is something she's dreaded since she first saw David, but it was inevitable. She shows up at David's room while Tess is there, and it's awkward and uncomfortable. Carrey almost seems startled to see Tess and says, "Hey, Tess, how are you?"

Tess responds saying, "As good as could be expected." Tess then asks in return how she's doing.

David interrupts, asking, "Is there any way I could get a hamburger smuggled in here?"

With that, they both laugh, and Tess says, "If you're really hungry for one, David, I would be happy to go out and get you one. Do you have anywhere special in mind?"

David says, "I think I would love one from George's, if that isn't too much to ask."

Tess considers it a break from the uncomfortable situation in David's room. She makes a call on her cell phone to Hayley, telling her that Carrey is there and that she's really glad that David decided he wants a hamburger, so that she could get out away from Carrey.

Hayley tells her that David has said, some time ago, that back taxes are owed on their mother's house, but Hayley thinks she may have a way to help. She has a friend who buys small houses and turns them, and he's interested in their mom's house. If they can agree on a price, he will buy it and pay off the back taxes, and that will pay for David's expenses.

Tess says, "That's great, but what about Carrey? She has to sign off on it too, and she's going to want a third of the money. I know David doesn't think she deserves it, and neither do I. She took all of mom's money and sold anything of value when mom died, and she doesn't deserve any of this money."

Hayley says," Greg has an idea, and I think you should hear him out." "OK, that's the least I can do, I guess. Can you get me his number, and I'll try and arrange something."

Tess arrives back at Carrollwood, and they tell her that David just got his morphine. He is starting to fade, but he sees her and tries to look attentive, so he can try and eat that "double-double" from George's. He gets about three bites down, then starts going into la-la land. He pushes the tray away and lies back into his pillow again, with his eyes half closing.

The weekend flies by, and there are a few moments, here and there, when Tess sees the David she knows and loves. Then there is the rest of the time, when he looks like a shell of the man she used to know.

The next thing she knows, it's time for her to fly back home. She's having a long talk with Jennifer about the situation, and she breaks down with the thought that she won't be able to afford to come back more than one more time. Jennifer tells her, "Tess, Mark and I were talking about your situation. We have a bunch of frequent flyer miles that we're not going to use, and we want to buy you a couple of flights to come and see your brother."

Hearing that, Tess is so touched by their generosity that she just cries. She tells them she has never realized there are such giving people in the world, and she will always remember their kindness. Jennifer continues, "You don't realize it, but you were there for me when I really needed someone. It was quite a few years ago, but you were there for me, and I've never forgotten it."

Later that night, when Tess is trying to sleep, she lies in bed and thinks of everything that's going on. She feels overwhelmed and numb, all at the same time. The same thoughts keep rolling around in her head. How is she going to solve paying for David's care and probably his funeral? And how lucky she is that her friends care and do so much for her? After looking at the clock almost every hour, she finally falls asleep between two and three. She gets up at seven and flies back home.

The next two visits get harder and harder, and each time, when it's time to leave, she feels her heart breaking more and more.

David has now been in Carrollwood for three months and is barely hanging on. The hospice nurses try to be realistic, providing facts that are as accurate as possible. They even tell Tess how to check his feet for signs that he is close to passing on.

David has told Tess, on her second visit, that he wants to be cremated when the time comes, and he wants his ashes scattered at sea near San Diego where he was born. Tess has told him that she has Mom's ashes, and asked whether it would be right to scatter both at the same time. He loved it. She said she would take care of everything for him, when the house is sold. His arrangements have been made in advance so there won't be any issues.

Tess is sitting in the only chair in David's room, because she's tired, worn out and emotionally drained. The previous day was all spent taking care of cremation arrangements with the local funeral home and handling all the documents that Carrollwood needs to take care of David when the time comes.

Carrey and a couple of his old friends are standing beside his bed. They are talking to each other because he's really groggy, fading in and out. Tess had been alone with him this morning and told him that he could let go anytime he wanted. She would be here and would always love him. He simply nodded like he understood.

These days, he can't really talk, because his vocal chords have been pretty ravaged by the cancer. If he can't whisper what he wants, he tries to write it down. When he wants to write, whoever is close to him tends to grab the "sign in" book that Jennifer brought a few weeks ago, and David scribbles something on one of the back pages.

They are having a chat about nothing, really, when he comes around and starts to whisper, "Write, write..." They grab the book, and he writes down "waiting for Tess." He tries to say it, but it's just an indecipherable whisper. But they understand him, and they look over at Tess, motioning for her to come to the edge of the bed. They tell David, "Tess is right here!"

Tess is standing by David, wondering what he needs from her. He reaches for her hand and just whispers, "Tess, I love you" and "Thanks." It's late on Sunday, and Tess is going to have to leave and go back to L.A. soon. She's wondering if that's his way to acknowledge her before she leaves. But he's still hanging on.

The time comes, and she reluctantly says good-bye. It's just the two of them, and Tess sits on the side of his bed and tells him softly how important he is to her. How she always remembers growing up together and all the things they used to do as kids—and all the trouble they used to get into together.

He has always been her partner in crime. She will always remember what a good person he is and how much he means to her. Because he's not awake much, due to the heavy doses of morphine, Tess manages to get him to recognize what she's trying to say to him. That is, he can let go anytime he wants. She wants him not to be in pain any longer, and the only way that will happen is if he lets go.

She's afraid that this is the last time she will ever see him, and suddenly she feels so heavy. And the goodbye is so final.

She flies home, and three days later, as she's getting ready to do some work for Courtney—setting up a catering job she has—the phone rings at six forty-five in the morning. When it rings, it makes her jump. She rushes to the phone, all the while thinking, the phone never rings that early in the morning, unless there is a death…

She picks up the phone with dread, and her worst fear comes true. The voice says, "Tess? This is Julie, David's hospice nurse. I'm saddened to tell you that we lost David this morning, at 4:10 a.m. our time." All Tess can do is stand there speechless.

Julie waits a minute, then asks, "Tess are you OK?"

Seconds seem like hours, and Tess finally says, "Was he alone?" Julie tells her that a nurse was with him. She had just gone in to check on him, because she had a feeling that he wasn't doing so well, and he went out peacefully."

Tess starts crying and thanks Julie for all her help and for keeping her informed. She says she doesn't really know what else to say, so she's quiet.

Julie finally says, "Tess please let me know if you need anything from me. And again, I'm truly sorry for your loss. I know David loved you very much."

Tess hangs up the phone and turns around to see Bear. He's sitting there, looking at her. She walks over and hugs him, and he just sits and doesn't try to wiggle away like he sometimes does. It's like he knows she needs him. Once she lets him go, he just lies down and looks at her for a moment and then closes his eyes.

Tess walks over to the sofa and sits down. She stares out the window for a long minute, then starts crying. She buries her head in her hands and just sobs. After a while, she calls Courtney and tells her what has happened. She stands up, goes back to the bedroom, and goes back to bed until Bear wakes her up again to go for a walk. For weeks, she only seems to be going through the motions.

She writes, almost every night, about seeing David die and what he said to her when they were alone. She's haunted by the time he turned to her, with tears in his eyes, and whispered, "I don't want to die, Tess." There was nothing she could say in return, because she knew he didn't have long.

She's thankful that she did get to spend that time, and they did reconnect. She was able to be there for him when he needed her most. And she was grateful.

Bear is lying on the floor at her feet, snoring. She rubs his back with the sole of her foot, while looking for jobs again on her laptop and sipping a cup of coffee. She finds a few ads and responds to them. After checking them all, she gets another cup of coffee.

Bear raises his head with the activity and then lays it back down again. She slides the notebook aside after a while, and pulls out a letter-size legal pad. "Dear Mom," she starts writing.

> Dear Mom,
>
> I know I have told you before how it's so hard at times to think that you're really gone. I still find myself, from time to time, reaching for the phone to try and call you. And I catch myself, and I feel that hole you left.

I'm still so thankful that we got much closer before you died, and I got to know what you were like when you were younger. I never realized that we had never talked about it before. It did seem ironic that we were a lot alike, and it explains a lot to me about why you treated me the way you did sometimes. But all I seem to know is that I miss you so much.

I'm looking for another job, and I think I'm going to accept Courtney's offer to work for her catering company, at least for a while. She said it's getting so much busier these days, and she's working for some pretty cool events.

Bear and I are taking longer walks these days. He seems to understand when I get so sad. I will find myself crying, just thinking about you and all the other changes—not being able to talk to Dad before he died, losing Uncle C, and breaking up with Greg, then your death and now David's death.

It just feels so overwhelming at times. Bear comes over and starts licking my face and distracts me enough to pull me out of the pit I find myself in, at times. I kept hoping that moving to California again would give me less reminders of you all. And that part has worked most of the time, but there's no comfort at times.

Thank God, Courtney and her family live here. Otherwise I don't know what I would do. She's more of a sister than Carrey ever was, and I would never have to question whether to trust her. She would never sell me down the river. She's the one ray of sunshine in my life, besides Bear of course.

You know I have often thought that, if Bear could talk, everything would be perfect. He can't—but I still understand him, and he seems to understand me. He's now sticking his nose in my arm, because he wants to go for a walk, so I'll mail this letter. I hope that tonight I can get some sleep.

Watch for David, because he is there somewhere.

I love you, Mom, and miss you still.

Me

Tess puts the letter in the envelope, puts a stamp on it, and addresses it to: Mom in Heaven.

She hooks up Bear's leash to his collar, grabs her keys, and heads out the door. They walk to the mailbox and stop so that Tess can drop off the letter, then continue on. She looks up to the sky, when the metal mailbox door slams shut, without even realizing it.

The sky is blue—again. She smiles thinking, how could blue skies ever get boring? It's gorgeous weather. Only low eighties during the day and cool enough at night to need a sweater. Just perfect.

When they get back from the walk, Tess calls Courtney's number. "Hey, girl, are you busy?"

"Never too busy for you. What's up?"

"Remember when you told me you might need help with a few of the upcoming events you have booked?"

"Yeah, and I still do. Do you want to do some work with me?"

"I sure would appreciate it. When is the next event?"

"I knew you were going to ask that, and I'm not at my desk. Hold on a second, while I get back there and double-check the calendar. In the meantime, when are you going to come over—and bring Bear of course? Oh yeah, here we go. Lemme see now...I have a big board meeting scheduled for a lunch to be catered, and I can use you then. That happens next Wednesday. Can I count on you?"

"That would be great. Would you e-mail me the details, and I can print them and let you know if I have any questions."

"That's a deal. So now, what are you and Bear doing tomorrow? Why don't you guys come over in the morning. We can hang out and have some lunch. You can go with me to pick up Natalie and then see how tired we are."

"Actually, that sound like fun. Why don't I call you in the morning and see how early we want to make it."

"Sounds like a plan. I guess I'll talk to you in the morning then. Bye, Tess"

"Talk to you tomorrow, Courtney."

Tess hangs up and sits back looking at Bear. "Well, big guy, are you up for seeing Maya and Courtney tomorrow? Well, if I didn't know better, I'd think you started smiling when I mentioned Maya! OK boy, let's go for the last walk of the night."

With that, she gets up and attaches the leash to Bear's collar. Bear walks to the door and stands there wagging his tail, while Tess grabs her keys and her cell phone. When they get outside the building, it's quiet, with just a couple of cars on the road. Tess thinks that, tomorrow, she'll bring her iPod, so she can listen to music. Maybe she'll take Bear on a longer walk that way.

The next day, Tess sits at Courtney's kitchen counter as Courtney pours her a cup of coffee. The two dogs have been put in the backyard to play. Courtney leans up against the opposite side of the counter and asks Tess how she's really doing. Tess says OK, and that she'll probably feel better once she's working and bringing in some money.

Courtney says that sounds good to her too, because she can use the help. Tess confides that the job market really sucks, and she's having a hard time looking for a new job. "I'm beginning to think that it's impossible to find a real full-time job. You know, I've been using Jobslist for as long as it's been around. All they seem to have, these days, are jobs that are bogus!

"I mean, every job I apply for wants you to join a membership to some kind of website, so they can get a copy of your credit report—which they say they have to have to schedule an interview. And no matter what their excuse, it's always bogus, and the company is bogus, and the job, of course, is bogus. So it's all depressing!"

"Geez, Tess, I didn't realize there was so much bullshit involved. I'm really glad that you're helping me though. Does that help any? "

"You know it does. It keeps me from thinking I'm crazy. And besides, things always have a way of coming around full circle—don't they?"

"I'm a witness to that. So yeah, you can't give up. Besides I won't let you."

"Well, let's get to work doing some arranging for this event. It really looks like they want it to be the big event for this year," says Courtney. Courtney and Tess walk in the garage door that leads to the great room in Courtney's house. They are chatting back and forth about plans they need to make to get the ball rolling on this project.

"I know the event after this one is an opening at a museum. It will be really busy and take two weeks of preproduction to get the space set up correctly. They didn't even know they were going to have a show for this artist until a couple of days ago.

"Evidently he's hard to get to commit. The owner of the gallery is having the initial showing at the Santa Monica Museum of Art and is really excited. It's a very important show, and she wants to do everything she can to make sure it's first rate, because the collection is bringing in big investors and collectors, as well as important art critics. So, Tess. This event could really put me on the map and bring in lots more customers. This could really make people stand up and notice."

"Well, Courtney, I know you, and you won't do anything but the very best. What can I do to help? There's only one thing that's questionable for me. In October, I'm going to San Diego and scatter my mom's and

David's ashes. They have it all set up, and it will be really nice to let them go."

"What date was it that you set it up? "

"October ninth. It was David's birthday."

"Oh no! That's the date of the opening. We have a couple of months to get everything planned. When will you have to leave to get to San Diego in time? "

"Well we're going to scatter them at sunset. They want to get away from the pier a good hour before sunset, so we have enough time to get to the spot that we're assigned. So I could help until I have to leave, and that would be around four or half past four or so. It will take about an hour to get down there and find the boat. But I could help you until then. Would that work for you?"

Courtney sighs. "It would help me so much if you could. I wish I could go with you, but obviously that won't be an option now. Are you going to be OK to go by yourself? Would you like to take Brad or Natalie?"

"That's such a sweet offer, but no. I think I have this one. The lady arranging everything will be there, and they have a small crew on the boat. From what I understand, they are really supportive. But I may not feel that way later, so I'll call if I need to talk. You know me better than I know myself."

"OK then. I'll need your help from the beginning, and we need to go to the gallery to check it out and make sure that the setup—and what they have in mind—are going to work together. The artist paints large canvases. I don't even know his name. We'll get all the details when we show up for the first meeting in two days. So why don't you plan on being here around eleven. We'll go to the gallery together, and you can help me game plan, OK?"

"That's a deal. I'll see you then. Have a good night, and tell Brad and Natalie, hi."

"I'll do that, and see you then. Bye!"

Together, they make the long drive from Courtney's house in Calabasas to the museum, which has a prime address and a wonderful open space that seems large and cavernous. On the drive, they talk about David. Courtney says, "You know you never gave me details of those trips you made to Waco, when you found out that he was sick. I didn't want to push you then, but how are you feeling about all of that now?"

Tess looks at Courtney with a sad smile, "I hope you know how much I appreciate you guys taking care of Bear when I made those trips. It was such a weird time, first finding out that he was sick, and then less than a week later finding out he's had a stroke and is in the hospital. You know he was two years younger than me, and I never considered that he would get sick like that. He seemed to go downhill so quickly."

"Yeah, it started in July, because that was when you made the first trip back for a few days. When you came back, I could tell it was not a good situation."

Tess looks out the window and continues. "Yeah, he was standing there talking to his neighbor who lived across the street, and he just collapsed. I don't think he really knew what hit him. He certainly wasn't prepared for it, and I don't think anyone can be ready for that kind of thing. It was so sad to see him like that."

Courtney straightens up in her seat, gives her head a shake, and takes a deep breath. "I remember that picture you showed me of all of you, when David was in the assisted living center. When was that taken?"

Tess says, "That was on my second trip there. After the first trip, Jennifer, Hayley, Lucy, and I arranged most of everything over the phone. They even helped him get me his power of attorney, so when Carrey showed up she couldn't do anything. David was at least coherent enough to make sure we weren't going to have any problems.

"I thought it was great luck, as well, that the girls were so helpful, going through the house with me before she hit town. We saw first-hand how he'd been living in mom's old house. The house seemed much smaller and colder, and it felt sad. They also knew someone who would buy the house from us, because he liked to buy property that needs to be fixed up and flipped.

"David hardly had anything in savings to pay for his room at the center. So selling the house seemed like the only way to take care of him and maybe get a little money to help with flight costs for me. Then we found out that Carrey had to sign off too, so she had to get a split of the money. She finally gave in, after a short fight against the idea. She insisted we could get more money, of course."

Tess looks back out the window and continues. "Yeah, it got so bad for David—the pain and, I think, the reality that he would never be able to leave there—that they were giving him large amounts of morphine. He would drift in and out of consciousness. Lucy brought him guest books that people signed in when they came to visit, and he was passed out. I would look through those books and read what they said, and it was comforting. Anyway, he got so thin, and he lost so much hair. I thought I could handle most of it, until one time we were sitting there, just the two of us, and he tells me 'I don't want to die,' and I felt my heart break."

After that last revelation, Tess sits quietly for most of the rest of the trip. When they get close to the museum, they start chatting again about the meeting.

They arrive at the venue for the event, and it turns out it's a beautiful large building. They walk in and find Audrey, who is their contact for making all the arrangements. One of the collections now showing includes sculptures and huge handmade weavings that are all really beautiful.

Tess looks around at the beauty, while following closely behind Courtney. She tries hard not to look like she's amazed at huge pieces.

Courtney walks up to the office door and knocks. A polished looking woman answers, and Courtney extends her hand and introduces herself. "So lovely to meet you Courtney, I'm Audrey, the coordinator for the event and owner of the Basil Grey Gallery. This event will move from the Santa Monica Museum of Art to my gallery after four weeks. Why don't you both come in and sit down, and we'll go over a few items that I think you need to know. Then you can put together your proposal, and we'll go from there. How does that sound?"

"I love working with people who know what they want and know how to ask for it," Courtney whispers to Tess.

They all sit down around a conference table that's set up with paper and pens, water, and a bowl of fruit. Audrey starts the meeting by handing out a bio of the artist and a few pictures of his last collection. She's waving her arms in sweeping gestures, while she describes how the event needs to come off as classy and irreverently elegant. There needs to be a lot of planning to make this one great, and she has a very nice budget to work with.

"Let me show you the area you have to work with, and we can discuss any limitations of the space," says Audrey as she stands back up, ready to walk Courtney and Tess out of the office.

While Audrey leads Courtney to a wing of the museum, Tess wanders in front of a very large abstract sculpture. She tries looking at it several different ways and cannot make anything out of it. She looks at the title and wonders how much it's worth.

Tess catches up with Courtney and Audrey, hearing Audrey explain further: "The opening will take up the entire south wing of the museum, and basically, all the important people in the world will be invited.

"Because the collection will be moved to my gallery to handle the sales, I have been fortunate enough to be chosen to organize the event. Oh, did I mention that, if all goes as well as expected, I'll want you to cater and organize another smaller-scale event, when the collection is transferred to my gallery? I hope you're interested in doing that one, if things go well."

"I hope they go as planned, because I think a second event would be lovely. Thank you."

Audrey smiles, and says "OK, then let's get started."

She leads Courtney and Tess to the middle of the first room and points at one of the corners, "Since the collection is quite large in scale, I thought we would have them hanging by wires from the ceiling. There should be a pattern, so the room has a flow, and your walk through is a sort of journey. We will have trees and large plantersaccenting the way, and I think we'll have a small cocktail area in the front, with a much larger area back there. What's your take on staff with roving appetizer trays?"

"I believe it can be done with little intrusion, with staff all in black with large white china trays, of course wearing gloves."

Audrey touches Courtney's arm and exclaims, "Oh my lord, you're thinking along the same lines I am. Yes, I like that. The only problem in choosing a tone for the event is that I haven't seen the collection yet. I was contacted by the artist's manager, and have been ironing out the details with him. So what I propose, for now, is that we come up with a game plan, and I'll run it by Maxwell, who is Nico's manager, and get him to sign off on it. Then I'll confirm it all with you."

Courtney finishes jotting down some notes, then says, "I suggest that we go with the starkness that this setting allows, as far as the staging, and have the appetizers be a subtle punctuation. That way everyone is paying attention to the art and not necessarily the food. The art remains at center stage."

Audrey smiles and nods her head. She walks to another room and motions with her arm, sweeping from one corner to the other. "That area will have the back bar with the dessert table beside it. And I think we should consider a cappuccino machine or two, added to the coffee area. The artist is of Italian descent, so I'm sure that would be a nice addition."

"I can set up a true espresso bar with a few baristas to handle it, and I think it would be great in the open-air area, with the brick walls on either side," adds Courtney.

Audrey smiles again, "That's exactly what I mean. I'm looking forward to hearing all your ideas—and to getting your proposal. Then we'll meet again, say in two weeks, and finalize everything. Just call when you're ready, and we'll schedule an appointment right away. Thanks so much for coming by. I can hardly wait for our next meeting. By the way, we'll have Roger sit in on that one too."

As Courtney and Tess walk back to the car, Courtney says, "I think that went really well! Thanks for coming along and being my second set of eyes and ears."

"No problem. In fact, I've never been to that museum before, and it was really interesting. I never realized that Santa Monica has such old money."

"Yeah, and I'm going to have some of that come my way for this event. This could be a great thing for my little company. The museum will be a terrific setting for what I think we can pull off. With Audrey as our contact, the decision-making should be a lot easier. When people can't edit down what they want or make a firm decision, it gets very trying."

The drive back to Courtney's house is really animated, with ideas thrown around and music playing in the background. Before they run out of ideas, they arrive at Courtney's.

Courtney says, "If you can work that day until three-ish, that would really help me. I think we will be able to start early in the day, and we'll be able to see the paintings before anyone else. Have you ever heard of this artist before…ahhhh…" She fumbles for the bio that Audrey gave her. "Oh yeah, Nico Moratelli? Have you ever heard of him?"

"Nope. But then again, I'm not big in the 'art world' either! Sorry, I can't help you there."

They go inside, walk back to the kitchen, and sit down. Courtney picks up the artist's bio and looks for a picture. "There's no picture of the guy, so what would that make you think?"

Tess leans over and glances at it. "I wonder if he looks like the typical artist, or if he just wants to be anonymous? So what does it say about him? Does it give any details?"

Courtney starts reading and laughs, saying, "It only says that he had another collection, and it sold really well, and that he is local, basically. No real details."

"Oh well, I always thought that artists are usually high-maintenance. Why would I want to be with someone who can only think of himself?"

Then they start discussing all the details that they need to cover to make the reception the most impressive gallery showing that anyone has been to in years. They cover the food ideas, presentation, staff size, the markets where they can get flowers and plants, and all the ingredients they're going to need. They have a couple of chefs in mind for different parts of the food presentation. Courtney then says she knows a couple of indoor landscapers she can use for the trees, planters, and whatever else they need—since they will probably have a big budget for this one.

As they discuss all this information and make the lists, their dogs are wandering in and out the back door. They play for a while in the backyard, then run inside for water and an extra pat on the head.

Courtney suddenly looks up. They have to pick up Natalie at school. So they jump up and close the back door, hustle the dogs into the car, and rush off to pick up Natalie.

They get there in enough time to sit at the light at the turnoff for her school.

The line seems long but goes by pretty quickly. They're still talking about the arrangements when they get to the school, and Natalie strolls up with one of her friends who wants to see the dogs. The girls giggle, then Natalie says good-bye to her friend and jumps in the backseat, grinning from ear to ear.

"Did you have a good day, Natalie?" asks Courtney.

"Yeah, Mom, it was great day. Got a B-plus on that math test we studied for last night."

They all chat on the way back to the house. After pulling into the garage, they get the dogs out and go inside.

Courtney asks Natalie, "Do you have much homework tonight, or can we have an early dinner? I'm making spaghetti tonight, so you can stay and have dinner with us, if you don't have something that you have to do…" With that Courtney trails off, looking at Natalie to support what she's saying, directing the invitation to Tess.

Natalie perks up and grins, saying "Yeah, Tess please stay for dinner. Dad won't be home for a while, and we can all hang out. Pleeeeaassse?"

"You're so persuasive. Of course I'll stay for dinner. Besides, Bear doesn't look like he's ready to go home yet either!"

"*Yay!* We won!! I'm going to put my stuff up and change clothes. I'll be back out in a minute." And with that, Natalie walks toward her room with both dogs following."

Courtney laughs, looks at Tess, and shakes her head.

"She always seems like such an adult in a little child's body. Do you see it?" Tess asks Courtney. "Or are you so accustomed to it?"

"Yeah, she's pretty cool. And you know she's always seemed that way, such an old soul."

The evening rambles on, and the three of them laugh and slurp "sketti," along with salad and garlic bread. Then they all help clean up the kitchen, leaving out a plate for Brad when he gets home. They sit around the kitchen island and laugh and talk for a while longer, then Tess says that she needs to head home.

They walk her outside to her Jeep and are saying their goodbyes when Brad pulls up. He parks his car, then walks over to say "hi and bye" to Tess, while giving Courtney a hug and kiss hello.

Tess gets Bear in the back seat, climbs in the driver's seat, and tells Courtney to call her when she gets up tomorrow. Then they can make the final decisions for the presentation that Courtney has to give to Audrey, so they can get the first half of the money and start making the big plans.

In the meantime, Brad and Natalie walk Maya back into the house. Tess drives away, heading home.

Tess is listening to her song, which happens to be just about any song by Bob Schneider. Right now, the favorite is "Changing My Mind." Her thoughts drift away, thinking it was a pretty good day.

Chapter Six

"What am I doing?" thinks Nico as he drags himself out of bed after only three hours of sleep. "What in the hell am I doing?"

He wanders over to the kitchen counter to make some coffee before he showers, mumbling to himself the entire time. "I'm too old for this! I can't do the staying up for all hours and get by for a full day."

He stops in front of the canvas that had him up half the night and sighs. What he sees before him is a combination of love and pain, with a dose of hope thrown into the mix. It's five feet high and four feet across, with images that spark the imagination with their bold strong colors. The shapes are like animal shapes in the clouds. And just like those images, which change as you look at them, this painting appears to move with the light but actually doesn't.

"Who *are* you?" He looks at the letter one last time, folds it, and puts it in the wooden box with the others. After a long pause, he smiles and mumbles, "And do you have any idea what your words have been doing to me?" He stares at his work while putting his shirt on and tucking it in his pants.

Then he sits while he puts on brown, scruffy short boots, the kind that change how people walk. Getting up, he strides to the bathroom, brushes his teeth, and finger-combs his hair. He grabs a jacket that's draped over the back of a chair and looks around to make sure he has what he needs.

It doesn't occur to him that the jacket looks like he slept in it. His overall appearance is one of someone concerned with more important things, something more otherworldly. Most people do not question his appearance, because it's just part of him. They are all accustomed to it, or get that way quickly.

It's just him.

He heads toward the front door, picking up his thermal mug of coffee and his keys, and flips off the light switch. He looks back and sees his iPod sitting on the dining room table. Walking back quickly to pick it up, he starts singing to himself.

His pace matches the song in his head, and he feels like he's on the right path and hopes it stays that way for a while. Driving to work, he starts practicing the answers he'll use when people ask him why he's still sorting letters, when he's about to have a showing and should be more positive about his future.

"How could you possibly want to do such manual labor, when you don't really need to any longer?" He hears the arguments against his actions playing out in his head and responds while still by himself in the car. He's afraid he won't sound genuine enough or honest enough in his response. There's no way he is going to give up the possibility of finding more letters, so he's really putting the pressure on himself to pull this off.

This has become way too important to him. He has *got* to make sure that he gets them all—or at least as many as possible. At some point, they're going to stop, or he won't be able to work in the dead letter office, and he wants to make sure he has as many as possible.

He's even dreaming about her, and every dream is much the same: He is approaching her from behind in a park, and when he reaches his hand out and touches her shoulder, she disappears right before his eyes. She's like a ghost and just dissolves away. He wakes up suddenly, after this happens, and feels startled that he has never gotten to see a face or hear her voice. She's gone into thin air just before her secret is revealed to him. With this realization, he lets go of a long wistful sigh.

Walking to the building doors, he straightens up a bit and takes a deep breath, bracing himself for running into someone who will ask him about his near-obsession with manually sorting the dead letters.

Fortunately for him, all anyone wants to say this morning is hello, and for that he's grateful. He takes the elevator to the basement, goes into the room, and starts in. Because they are getting closer to Easter and the spring holidays, there are a few letters addressed to the Easter bunny and a couple of other imaginative characters. It makes for an interesting morning. Before he realizes, it's lunchtime, and then the afternoon goes just as quickly.

When his quitting time is close, he realizes that there may not be a letter today, and he's disappointed. But not so disappointed that he won't show up again tomorrow. A couple of coworkers are off to the side, talking, as he exits, and they both chime in: "Good night! See you tomorrow."

He responds in kind and keeps smiling all the way to the parking lot. He sits down and looks out the front windshield. There's a wonderful sunset happening, and he almost didn't notice, he was so wrapped up in thought.

On the way home, he sings along with Bob Schneider's "40 Dogs (Like Romeo and Juliet)," swaying his head from side to side, in slow motion, like a bobblehead doll. He doesn't mind all the traffic and just lets his mind wander to the painting he started last night. Seeing shapes and color in his imagination, he's letting his thoughts drift. And he finds himself wondering, once again, who this person is and starts comparing himself to a Peeping Tom. Even though he's uncomfortable with the idea that he reads about this woman's innermost thoughts, fears, and joys, he wants to see more—wants to know more.

Out of nowhere it seems, he gets hunger pangs. He doesn't want to take the time to cook and is not really in the mood for fast food. He smiles to himself and places a call on his cell. He calls his mama's restaurant and places an order to go—Portobello ravioli with extra garlic bread and, of course, they make sure a salad is thrown in the bag. Nico grew up in front of most of the people that work for his mama and considers a lot of them to be like great aunts and uncles.

Then he gets sidetracked again and remembers that he needs to call his manager, Maxwell, and find out what details have been decided for his showing and when it's being set up. The last he heard, the opening was less than six weeks away, and he wants to make sure he's ready for it.

This one is more important than the first one. There are so many more expectations this time, and he's really feeling the pressure. The only good thing is: he feels like this showing will be better because of his inspiration.

There are still times when he wishes he knew who to thank, but he may never know that. He thinks to himself, there's no way to thank her because she would probably never understand why he needs the private observations and notations of her pain and her personal growth that he sees revealed in each new letter.

Maybe someday he can give back—somehow. This is the convoluted thinking he goes back to so that his conscience is relieved. He knows he must just go forward and make the best of what's going on and try not to feel so guilty. He feels like he's using her, and he is, in a weird way.

He wonders, what she would think if she saw what her letters inspired? Would she recognize them? Would they strike a chord in her, or would she walk right by them never knowing or realizing what they are? He smiles to himself.

He gets to his place, arms loaded with his dinner, his satchel, and the bottle of wine he grabbed on the way out of the restaurant. Once inside, he drops everything on the kitchen counter and spins around with a purpose in mind. He strides over to the stereo, puts on music, and starts dancing on the way back to the kitchen. Opening the wine and pulling the food out of the bag, he starts singing along. "We've got to carry each other, carry each other..."

He finds himself swaying to the music while fixing himself a plate of food and pouring a glass of wine. He takes his food over to the table where most of his paintings are lined up against the wall. He quickly eats while looking around the room at his work and wonders if it will be enough—and if it will be good enough.

Shaking his head, he talks to himself. "I cannot start to doubt this thing. I just need to go on and continue. Good or bad, it's the best I can do at this point, and I've got to let it ride."

He eats his dinner, contemplating what he will work on tonight, because he did not get a new letter today. But he remembers a past letter with a page describing a beautiful day she spent hiking with her dog, Bear.

That excerpt seems to ring out differently than the rest of the letter. He doesn't know if it's because it's about her dog, or if she's starting to feel differently about her life.

Nodding his head in agreement with himself, he decides he will bring that to life. With about half his dinner eaten, he takes everything back to the kitchen and puts it away in a hurry, so he can get to work.

Then he cranks up the stereo and starts dancing around the room, while he places a new canvas on the rack. He grabs a pencil and starts sketching what he sees in his head—the mental visualization of a hike in the hills, with tall dried grasses and a small pathway, created by man or animals, that leads to the top of a hill. The sun is out and bright and not one cloud. The rough-looking trees that are encroaching on the pathway have been neglected and overgrown, just like all the weeds and grasses that almost cover the path.

He feels like he has seen this kind of area before in real life, but he doesn't remember where. It just seems so familiar that the painting he's creating seems like something from his memory, rather than something he has only seen in his mind, conjured up from someone else's words. He doesn't take the time to marvel at how serendipitous it all seems. She is providing so much imagery to him, and it seems like she's becoming a ghost of a companion to him.

He's so wrapped up in expressing his reactions that he's starting not to notice how much he has needed this to happen. It's not that he's taking the letters for granted, but that he's accepting and not fighting his reaction to them.

As old as he is, surely he should have had his heart broken a couple of times by now—and possibly be in a solid committed relationship. Instead, he's a loner and seemingly not concerned by it.

He has always seemed to be that way. He's never had a dog or a cat, and he's starting to wonder what Bear would look like. Maybe that might be the key to finding her somehow.

His mind is blank while he works. Then suddenly he pauses and starts thinking about how she describes going down to the beach and taking her dog.

He remembers that she never mentions the beach by name, but she does take Bear and sits and reads or watches people go by. She does mention being able to see a pier, and there are only a couple of beaches that allow dogs where you have a pier in the view.

Maybe he should go to the beach on Saturday. He starts mulling the idea. How many females with a large dog could there be on the beach? There might not be that many, and he could strike up a conversation and see if something stands out. Maybe he could figure out who she is. But then what would he do? He can't say, "I read your letters, and I'm sorry" or "I can appreciate your pain and what you have gone through…"

Nope, none of that would do.

He thinks, "If that was done to me, I don't think I could be generous enough to understand, and forgiveness would be hard to imagine. But if I don't try something, the picture will always be incomplete."

With that, he walks into the kitchen and pours himself another glass of wine.

He takes a sip as he walks back toward the canvas and stares at it for a minute. He sets his glass on a table that's close, picks up his brush again, dabs it in paint, and starts again, turning his head at an angle as if looking at the canvas differently.

Nico continues while letting his mind drift, occasionally singing along with familiar parts of the song playing in the background. He pauses, here and there, only to step back and look at the entire canvas. Then he takes a definitive step forward to work on a part that has caught his eye and needs some attention.

This little dance he's doing unconsciously goes on for hours, and the next thing he realizes, it's 3:25 a.m., and he has to get some sleep. The silver lining is that tomorrow is Friday. But for now, the most pressing thing is Friday morning and getting to work—and not looking like he has pulled another all-nighter! When people notice at the post office, they give him a hard time, and he really doesn't want to call that kind of attention to himself right now.

So he turns off the lights and gets undressed and into bed. It doesn't take more than two minutes for him to be sound asleep.

Later that morning, when the alarm goes off, he does the same routine as always. He jumps out of bed and pulls on his pants, then his boots. He does his same bathroom routine, finishing with finger-combing his hair, putting on his wrinkled jacket, grabbing his coffee, and getting out the door in record time.

He seems preoccupied driving to work and doesn't sing along with the music playing in the car. His mind is elsewhere. He remembers thinking he should try and figure out which beach "she" goes to with her dog. Her dog...that may be the key.

He'll go through the letters tonight and see if he can find any other clues he has missed about the dog. Bear was his name, and he's a big dog.

He gets to work and sees only a few people on his way downstairs, then starts sorting letters. The morning flies by, and after he goes to lunch, he comes back and settles in once again.

Just as the afternoon seems to bring a lull in his energy, he spots another letter from her to her mother. His whole body tenses up. He looks around to make sure no one can see him, and then stuffs it in his pocket.

At this point, his whole demeanor changes, not only with better posture but a more positive tone. He can hardly wait to get the letter home and see what it says. Even though it's Friday, he has decided he will get out all the letters and see what they say about Bear and the beach. He may not even paint because it's important to find clues.

He can't remember if the letters have said which days she goes to the beach or what she takes with her. It seems like she's said something about getting a new chair to take along. Now if he can just find that letter, maybe she gave more details about it, like a color—something more to go on.

He doesn't realize it, but his afternoon has flown by, and it's time for him to leave. He double-checks his pocket to make sure the letter is safely tucked away and is not showing.

He strides out of the building nodding, here and there, at people saying "Good night" or "Have a nice weekend." Once he gets in his car, he sighs from relief and drives home. He picks up some dim sum and fried rice on his way home.

At home, he gets all the letters out, sits on the floor with his dinner and chopsticks, and goes through the letters one by one, combing them for any clues about the beach or Bear or something else to go on.

He sorts them out by what she seemed interested in at the time and what was bothering her. They are also pretty much in the order of when she mailed them. Guided by the dates, Nico remembers the sequence that she spoke about things, and he picks up three letters that might include details he's forgotten about her going to the beach with Bear.

By the end of the night, he has found a few clues. Not many, but he thinks he has enough to go on. The clues are that Bear is a big dog; the chair she's got is striped; and she goes to the beach two or three times a week when she's not working. She likes to go to parts of the beach that aren't so crowded, and she goes in the morning and leaves early in the afternoon.

So he's going to try and go tomorrow morning. If nothing else, it's good for him to get out and take a good walk along the shore.

Nico thinks that, with those clues, he might have an idea of who he's looking for. But what he doesn't know is how tall she is, what color her hair is, or even the color of her skin or eyes. Is her hair long or short? What color could Bear be? What kind of striped chair would she have? How old is she? Now the doubts are creeping in, and he wonders if he knows just enough to discover too many girls who might fit the same description. Oh well, he's going to try anyway, and maybe he'll get a couple of answers to his burning questions.

He used to hang out at the beach when he was teenager, and then he started working and painting, and that took priority over going to his old haunts. Even before that, he can remember his mother bringing him and his sister to the beach when they were kids. Those days always seemed like perfection. She would pack a picnic lunch, and his favorite aunt would join them, and Sunday afternoon became a time of easiness and bliss for him.

The beach described in her letters sounds familiar to him, and he thinks he knows the general area. At least, he hopes he does. So many questions about her, and he may find out tomorrow.

He puts the letters away and closes the box they are all held in with an odd kind of reverence and respect. He then put all the leftovers and dinner remnants away, realizing that it's much later than he thought.

He's much more tired than he thought as well. He falls asleep before he can run his day back through his mind, dissecting it as he goes.

The next morning is beautiful, and a stray ray of sun shoots through the blind right in his face and wakes him up. Instead of being grumpy, he stretches and starts to smile, then rolls out of bed hoping he hasn't slept too late today. It's important to try his plan today.

Walking into the kitchen to make some coffee, the clock says it's twenty past eight, and he nods his head, thinking it just might work. With coffee brewing, he heads to the bathroom to get cleaned up.

The buzzer for the coffee goes off, and he shuffles in to fill a thermal "go" cup, then sets it on the counter. Nico grabs a large towel, his phone, and keys and heads for the door. He picks up his coffee cup and sunglasses while heading out the door.

He drives to the beach by the pier, where they allow dogs, and finds a parking place. He walks down to the beach and sits on his towel and starts looking around.

There are not many people on the beach this morning, but it's still kind of early. Nico doesn't see any large dogs with anyone, much less "his" lady. He lies back to rethink this situation and winds up dozing off. He's only asleep for about twenty minutes, but it's long enough for the people around him to change. It kind of startles him that it seems so different . What if he has missed her?

He sits up and decides he should probably take a walk down the beach and see if he can spot her. He puts his shirt back on while he walks along the shore, and when he gets to the end of the dog-accessible beach, he turns around and starts walking back the other way.

He looks for a striped beach chair and a female with a large dog. In fact, he still doesn't see any large dogs this morning, which he thinks is kind of weird.

After walking to the other end of the dog-friendly beach, he walks back to the area where he first took his nap. He sits down again and looks down the beach in both directions, then glances at his phone for the time.

This is past the time she says she's at the beach, so maybe he has missed her or maybe she didn't come today. Hearing his stomach growl, he gets up and smiles because he has just decided to go to his mama's house and see if she will feed him.

After a very short drive from the beach to his mama's, he parks a couple of houses away and walks up. Mama Mortatelli's house is in Santa Monica, and could be described as a bungalow. It's a small three-bedroom, one-bath house with an added-on second bathroom and a sunroom facing the garden. She has also changed out the small front porch with one that hugs the corner of the house with a hanging bench seat and some wicker chairs.

Her garden has become her delight, and because she works so much in her restaurant, she has made a deal with the widower who lives across the street. He takes care of her garden for free meals at the restaurant. They don't keep tabs of who does what but use it as an excuse to see and talk to each other. They're nothing more than good friends who understand that they both feel they've had the great loves of their lives and are comfortable with just having a friend.

Mr. Edgar Hightower used to keep to himself, after his wife died in 1976. They never had kids, and he never felt much need to find comfort in the company of other people. He has a lovely garden in his yard with a very nice wrought-iron fence that goes around the parameter.

He created his garden for his wife, Emma, when she first got ill. He wanted her to be able to look out their window and see the garden filled with pink and white flowers that smelled so good. She talked about such a garden when she was a child in England, and used to play hide and seek. The look on her face, every time she spoke of that garden, was translucent joy.

When she died, he focused on her garden, making it a memorial to her and their love. He got enormous joy from working there and making a statement with it.

One morning, he was working contentedly, and he heard a voice say, "How lovely." He looked to see where the voice was coming from, and it was Mama Mortatelli. She was taking her morning walk around the block and was walking by his gate. He slowly got up and walked over to her and said, "Thank you," while taking his floppy canvas hat and glove off to rub his head.

They'd met years earlier but saw no need to be in touch, so each had forgotten the other's name. Once reintroductions were done, Mama Mortatelli, admiring his garden again, said she tried to make some herbs and flowers grow in her garden, but they didn't do half as well as Mr. Hightower's were doing.

"Mr. Hightower…" she began.

"Edgar, please call me Edgar," he said.

"Then please call me Annamaria. I don't have time to have the nice garden I would prefer, because I need to be at the restaurant most of the time. But I would like to extend an invitation for you to come down and have dinner, on me."

Edgar responded, "To what do I owe the honor?"

"Just being neighborly!" she said as she starts walking off. They both smiled as they continued on with their day, not realizing that they had just started a wonderful friendship.

At that time, Edgar's brother lived far from him, but in the same city. He talked all the time about how his life was so wrapped up in his son and his wife and their daughter that he didn't get to see Edgar much. They talked on the phone every two or three days, but that meant that Edgar spent a lot of time on his own. He probably wouldn't have admitted it, but having a friendly face in the neighborhood would be nice, he thought.

One evening around six, Edgar took Annamaria up on her offer and went to Mortatelli's for dinner. She put him at a table she could wait on, just to make sure he enjoyed himself. Right before dessert, Annamaria sat down with him for a minute and asked him if he was enjoying himself.

He said he was.

She asked him if he enjoyed the food.

He said he did.

She got a sly smile and asked him if he could possibly help her with her garden.

He said he didn't know if he could, because he hadn't seen it, but he wouldn't mind trying. Since he knew she was usually off on Saturday afternoons, he said, "Why don't I come by this Saturday, and we can walk around your garden and make a plan. That way, I know what would make you smile when you look at it."

She was delighted. She was amazed because she had really enjoyed Edgar's company, especially when he spoke to her about her garden, because then he had just seemed relaxed. It was nice.

So the plans were hatched for the new garden and for the payback of wonderful homemade Italian food.

They began plans for the garden in February. By the end of March, she and Edgar had the basic layout in place, and he was starting to gather flowers and herbs to put in Annamaria's plant beds.

Annamaria's kids started treating him like one of the family and were glad that Edgar and Annamaria were friends. The staff at the restaurant would tease Annamaria about her gentleman caller. Edgar still had most of his hair, even though it was silver grey, and with his faint British accent, he seemed quite the gentleman. Even with the teasing, they still liked Edgar and accepted him as part of their lives. He was quite a calming influence, no matter who he was around.

As Nico walks up the street to his mama's gate, he sees Mr. Hightower in the side yard, pulling weeds and planting new basil and cilantro in the plant beds by the kitchen door. He waves and catches his eye.

"Good morning, Mr. Hightower. I think the garden is looking really great. Are you pleased so far?"

Edgar responds, "It's looking fairly right, I believe. Your mum is quite appreciative of my work, thank you."

Nico smiles, walks to the front door, and knocks while opening the door. "Mama, are you decent?"

"Nico! I'm in the kitchen. Come on to the back."

Walking into the kitchen, Nico notices his mama at the stove, stirring something in a pot. "Mama, I was missing you and thought I would just come over for a visit. Have you heard from Sera? What is she up to today?"

"Well, it seems that Sera and Roger are going to the farmers' market, and then they said they will come by here. So can you stay a while? I think we're going to cook up an early dinner."

"You and Sera cooking? Of course I'll stay. Maybe we can ask Mr. H if he wants to join us after he gets his plants in the ground." He looks out the side of his eyes, and his mama swacks him with the dishtowel in her hand.

Nico laughs and says, "What was that for?"

"You don't need to read anything into our respectful friendship. He is nothing but a gentleman, and quite honestly he's still madly in love with his dear departed wife."

Nico plops down on the stool in front of the kitchen bar and says, "Honestly Mama I'm just happy you have a friend, and if you have found more than that, well, I wouldn't knock it either."

"That's better. Now would you like to walk out and invite Edgar to dine with us?"

"Edgar, huh? No problem, I'll be right back."

Nico walks back into the kitchen about five minutes later and says, "We have another guest for dinner, Mama".

And without turning around, his mama keeps stirring the tomato sauce she's making. They hear the front door open, and Sera yell, "Mama we're here! Where are you?"

Nico and his mama chime in at the same time, "In the kitchen!"

Sera and Roger walk in, with their hands full of bags of fresh vegetables and bread. Roger hands one of his bags to Mama and says, "We also stopped at the butcher shop for you."

She looks in the bag Roger is holding and lets out a squeal of delight. "Oh good, I was hoping you would get some of their prosciutto. Just put that one over there, and I'll start with that one right after I finish this."

Nico grabs one of the bottles of wine off the counter and picks up the corkscrew. As he opens the wine, he says, "It's been too long since we've done this. This way I can find out what you two are doing these days. I haven't seen you for a couple of weeks now. So tell me everything."

Nico picks up five wine glasses and walks back to the open wine bottle. Choosing one of the glasses, he tilts it slightly, while putting the dark green wine bottle to the rim—and pours in a very dark red wine.

Sera pulls away one of the glasses, walks to the refrigerator, and lets the icemaker drop odd-looking cubes into the glass. "Yes, dear brother, you're going to be an uncle!"

Nico stops in midpour, putting both the glass and the bottle down abruptly. He looks at Roger, "Really?. . .*Really!*"

Roger, smiling back at Nico, says, "Yes I'm the luckiest man in the world!"

Nico lets out a loud whoop and rushes over to grab Sera. Picking her up, he twirls around the room, with her laughing at him. "This is wonderful!" Nico, still almost yelling, turns to his mama. "How long have you known?"

She replies, "I found out last week, but she made me promise not to tell you, so she could."

Nico asks "Is this why you guys are over her now? Or did this happen spontaneously?"

Sera sits on one of the high stools next to the kitchen counter, and says, "Well, Nico, since you were finally able to start working again on your paintings, we wanted to wait until you seemed to come up for air. It's so important to me that you have finally gotten through that creative block. And I knew if I told Mama, I would have to tell you, so we kept it quiet, even from her, for a little while. This whole get-together just sort of happened. But I'm really glad it did."

Nico starts pouring wine again. "A celebration, then, is what this is!! This is wonderful. And might I add, I really needed it. Mama? It's getting kinda late in the afternoon, where is Mr. Hightower?"

"He went home to change clothes and wash up. He should be back any minute."

Nico turns back to Sera, "So tell me, how much longer, and what is it? You look wonderful, by the way. I think it agrees with you." Nico looks back at Roger. "Couldn't have happened to a nicer guy."

Sera smiles widely again. "I'm four months along, and we're waiting to see if it's a boy or a girl until the baby is born. We do have some names in mind, but we both really think we need to meet him first."

Roger pipes up, "Or her! You cannot choose, because it has already been decided and not by us."

"I think, when she starts showing more, I'll be able to tell, because the shape just gives it away," Mama adds. Then she opens the back door for Mr. Hightower who has just knocked.

"Mr. Hightower, here have a glass of wine. We are about to celebrate my sister bringing a new life into this world." And with that, he hands him a glass of red wine. He hands one to his mother and one to Roger, before grabbing the last glass for himself. He raises his glass and says, "To the new life, the new addition to our family, and to the lucky kid who gets these two great people as parents. Salute!"

All the glasses clank together. After everyone takes a sip, Mr. Hightower says, "A new life is always exciting news."

Mama has been working on some bruschetta with tomatoes, basil, garlic, and olive oil on day-old homemade bread that she has slightly toasted in the oven. She knows it's one of Nico's favorites. She takes one of the pieces and, when she finishes sampling her work, takes another sip of wine.

She walks back to the bag with prosciutto in it. She pulls down another platter from the cabinet and assembles the bread that has been rubbed with garlic and toasted in the oven. She adds cheese and returns it to the broiler for just a minute, then lays the prosciutto on top. She piles some spicy red pepper in olive oil in the middle of the plate, with the bread covered in prosciutto all around it.

As she puts it down, she turns to Nico and says, "One day, my son, you will buy your mother a brustolina grill, and then your mama will make you the best bruschetta you have ever had."

Nico grabs his mama around the waist and hugs her from the side. "Yes, Mama, I will. But the problem really is, if you start cooking any better, we're all going to eat too much."

Nico quiets for a bit, looks around the room, takes a sip of wine, and smiles at his family. He wonders, why haven't I done more of this? He has taken this love and his family for granted. He looks at each one of them and really sees them.

His lovely sister, Sera, who is now pregnant with her first baby, never thought she would find someone to date, much less marry and start her own family. She chose Roger, who came into her life with what seemed like chance, but then, to hear them speak of it, there's no such thing as chance. It was all meant to be.

Watching his family, he feels—more than ever—that he needs to make this show the best it can possibly be. He needs this one to be very successful. As everyone is snacking and laughing and drinking wine, he turns to Sera and says, "So how are you feeling these days? Are you working at the restaurant?"

Sera laughs and says, "Mama took me off the schedule as soon as I told her I was pregnant. You know Mama. She's being protective and is just trying to take care of me. But I'm feeling pretty good. Actually I'm starting to get a little bored."

"Sera, you seem have some free time, at least until the baby comes. I could use your input, in a couple of weeks, during the walk through of the gallery setup. I respect your judgment and would appreciate your take on things. Especially now that you have time on your hands!"

"Sure, just let me know when you get a date and time, and I'll be glad to go along. Is there anything in particular that you need help with or just another pair of eyes?"

"That's just it. I'm trying to take in everything, and I'm sure there are details that I'm going to miss. The gallery owner is very involved, and she's great. They have someone named Courtney who's handling the catering and the set up and is hiring waitstaff and all that. But, I'm sure there are things I'm going to miss. I want to show you the collection as it stands now and see if you have any ideas as well."

"You mean I'll get to see your work? I'm honored, Big Brother! And I bet you haven't even shown Mama yet, have you?"

"No, not yet, but I plan to. She's just been so busy, and I wasn't ready to show anyone but Maxwell. And I didn't even show him until a few weeks ago, right before he set up the meetings with the gallery. It has all been a really well-guarded secret."

"Why is that?"

"I wasn't ready to show what was going on in the studio yet, and I wasn't really sure how I felt about them either. But now, like children who are old enough to go out into the world, I'm ready to have them seen." Nico smiles as he watches Sera's face for her reaction.

"The one thing that I'm really glad about is that you're back to being your 'old self,' and you seem like you have that old feeling that you used to have. Do you want to tell me what happened? Or is it another one of your secrets?" asks Sera.

"Well, I want to tell you that it had a lot to do with going to work with Roger, and getting the time to think about a lot of different things." He thinks there's no way she would ever understand his using those letters and putting Roger and himself in any kind of jeopardy.

Sera smiles and reaches out and touches his arm. Then she turns and starts listening to the other conversation going on in the kitchen. Mr. Hightower and Annamaria are discussing her garden. They're getting so focused on their conversation that they don't realize Nico, Roger, and Sera are no longer talking and are just looking at the two of them, smiling.

Edgar and Annamaria suddenly stop talking, and both turn at almost the same time to look at Annamaria's three children. Suddenly, they all start laughing. Annamaria then turns to Nico and says, "Why don't we start on the chicken piccata, and Sera can start on the salad. I think the artichokes are almost ready, and Roger you can make the stuffing for them." With their marching orders, they all get busy in their mama's big kitchen.

Once dinner is made, they take a seat at the table in the garden, which is loaded with food. The conversation is lively, and a couple of bottles of wine are consumed, along with almost all the food. The conversation continues, and after they finish eating, everyone helps clear the dishes from the table.

Nico and Sera find themselves in the kitchen by themselves, loading the dishwasher. They're glad they told everyone to stay at the table outside in the garden and relax. Since the weather is so mild, they chose that table for dinner, instead of the one inside. The dining room is lovely, but the garden table is like something from an Italian garden, complete with strung lights, an old tablecloth, and lots of candles.

Sera pauses while putting a bowl in the dishwasher, asking Nico, "Did you know that Edgar has been working on the area of the garden where the table is now? He told Mama that she was right about what she wanted because it turned out well."

"Considering that he doesn't give up a whole lot in conversation, that was probably quite an admission. Don't you think?" Nico says.

Sera laughs and says, "I'm sure it is!" They both start laughing and continue cleaning up the kitchen and loading the dishwasher. Sera turns to Nico and asks, "Do you have someone new in your life, or is that a dumb thing to ask?"

Nico looks at her for a long minute, and then says to her, "Now even if I've been seeing someone, you will know when you meet her. Let's just say, right now, there's the promise of someone." And with that, they continue cleaning the kitchen, then join the group outside with a couple more full wine bottles in hand.

Chapter Seven

"Bear! Hold up! I need to mail this real quick." Bear turns around, and Tess reaches for the mailbox handle. She pulls it and drops a couple of envelopes in.

She says to Bear, "OK, boy. Now that we have that taken care of, we can go for a walk."

They have taken this same route two or three times a day since they moved into this apartment. So when they walk around the neighborhood, Tess thinks she notices even the smallest details. In fact, most of the time they are walking, her mind is somewhere else.

She still thinks about David's last three months and tries to make sense of it and tries to assimilate what it means in her grand scheme of things. As much as she tries to absorb and understand it, her emotions are like a huge old house, and each room has a different memory, a different emotion and feel. A song can make her remember a certain time in her life. For example, she feels like she can revisit those last days of David's life and then get up and close the door on that emotional room.

She can open another door of memory and think of when she was married, with that whole complex of emotions. She wonders if she will ever be able to understand what it all means, but right now, they all seem separate. She often wonders if this is her coping mechanism. Because she sometimes fears that, if it all hit her at once, she wouldn't be able to get over it and hopefully move on.

She lets her mind drift to a summer long ago, when she and her brother would walk to the public pool not far from their house. That park had three baseball diamonds and a small-scale train that looped around the entire park. Of course, it stopped and started in front of a snack stand that only sold fried food, candy, or soda. That soda was always called "Coke," unless you wanted a Dr. Pepper.

That Kiwanis Park had a miniature golf course, four tennis courts, and a fairly big L-shaped pool, which they practically lived in during those long, hot Texas summers.

They didn't install the batting cages until years later. It was always the pool that had everyone's interest in the summer. You walked through the turnstile, checked in, and rented a wire basket to put your things away, so you didn't have to worry about them. The changing rooms were behind the desk, with the girls on the left and the boys on the right. It smelled like chlorine no matter where you went. It wasn't until seventh grade that they'd figured out why the shallow kiddy pool, on the right as you walked in, was always warm, no matter how cool it seemed outside.

There was a high diving board and a low diving board, and the lifeguard sat in the indentation of the L. When the pool was really crowded, there was a second lifeguard who sat on the opposite side. A concrete deck went out eight feet from the edge of the pool, and then there was grass.

Everyone had a favorite place to sit, and Tess's favorite was away from the shallow end because the younger kids always played there. She wanted to be where the "older" set hung out, and it wasn't too far from the snack bar either.

Those were the days, she thought. She would get there around ten and would read her book all morning, lying on an extra-large towel, in the cutest two-piece swimsuit she could afford, with sunglasses and her hair pulled up in a ponytail. Her blue-jean cutoffs and shirt would lie on top of her sandals beside her.

By noon, she'd have been in the pool a couple of times to cool off. Floats were not allowed in the pool. Otherwise, she would have floated on one for hours. She was usually so hungry by two that she'd order onion rings and a large Dr. Pepper from the snack bar. All the swimming and walking to the pool from the house and back was apparently enough to work off anything. She smiles to herself, thinking: that's the kind of exercise I like. Something that doesn't feel like exercise is the only way to go.

Bear suddenly pulls on the leash and yanks Tess out of her daydream. She's right in front of the building they live in, and Bear wants to be on his bed for a midmorning doggie nap. Once inside the door to the lobby, Bear quicksteps it toward the elevator. Tess usually likes to take the stairs for exercise, but the elevators are easy if they have just walked further than usual.

Once inside their front door, she notices the answering machine and then looks at the cell phone in her back pocket. She's missed a call from Courtney. She hits the play button on the machine. "Hey Contessa! What 'cha up to this morning? Guess you're out with Bear, so I'll call your cell. If I don't get you for some reason, please call me back. I need your help. Talk to you soon." Tess pulls her cell phone out of her pocket and realizes she missed that call too, so she listens to the message, and Courtney says about the same thing. So she calls Courtney back, "Hiya, what's going on?"

Courtney responds, "Good morning! Were you walking Bear?"

"Yeah, we had a nice walk this morning. The weather is getting nicer every day it seems, and every morning lately, we smell the orange blossoms in the air. You know how heady that can be. Sorry, I didn't hear my cell when you called but..."

Courtney stops her with, "You want to make some quick money?"

"Of course! What do you need me to do?"

"I need an assistant for the day. I need to give my proposal about the opening at the Santa Monica Museum of Art. The director, Audrey, who you've already met will be there and a couple members of her board of directors, along with the artist's manager.

"Evidently, word of mouth about the artist is spreading, and the exhibit is becoming more and more important. This means that my mark in this business could be much better, if I can make the party for him just as spectacular. So, short of just recording the meeting with them, I want another set of ears with me to write an extra set of notes, so I don't miss anything. Are you in?"

"Sure Courtney. I'll do my best to help you. When is your meeting?"

"At half past ten tomorrow morning. Is that too soon for you?"

"No that's fine since I'm not working. What time do you want me to come over there? I'm guessing you want to leave from your house."

"Why don't you come over around eight? We can have coffee and go over my notes of what I have so far, and we can talk about what I need to fill in using details from the notes."

"Sounds great! See you in the morning."

Tess hangs up and walks to where Bear has plopped down on his large dog bed. She sits down on the floor beside him and starts talking, while she rubs his head. Bear just looks at her and acts like he's listening.

"Well, Buddy, it looks like you get to hang out with Maya tomorrow morning for a while. Courtney and I are gonna go to an appointment, and I sure hope I can help her. This could mean a lot of new business and could really put her on the map. This could be really good."

Tess spends the rest of the day looking online for a job, talking to Bear, or complaining to him about the job market. They take at least two more walks before nightfall, and as the sun is setting, Tess sits out on their tiny balcony.

It's just large enough for two simple chairs, a small table, a couple of plants, and a rug for Bear to lie on. She put small white lights in the ficus tree behind the guest chair, which always has something sitting on it, because she rarely has guests. The two of them relax and watch traffic or the sunset behind the buildings across the street.

Their building is on a corner, with a traffic light and a big grassy median strip in the street. She asked about that median a long time ago and was told about the trolley cars that used to run there in the twenties and thirties. Now they're building a busway for nonstop express buses. They always stop working around six, so by sunset it's much quieter, and sitting on the balcony can be relaxing.

In this quiet time, she wishes she had a partner to talk to or just enjoy the quiet. It's also times like these that strengthen the bond she has with Bear. He's such a good listener.

She remembers a time, when she was watching a show that was almost over, and Bear wanted to go for their walk. She looked him straight in the face and said, "Ten more minutes, Bud, when the show is over we'll go out. I promise."

The show ended ten minutes later, and Bear was right back in her face, seeming to say, "Your ten minutes are over. Let's go!" Tail wagging and tongue hanging out, he wouldn't get out of her face. Tess laughed and said OK, getting up and heading to the door. She grabbed a sweater, the leash, her keys, and her cell phone and met Bear at the door.

Next morning, the alarm wakes them at six, and she gets up and gets dressed to get Bear outside. It's still just turning light outside, and the air is really cool and smells like orange blossoms and eucalyptus. A couple of other dog walkers are out. Each seems in a quick pace to get the "business" done, so they can get home to their coffee.

Before they realize it, they are back in the apartment with Bear plopping down on the couch, while Tess gets busy making coffee in the kitchen. They are not going to hang out this morning, because they're going to Courtney's, so Tess puts on her iPod and sings along. She has the coffee pot ready by the second chorus. By the next song, she's heading to the shower.

She's ready to leave by seven thirty, and she and Bear are in the Jeep heading out of the underground garage to Courtney's. She's thankful that Courtney lives in Calabasas, so she's going against traffic. The morning is starting to warm up, and the sun is out with a lonely sky. When she gets there, Courtney meets her at the door with Maya, and they walk the two dogs to the backyard.

Tess sits at the kitchen counter on a wooden barstool, while Courtney is in the kitchen pouring two cups of coffee. "This is that Italian coffee that we like so much," she says as she pours.

Tess is flipping over the cover of her notebook, so she can start taking notes. Courtney starts talking about how she wants to feel them out on her plan for the party. At first, she was thinking about doing champagne and canapés, with all the waitstaff in white shirts and black slacks. A minimalist approach, so the true center of attention would be the artwork.

But now, she's thinking that she might give them a couple more options, such as waitstaff in black, with the music and theme like a coffeehouse, slightly "beatnik" in tone. They could serve coffee drinks and sweets like warm cookies, because part of the patio is open-air, and a couple of baristas could be there.

Then she starts talking about the third choice, with very sensuous foods and a table of sweets, with a lot of Italian chocolate served in various ways. Italian red wines, Bellinis, and Americanos would be served in an atmosphere much like an Italian garden or a courtyard in a small Italian town center. And the hors d'oeuvres she suggests are bruschetta, stuffed mushrooms, and melon and prosciutto. It would be nice to add a fountain for the real courtyard feel.

"Courtney?"

"Yes."

"What's an Americano? I've had Bellinis before, but not an Americano."

"Well, an Americano was created by Campari in the mid-1800s with sweet vermouth, Campari, and club soda. The Americans made it popular in Milan in the early 1900s, so they renamed it. I don't want to make the Bellinis with champagne but the Italian way, using Italian Prosecco instead. Since Nico, the artist, is Italian, I'm thinking this may go over better. But I want you to help me judge their reactions with each suggestion. OK?"

"Got it."

"I just think that the Italian vibe is the one I should concentrate on. So let's pack up here and head that way, and we can discuss the waitstaff clothing and other details along the way."

"Yeah, it does sound great. If we can fine-tune your idea to give them more details after you introduce it, I think they'll probably go for it."

They pack everything up, give the dogs a treat, and head out the door. They pile everything into Courtney's car, and start talking up the evening in Italy—bringing up sculptured topiaries and, instead of just a coffee bar on the patio, an espresso bar with Godiva chocolates next to it.

Courtney mentions that she wants to check the flooring in the gallery where the party will be, as well as the patio. She's really sold, now, on the "Milan evening" theme for the party and hopes that they agree.

Tess notices a big smile on Courtney's face and that she's preoccupied and actually sitting up a little straighter. She only mentions a couple more things for the rest of the ride.

They pull up, park next to the Museum of Art, and walk in the front door. At the information desk, Courtney hands the girl her card and says, "Good morning. My name is Courtney Williams, and we have a meeting with Audrey at ten."

Audrey's assistant comes to the information desk and takes Courtney and Tess to a conference room that Courtney remembers from her last meeting. Audrey is sitting at a conference table, and she introduces them to Mr. Rodney Bingham, Mrs. Li Wing, Mr. Edgar Hightower, and Mr. Maxwell Gibbs. They all sit down and start the meeting.

After Courtney introduces Tess as her assistant, they go over ideas and start discussing the options. Tess watches as Courtney pitches the three ideas and notices that they perk up a little, when she talks about an evening in a Milan courtyard. They really seem receptive, and one of the gentlemen is quite positive in his reaction. And he seems to start rolling detail questions in that direction.

Since this is their second meeting, and they have asked for more concrete ideas, Courtney starts giving more and more details of what they could do to bring Milan to the museum, making it an evening that everyone would remember. She describes her vision as being a late summer evening in an old courtyard that's upscale and completely refined.

They start responding to what she describes, asking more questions about details of the décor, the layout, the food and drink, and even what the waitstaff would wear. When they finish all their questions, she knows that she has been on the right track with her proposal.

About an hour into the meeting, Audrey says, after a pause in the discussion, "Well I think that we can agree whole-heartedly that we want to make it an evening in Milan. Could you e-mail me your written proposal by Friday, including all the details and cost projections?"

"Absolutely!" Courtney says. "Should we go ahead and lock in a date and time for the meeting, or do you need to get back to me about that?"

The other participants say they need to check their schedules and will firm up a time by tomorrow. They are all smiling and take their time leaving the conference room.

Courtney and Tess walk with Audrey to the door, and Courtney asks, "Audrey, would you mind if we discreetly take some measurements of the gallery space where you want the launch to be set up?"

Audrey says, "I have a couple of floor plans copied and ready for you, and they provide measurements. What I can do is have my assistant, Sophie, show you the wing and answer any questions you may have. The plans even have all the power outlets marked, so your plans can be complete."

Courtney says, "That's terrific, Audrey, I'll definitely take you up on that."

They meet Sophie in the lobby, where she hands the plans to Courtney. The three of them walk into a cavern-like space and start looking around, taking notes. Tess tries to take the best notes she can, walking around behind Sophie and Courtney.

Courtney is taking pictures with her iPhone for later reference, and after another hour, they are ready to leave. They say their goodbyes, and Tess and Courtney walk back to their car.

Once inside, Courtney turns to Tess, grins really big, and exclaims, "That couldn't have turned out any better, I don't think! They really seemed to like the whole Italian angle, and that one guy, Mr. Hightower, seemed really enthused. He really seemed to turn the tide for us. What are your thoughts?"

"Courtney, it's too bad we couldn't have recorded it for posterity! That was such a great meeting. Lucky you. Do you want to go back to the house and write everything down?"

"Get out of my head. Yeah, I was thinking the same thing. Can you write while I drive, or would you have motion sickness?"

"Sure, we can start now. Let's get on the freeway, and I'll write as we go."

On the road, Tess starts making lists of things that Courtney wants to check into and include in her proposal. She's so excited that she's rattling off things, one after another. Tess just smiles.

Courtney stops talking after a while, looks at Tess, and says, "Here I've been, babbling on, and I wish you could have something just as positive in your life. I try not to press you, because of all that you've been through in the last couple of years, but there are times when I wish I could do more for you."

"Well, I think we can take the list we have and go over it again, when we get to your house, and see what we want to add or change. And my life is getting better all the time," Tess adds while looking out the window. Courtney notices the change in Tess's demeanor.

At Courtney's house, they drop their purses and notebooks on the bar. "By the way I really appreciate you going with me to the museum today," Courtney says. "That really did help me out. What did you think of the whole set up? Is there anything that stands out to you?"

"The bones of the museum are great, and you won't have any trouble making it an outrageously great opening. Whatever you need me to help with, I'll be happy to help." Courtney sets a cup of fresh coffee in front of Tess, who's sitting on a chair by the kitchen counter.

Courtney is busy in the kitchen, putting something together for them to snack on, when she looks over at Tess and stops in her tracks. Tess is looking out the kitchen window with a far-away gaze, not saying a word. After a minute, Courtney softly says, "You wanna talk about it?"

Tess sits up a little straighter. With a sigh, she tells Courtney that she didn't realize she wasn't present—and apologizes.

"There's no need for an apology, sweetie, but maybe it would help if you talked to me. Even if I can't help, I can listen. I know that sometimes, if I can talk about something to you, just talking helps me figure it out."

Tess smiles at Courtney and says, "Yeah, I remember you saying that sometimes in mid-conversation. And I can remember doing it while talking to you. But this time, it seems like I just can't put my finger on it, or maybe I don't know where to start."

Courtney sits on the other side of the counter with a cup of coffee and a small plate full of kolaczkis, all warm and ready to eat. Tess takes one, puts it in front of her, and takes a sip of coffee. She looks at Courtney, smiles, and sighs.

"I don't know how to start. But a lot of it's a weird feeling I've been having, and it makes me feel like I'm waiting for something to happen... like there's something around the corner, and I need to be prepared for it, but I don't know what it is. And I feel like I'm in limbo, like I can't get anything done, can't find a job, don't feel like I should invest any time or energy into anything, because this "thing" is going to change everything. There's no rhyme or reason why I should expect anything. I mean Publisher's Clearing House is not going to knock on my door or anything."

"That's understandable in a way..."

"I think about my mom and David all the time. I'll watch a show on TV, for example, and it shows a mom being a great mom, and I start crying. Or they show a brother and sister doing something together, and I get so upset and depressed that I don't know what to do. And the next thing I know, Bear will come over and remind me that he's my family, and he loves me no matter what. Since I'm being honest with you, there have been times when I think nothing matters—that I don't matter and that no one would miss me if I was gone...but then there's Bear. And I don't think that anyone could love me as much as he does, and I like to think that nobody would love him as much as I do."

Courtney just sits there, kind of dumbfounded by the revelation that Tess could feel so alone. Then she realizes part of what Tess said and slowly starts to say, "You really wouldn't hurt yourself or anything, would you?"

"Since I'm being so honest, yeah, I thought about it, and then Bear will remind me that I'm really there for him, if nothing else, and there's no way I would ever leave him voluntarily. And speaking of my "child," where is he?" She gets up and checks on him in the backyard, with Courtney following.

"There's my baby!" Hearing her, Bear comes running. Maya is running alongside him, and they can tell they had a nice time hanging around in the backyard together. They all walk back into the kitchen, with the dogs taking turns at the water bowl, then going over to sit beside Courtney and Tess who are back on kitchen stools.

Tess looks down at Bear lying on the wood floor, and reminds herself how lucky she is to have such unconditional love. He's the perfect companion. Tess glances back at Courtney and says, "Did I ever tell you Bear was the perfect puppy? He was house-trained in a week. He never chewed on anything that was not his toy, and he always, always loves me."

"That he does! Anyone can tell that. He's a sweetie, and it's really great how he and Maya get along so well. It's really nice to be able to leave them together and know that everything will be fine. And you, my friend, what can we do to change your situation?"

"Well, other than finding me a full-time job or a man I could love who could love me as much as Bear does...just being a good friend is the best thing, and the only thing, that I need. So, thank you."

"Well, I don't know about you, but coffee just isn't what I think this situation calls for." Courtney goes to the bottom kitchen cabinet for a bottle of wine. She brings it out, swinging it by its neck and says, "I don't have to pick up Natalie from school this afternoon, because she isshe's going to her dad's house for the night. I think you and I both could use a glass of this, for no other reason than just to celebrate life. What do you say?"

Tess smiles slightly and replies, "As they say, its five o'clock somewhere, isn't it? Yes ma'am, I think I could use a little. Do you need any help?"

"No, I've got it. But I just thought of something. We have a loaf of Italian bread and some tomatoes, fresh basil, and garlic. Would you mind making some of that bruschetta that you make so well? Brad will be home in an hour or so, and I know he would love some too. Would you mind?"

"I would love to! I think that's a great idea." In the kitchen, Tess opens the refrigerator and gets all the things she needs. The she pauses, looks at Courtney, and thinks—you, Bear, and Aunt Barbara—you're my family. I don't know what I would do without you. She smiles and gets busy helping Courtney in the kitchen. They sip wine and make the bruschetta, and before they know it, Brad is home. He joins right in the conversation. It's comfortable. There's some laughter and some excited conversation, and the late afternoon rolls into early evening.

After a while, Tess sighs and says she needs to get Bear home, and she's getting a little tired. She's only had one glass of wine the whole evening, so she knows she's OK to drive.

Courtney, Brad, and Maya walk Tess and Bear out to her Jeep. The two of them pile in and wave good-bye. Tess promises to call Courtney the following morning. The whole way home, Tess thinks about how wonderful it is to have Bear in her life. She checks on him in the rearview mirror a couple of times, only to see him lying comfortably in the back seat.

Back in the apartment, Bear jumps on the couch, flops his head, on Tess's lap, and looks up at her, almost to say, "Yeah, mom, I'm right here."

Tess rests back and absentmindedly strokes his head, while zoning out looking toward the TV. She looks down every few minutes to smile at him and feels grateful.

After a while, she finds herself dozing off and waking back up. After a few times, she decides it's time to get into bed. Bear follows her to the bedroom and plops down on an overgrown pillow, watching Tess's every move until she gets into bed, then lays his head down and closes his eyes.

The next morning, as usual, Bear wakes Tess up by dropping his head on her side of the bed, just watching her until she wakes up. He used to get impatient. When she didn't wake up within thirty seconds, he would start nudging her or licking her hand or her face. But that seemed to startle her, so she would jump, and he didn't like that. These days, all it takes is watching her, and she wakes up to see his smiling face first thing.

She looks at him and says sleepily, "Good morning, Sweet Face! How are you, my honey?" She gets up, all the while talking to him, almost expecting to get an answer. She gets dressed and goes to the bathroom quickly, so she can get Bear downstairs, and he can do his business.

This morning, there's no letter to send to her mom. She's still going over part of the conversation she had with Courtney yesterday in her head, still thinking about some of the things they talked about—still having loose ends of thought.

The morning is a bit foggy and cool, with the sun just starting to show. Bear is not walking as fast as he used to, and Tess notices that he's getting a bit slower in general. I guess, for a dog that old, it should be expected.

Tess starts thinking about how important he is to her and stops for a minute to just love on him, and he perks back up. It seems that he would do anything for her. She reaches over and starts scratching his head while they finish their walk.

They get upstairs, and the coffee is finished brewing, so she pours herself a cup and puts a little milk in it. Taking a sip, she walks over, next to Bear, in front of the TV. She sits down, and he picks his head up off the floor for a second to see Tess beside him. He plops his head back down, and scooches his back next to her leg. She sits for a minute, just looking at him scratching his back.

She pauses, takes another sip of coffee, and watches Bear as he sleeps. "You're such a perfect companion. Always have been. I think I've loved you from the moment you picked me…yeah, I know you picked me. It was all part of your grand plan, wasn't it Bear?"

He picks up his head again and looks at Tess, then plops it back down and rolls over on his back, with his legs folded in the air. Tess laughs and scratches his belly for a while, until he turns over and goes back to sleep.

Tess sits there for a while, just thinking and watching TV. She doesn't even know what's on, because she's deep in thoughts, trying to figure out why she should feel so uneasy. She's been at lots of crossroads in her life before, and they have not made her feel so apprehensive—so unsettled. Every time she starts feeling overwhelmed, she starts trying to break it down into smaller pieces, seeing if she can make sense of at least part of it. Maybe if she can do that, the big picture won't seem so blinding.

Didn't some Middle Eastern mystic once say that the path to enlightenment starts with questions?

"Well, Bear…all I know is that I miss being able to call Mom and ask her questions, and if I didn't have you, I don't know what I'd do…" Her voice trails off, and she just looks at Bear and sighs. As she smiles at the way he makes her feel, she starts to get up off the floor and says, "OK boy, it's late, and tomorrow is another day. Let's go night-night and see what tomorrow brings." And they both get up and go into the bedroom and go to bed.

Chapter Eight

"Knock-knock..." Nico opens the kitchen door to his mama's house. "Good! You're up I see," he says to his mama, as he walks over to give her a hug and a kiss on the cheek. "I didn't think you would be sleeping in on a beautiful morning like this. What are you up to?'

His mama gives him the once-over as she gets another cup to pour him some fresh coffee. "I just made this, 'cause I guess I knew I'd be having company. If you want a cappuccino, you can go to the coffee shop for that. So tell me, what are you doing up and around this early in the morning, all cleaned up and ready to go somewhere? I mean it's Saturday, and I know you're not working today."

"Well Mama, actually I have been down by the beach already scouting around. I woke up on my own and got restless, and thought I would see if a friend of mine was taking her dog to the beach, but I didn't see her."

"Oh? And do I know of this friend of yours? Is this someone I've met before?"

"No, Mama you haven't met her. So what are you going to make for breakfast? Anything?

His mama laughs at him trying to change the subject and turns around to open the refrigerator to see what she has in the way of ingredients. "That's OK. I'll let you get away with that for now, but you know I always find out. So let's see here...Are you hungry for anything in particular? Or would it be OK with you to just have one of these fresh croissants that I picked up earlier with fresh strawberries and blueberries I happen to have?"

"Oh, Mama, that sounds perfect. And while you're getting that out, why don't you tell me where Mr. Edgar Hightower is?"

"Well, for your information, Edgar has gone to the plant nursery to get some more flowers for my garden. He thinks a couple of places are not growing in as quickly as they should, so he wants to add some depth and color to those areas. And while we're at it, why don't you tell me your thoughts about him?"

"Mama, if he makes you happy, I'm all for it. He does kinda dote on you though...

"I know that's not a bad thing, because if it was, you would have said something a long time ago. So why don't you tell me what is really on your mind, and then we can get on with important things—like breakfast." With that remark, she turns around to the kitchen counter.

Smiling to herself, she glances at her son. She watches him as he looks out the window like he's a million miles away. Still looking out the window, he watches a couple of birds playing on a bush. They chase each other in and out of a hydrangea bush, making a lot of noise. He watches until they fly away. He stops for a minute, turns around, looks at his mother, and slyly smiles.

She laughs, and says "Nico, I know you better than you know yourself sometimes. Do you want to tell me what's really up with you, or do you want to continue telling me that nothing is going on?"

"I don't know what you're talking about, Mama."

"Do not toy with me Nico. I'm your mama, and I know when something is going on and when something isn't. You're preoccupied, and I want to know about it. What's going on?"

"Oh Mama. Where do I begin? The weirdest thing is that I don't even know her. I just know of her. And what I do know absolutely fascinates me. She hasShe's seen so much tragedy, and yet it seems like she looks for the good in it. She still tries to find something positive."

He trails off, staring at some flowers in his mama's garden—outside the window, just swaying in the breeze. He sighs and looks down at the countertop in front of him.

He looks over at his mama, and starts talking to her again—amazed at himself, that he's running off at the mouth all of a sudden. He grabs his mama's hand and says quietly to her, "I don't know what I would do if I lost you and Sera and Roger, and my world was turned upside down. I don't know if I would be able to make sense of things. Mama, I just don't know what I would do. It all seems too much—to lose your whole family and expect to go on with your life. It seems like you would have to create your life all over or wind up just grieving the rest of your life. I don't know how you would get over it."

"Well now, that was quite a story. She sounds pretty levelheaded to me, to go through all that and still try and find the good. But, my piccola, what about this has captured your thoughts so strongly?"

She turns and tries not to look at Nico, in hopes that he will talk more about this young woman he seems fascinated with. She knows that the less attention she pays to what he's saying, the more likely he is to over-explain. That way, she gets all the information, often more than she really wants to know!

Nico finds himself wanting to tell his mama everything he knows, but his thoughts trail off when he remembers that he can't give it all away. He wants to share this with her, because it has become so important to him. So he picks up another strawberry and starts talking slowly. "She also has this dog that she takes almost everywhere, a really big dog." His voice trails off again, as he smiles, going deeper in thought.

His mama smiles and continues making their breakfast. They work quietly on the meal at hand for a while, until she says, "So what else do you know about her? What's her name, for example?"

Her questions are falling on deaf ears, because Nico is miles away, trying to figure out what he should do next. His mama only smiles when he gets like this and lets it go. She busies herself with finishing their breakfast, and they sit at the kitchen counter and eat, talking about his sister Sera and her pregnancy.

When they're done, he helps clean up the kitchen, kisses his mama on the cheek, and leaves. His only thought is to see if he can find her at the beach and beelines there. He spends all afternoon looking at women that he thinks might be her, but nobody fits the profile he has in his mind.

But by the time Monday rolls around and he goes back to the post office, he's hoping that he can find another letter from her. He has such purpose and single-mindedness that he doesn't notice how fast the day goes by. When he realizes it's time to quit for the day, he slumps his shoulders as he leaves, because he has no new letters.

Disappointed, he gets in his car and puts on some music to lift his spirits. He gets lost in the music, and before he knows it, he's pulling up in front of his house. He goes inside, grabs a beer from the refrigerator, and puts a medium-sized canvas on the easel. He hits play on his stereo, not caring what music comes up. He stares at the canvas for a couple of minutes, picks up a large brush, puts several shades of blue on his palette, and starts attacking the large white area with large swipes of blue. Nico continues until the early hours of the morning, and finally feels content enough to fall in bed.

Morning crashes in before he's ready for it, as usual. He gets up and goes back to the post office, hoping again to find another letter.

It almost startles him how quickly he finds one this morning. Then his day seems to drag, because all he wants to do is get out of there to read it. He keeps working and finds a second letter.

Now he just wants to feign sickness, so he can leave and see what's going on. But he does the responsible thing and keeps digging through the buckets of mail, sorting as best he can. This job has reminded him that he's a responsible guy, and on a very elemental level, he likes this job. It has provided him with the comfort of doing something worthwhile when he had been feeling like his days were not productive. There's a basic joy in that.

So when his day is finished, he almost runs out the door to get home to his new finds. Once he's home, he sits on the floor with the box he keeps her letters in, takes the two new letters out of his pocket, and looks at the postmark on the envelopes. He decides to open them in the order of these dates.

Reading the first letter, he stops after getting halfway down the page and drops his hands, with his forearms now resting on his knees. He looks up and sighs. Talking out loud to himself, he says, "This has got to be a really hard thing for her to do." He pauses for a minute, then starts reading again and slyly smiles. "This may be my chance! Maybe I can figure out more details…" His voice trails off as he goes back to reading.

She is going to scatter her mother and brother's ashes in San Diego, and Nico knows that only a few companies help with the burials at sea, as they call it. He has purpose. He used to hang out in San Diego when he was younger, because it seemed so down to earth around the bay area of that city.

"I can make this happen," he thinks to himself. "All I have to do to meet this letter writer is hang out in that area. I'm sure there aren't that many scatterings that happen on a daily basis. This just might work."

He combs the letter for clues on the date, and it's not until the second letter that he finds one.

"Ah, man!" he says out loud. "It's the same day as my opening. How in the world am I going to pull this off? Hmm…let's see here. The opening doesn't start until eight, and they have to do this during the day." Re-reading the second letter, he realizes that she's going to do it at sunset.

He goes to his computer and pulls up the calendar to get the time of sunset on that day, checking for how much wiggle room he has between being at the dock when the boat goes out and getting to his opening. Nico laughs to himself that he may be late to his own gala. But aren't all artists supposed to be fashionably late?

He neatly folds up the letters and puts them in the box with all the others. He locks the box and puts it back on his dresser, then walks over to the canvas he's currently working on. He tilts his head, trying to get another take on what's there, turns on his heel, and walks back to his stereo.

Now is the time for some inspirational music. He puts on some more Muse, this time it's "Starlight," and he starts dancing around the room, heading in the direction of the canvas. He loads more paint on the palette he was working with the day before and, picking up a wide brush with pure joy, starts working. He has solid hope, he feels.

He falls into the same pattern as the night before and exhausts himself. He falls on his bed only to have his alarm go off way before he's ready for it. He drags himself up, gets cleaned up, and heads back to work. But unfortunately, today is not a letter day.

He's fine with that, because he got two yesterday. He believes that he'll be able to figure out when she's going to be in San Diego, so he can meet her—or at least see who she is. He thinks to himself, "I can make this happen!" That day at work goes smoothly, and once he gets home, he gets a phone call from Maxwell.

"Maxwell! I'm glad you called. What's going on?"

"Well, Nico, I wanted to give you an update on your event and let you know the plans that have been made so far and what you can expect."

"Sounds great. I'm going to put you on speakerphone, because I just got home, and I want to open a bottle of wine while I talk to you. OK?"

"I like that idea. Go right ahead. And you might want to grab a pen and some paper, so you can write down some details. So let's see, where do I begin? Ah...yes. Here are my notes. The opening is October ninth, a Saturday night. It's at the Santa Monica Museum of Art. But I think you knew that, didn't you?"

Nico reaches for a glass and fills it halfway up with wine, turns, and starts looking for a pad of paper. He knows where a pen is. "Yeah, Maxwell, I know where and the date, because you cleared that with me some time ago, it seems. And you also said, if I remember correctly, that we're using a new catering company, right?"

"That's right. And they're going to start setting up the wing of the gallery where your collection will be housed for a while—three weeks I think we said—the weekend before. The caterer will come in on the Friday before the Saturday showing to set up the final layout. Everything should be good to go by that evening. I think you need to deliver your artwork the weekend before the opening. When you deliver the paintings, you should go ahead and place them like you want them to be shown, so they don't have any question on where they go. Do you agree?"

"That would probably be the easiest thing to do, yeah. Are you going to be there to help me block it out?"

"You can count on it. It's probably the most fun part of my job. And I'll just be there to support you, and make sure your decisions are the ones that are adhered to—and that the showing plays out exactly the way you and I want it."

"Maxwell, that's a big help. But you know I'm going to want your input, and if you have any suggestions you need to speak up as usual."

"No problem there. Now let me know if you want to get invitations and if we need to make any special arrangements for anyone."

"Oh yeah, Maxwell, did they decide to use the open-air patio area that's just off that space?"

"Ahmm, let me check my notes....patio area...Yeah, here it is. They're using it and putting a full cappuccino/-espresso bar with desserts. It should be a really cool and pretty evening, and it will also be a great place with the other things the caterer has planned. I think I told you that it will be themed an evening in Milan, more or less, didn't I?"

"Right. I think you did tell me all this. I really liked that idea and was hoping they would find a way to use that space for us. Just so you know, I have something that I must do earlier that day in San Diego, but will definitely be back in plenty of time. Now, I'll get a list to you of the people I would like to be there, and we can make sure we don't duplicate anyone. Do you have a list of who in the art world will be invited and how many we expect?"

"Actually, as far as the list goes, I know that at least a dozen contacts in New York plan on being out here, because they have been asking for details. They're very excited about this collection. But don't think you flew that comment about going to San Diego right by me! What in the world could be so important that you're going to San Diego the day of your opening? You better not be a no-show—that would kill us."

"Like I said Maxwell, it's not going to make me late. But this is definitely something that I *have* to do, and there's no debate about it."

"Sometimes you scare me, Nico. But I'll trust you. Are there any concerns you want me to address about the showing before we get down to your delivery date?"

"Are they going to have someone there that Saturday to show me where they're setting up tables and such?"

"I don't know if they've planned that, but I can ask them to. I don't think they will mind, because they have been really great so far. I'll ask and get back to you with a name and a time. Anything else?"

"Not that I can think of. But I've done a few more paintings since you last saw my work. I think, maybe one night soon, you should come over for dinner and help me group them and make sure there's nothing I should edit out. Can we do that?"

"Sure, I would be happy to. You're not starting to doubt this collection are you?"

"Maxwell, I guess I'm starting to get a case of nerves because it seems like so long since the last show, and there were no expectations then like there are now. I feel pretty good about it, but I'm feeling the pressure of the build up."

"That's easy to understand, Nico, and I can't say I don't feel the same way. It's really important to me that this show and you are a success. It has been such a difficult journey, and sometimes it's hard to process. But I think this is going to be great, and we'll both be happy with the end result."

"OK, I'll try not to be so anxious. When do you want to come over for dinner?"

"Hang on a second, and let me get my calendar and I can give you a day....hmm, let's see here...OK. It looks like next Tuesday night is clear. Do you have plans then?"

"Nope, let's make it Tuesday night. Why don't you come over when you get off work, and if you're going to be later than seven thirty just call? Do you know what you want to eat, or do you want to just pick something up on your way here?"

"I think I'll just pick something up."

"Sounds great to me. I'll call you if anything comes up between now and then, OK?"

"Great, Nico. It will all be great, and we will catch up on Tuesday night."

After they hang up, Nico sits for a few minutes looking around the room, takes a deep breath, and hangs the handset up in its cradle. He walks over to the easel in the corner, looks at his most recent work, and stuffs his hands in his pockets. He tilts his head slowly to the side, while staring at it for a while, and smiles slightly, then walks over to the stereo and turns on music. He bobs his head back and forth to the beat and picks up the paint palette. He puts more paint on top, picks up a brush, and starts in again on the one he half completed last night. The same routine happens night after night, and he's so relieved that his creative block is over that he doesn't care how much sleep he's missing. He gladly accepts this over the drought any day.

The next morning, he goes through the same routine he has gotten used to, and while driving to work, he notices people. They're not anything special but he notices them. They are doing their everyday things—walking their dogs, waiting for the bus, going to and from their houses. A whole world of individuals who have their own lives, worries, fears, and happiness. It seems like he's becoming aware of this intricate fabric, in which each thread is a person's life, and it's all woven together in this amazing tapestry.

It's almost like he has been seeing everything in black and white, and now suddenly it has turned to color, like an old movie that wants to make a point. It's almost confusing. Surely all this has been here all along. Surely he has not been that blind to everyday life, taking it so much for granted that he has had such tunnel vision—too absorbed in his own wants and needs. And has he even been aware of his own needs? Has he been so numbed by cynicism that he became blinded to the world?

Nico starts looking at everything now, not wanting to miss anything. His eyes wander to everything along the roads on the way to work. He sees a mother and very young daughter walking down the street, probably on the way to school. That little girl is so cute, and she's maybe in the first or second grade.

She has a lunchbox and a pink sweater over a little dress. She has hold of her mother's hand and is looking up to her, smiling. She looks so innocent. It's hard to remember when he has felt innocent, or if he ever has. Maybe that's his problem. Maybe he lost his innocence too early. He just remembers that he has felt a sense of protection for his family since his father died. He has never taken the time to wonder what his life would have been like if he had lived.

They would probably still be in Brooklyn. And he's sure that his life would not have turned out the way it has. All he knows is that, if he ever has kids, he wants them to keep their innocence as long as possible.

Sera's child will hopefully grow up to have the kind of childhood that she and Nico deserved. He wants to be that child's godfather. He wants to make sure that he can help with its childhood, making sure that it knows that so many people love him and want to protect him. This is really important. He can only imagine what Sera and Roger are going through. They must be starting to go crazy! His blinders to the world are gone, and previous details of everyday life are suddenly visible. He's starting to realize how he has changed.

He drives up to the post office parking lot, gets out of his car, and goes in. He beelines to the basement. He glances around on his way there and sees people in their own little worlds, not really noticing anything else. Maybe it's because it's a Friday, and everybody is ready for the weekend. Or maybe they are all just wrapped up in their own lives. He shrugs his shoulders and keeps going.

He lets his mind wander as he goes through the continuous mountain of mail that holds no surprises....at least not so far.

Lunchtime with Roger comes and goes, and it's late in the afternoon when he finds another letter from her. He puts it to the side, and when he feels comfortable enough, he stuffs it in his pocket, excited that he has another piece of the puzzle.

He finishes up his day and heads home, not wanting to do anything but get home. Once inside his place, he realizes that he only has bread, peanut butter, and jelly. He laughs at himself because he's fine with that. He only wishes he had milk to go along with it. Instead, he makes a cup of tea, sits on the floor, once again, with the wooden box of treasures, and pulls the latest letter out of his pocket.

He opens it gently and reverently and starts reading. The room is quiet while he reads. He gets about halfway through and drops his hands and looks up, with his eyes watering. "How does she do it?" he says out loud. "Where does she find the hope and the strength? She's gone through so much..."

And he picks up reading it again. Once he has finished, he takes a sip from his cup of tea and looks down at the letter lying on the floor. Amazing. Or maybe she's still in the middle of it and doesn't realize how strong she really is. She's just trying to get through whatever it is—to a level place where she can catch her breath and see ahead.

With that last thought, he puts the new letter in the wooden box, shuts the lid, and locks it. He puts the leather cord holding the key back on his neck, dropping the key down his shirt. Getting up off the floor, he picks up the box and puts it back on his dresser.

He turns on his stereo and starts shuffling to the studio in the next room. He places a new canvas on the easel and, thinking of the letter he just read, starts to paint another new vision. This one starts off dark and moody. As he progresses, a light seems to come through in the upper right section, almost like a starburst. It winds up being mostly abstract and, to him, looks like a train coming out of a tunnel in the darkness.

Before he knows it, it's again close to three in the morning, and he's finally heading for bed. But tomorrow is Saturday, and he will once again try and see if his letter writer is at the beach with her dog. He knows he must keep trying.

Morning comes, and he gets up and dressed, not wanting to take the time to make coffee. He will just get some down there. He jumps in his car and sits on his towel, in his shorts, with his sandals and shirt off and sunglasses on. He starts watching for a girl and her dog.

The sun is so warming. With the breeze off the ocean in his face, the waves lull him into a meditative state, and his eyes get heavy. He drifts off to sleep lying on the beach, but with his sunglasses on, nobody notices or cares.

About forty minutes later, he gets startled awake by young kids running and playing in the sand not far from him. He smiles to himself that he will have a nephew or niece before the end of the year. And then he'll take the child to the beach with him, and that will be so much fun.

He's just thinking and watching people go by, looking for any female who has a large dog with her. It's a beautiful day, and it's really interesting seeing so many different kinds of people out for the same thing—just to enjoy an afternoon. He, on the other hand, is doing more than just enjoying an afternoon, he's actually getting more ideas he wants to try and paint.

He has started watching a couple with a young child who is so joyous. He must be about three or four, and has a little pail and shovel, trying to make little piles of sand around him. Once he builds them up, he tears them down, then runs and plays with the waves lapping up on the shore. His parents are sitting in sling-back striped beach chairs under an umbrella, with eyes only for him and what he's doing. His father content just to watch until the boy cries for him to come and play.

"I wonder if that could have been me, had things been different?" Nico is thinking. He shakes his head, knowing his mother never wound up being much of a beach person. This makes him smile, realizing that he likes things they way they are. He's starting to like himself again too. He's taking on a new appreciation for his life and the way it's turning out, and it's a surprise.

Its getting to be too late in the afternoon for her to show up, so he decides he will just head home. He puts his shirt back on, picks up his shoes and his towel, and starts walking back up to the street to find his car.

Stopping at the dim sum place around the corner from his house, he picks up some dinner, so he can try and do some more work. The beach was really inspiring today, and it would be nice to see a portion of that.

At home, he puts on the stereo and gets busy in the kitchen, getting dinner together. He unpacks the dim sum and gets a plate and chopsticks out, while he's warming some sake in the microwave. All this is then transported to the table in the dining room-studio.

Before he sits down to eat, he puts a blank canvas on his easel. It's about three feet tall and six feet wide, and he tightens the clamps in place. Back to the table, he sits down to eat facing the easel, staring at the blank slate.

After dinner, he walks back to the stereo, turns it up, and shuffles back to the canvas. He picks up a pencil and sketches the horizon, dunes, an umbrella, and two beach chairs. There's a food basket, a pail, and a little shovel sketched in as well. He puts an array of gold and brown paints on his palette and starts blending and painting and gets lost with the music and the picture in his head.

Since it's Saturday night, he doesn't have to worry about the time and can just go until he gets tired. He doesn't realize what time it is, until he starts seeing daybreak and realizes it's Sunday morning. What a great night, he thinks.

With daylight starting to stream in, he decides to take a break and make some coffee, so he can possibly finish this one today. Sunday flies by, and suddenly, it seems it's Tuesday night, and Maxwell is coming over to sort through the pictures, because Saturday is delivery day to the museum. Nico is starting to get a little nervous.

Maxwell gets there with Chin Chin's Chinese chicken salad, which is one of his favorites. He also brought some great Japanese beer to go with it. They stand while they eat, both of them unable to sit. They walk around the studio pulling paintings from behind other paintings, Maxwell grinning while he eats his dinner, following Nico from one leaning pile to the next.

After a while, Maxwell goes over and sits down, setting his salad bowl down on the table with his fork lying on top.

"Nico, you have truly outdone yourself, and I'm proud." Then he just sits for a couple of minutes in silence. Nico is only partially acknowledging Maxell's amazement at their situation. He may have too many for this show, and he might have to hold some back.

This makes them both happy. With that decision, they must go through and divide the paintings up, for this show and then possibly a second show within the next six months or so. They decide not to let anyone know that they have more, just waiting.

They think the group they've decide to take speaks volumes and can be shown in a real story. They're happy with the end result and sit down to toast to good health. Things are finally starting to feel right again.

Saturday rolls in, and they're at the museum delivering the first half of this showing's paintings in the rental van. He drops them off to Maxwell and has Sera with him. Courtney from the catering company and her staff are buzzing around. They interact with Audrey and her assistant, and then the chain of command goes to Nico and Maxwell.

Nico and Sera leave to get the second half of the collection, and Maxwell starts to place them in the groups that he and Nico chose earlier in the week. The museum curator follows with white gloves, picking up and placing the paintings, one by one, in the appropriate areas. A few of the event staff are looking at the pictures in pure pleasure as the covers come off the canvases.

Nico barely notices because he's too involved in getting all the canvases out of the van and getting them in the right place. He's thinking that once that's done, with the paintings in a different environment, with different lighting, he will understand whether they stand on their own or not.

So he keeps busy not only with placing his work but with watching after his sister. At this point, she is over seven months pregnant, and he's definitely the protective brother. He's so protective, in fact, that everyone except Maxwell thinks they are not brother and sister but husband

and wife, although no one says anything. And with nothing being said, nothing can be denied, so it's just accepted as truth.

And with everyone thinking this very pregnant lady is his wife, no respectable female will flirt with him. And with them all being very polite, Nico figures they are lukewarm to him and to the collection, so he's just polite as well. And with everyone being so polite, he wants to get this done as quickly as possible.

That way, he can take his pictures of the placements and study them more at home. He's not realizing that the looks he's getting are because every person helping with the set up of this exhibit is astounded with the raw beauty and amazing depth every canvas is showing.

Maxwell is still running around, getting an odd feeling because no one is saying much, and there's an odd energy that he can't seem to put his finger on. So he's trying to engage someone to get an opinion, and everyone is realizing that they're part of something special—and that this exhibit is going to make waves. Everyone is realizing this, but Nico and Maxwell don't understand that they are all having difficulty verbalizing their awe.

Each team is working diligently, and time is flying by as everyone stays busy, doing what they're supposed to be doing.

Nico is only picking up on a weird dynamic, and Sera is getting tired and uncomfortable. He calls Maxwell over to the open patio. This is where they're going to set up the espresso bar, but they won't do it until the day of the opening. It's cleaned off and empty, and the perfect place for a short confidential conversation.

Maxwell shuts the door after following Nico out, and they go over last-minute instructions. After ironing out the last details, Nico tells Maxwell that he needs to get Sera home. Maxwell smiles and says, "This is going to be great—just you wait and see!"

"I hope so, but I'm getting a weird feeling and I don't know what it is. Are you feeling it?"

"Yeah, Nico, I sure am. But I tell you what, I'll check it out and see what they say and let you know. Go ahead and tend to your sister, and I'll give you a call later with any questions or any updates. How does that sound?"

"Sounds like a plan, my friend. I hope it works to our favor, but you must know that I'm really nervous now! OK, I'm going, but don't forget to call and let me know if you need anything."

"Will do. Go on now and be careful. I'll let you know if you need to come back after you take Sera home. Now get out of here, and don't worry."

With that, Nico returns to Sera. "You ready to go? Maxwell said he has it covered, so we can leave if you're ready."

Sera smiles and says, "Sure we can go. That sounds like a great idea to me." They stride out the entrance arm in arm, chatting about how it all looks, hung around the gallery, and what they need to do next.

"Now, Big Brother, we have to find you something suitable to wear. You cannot wear your old jeans and think you can get away with it. We need to go shopping and get you something that's equal to this showing. And I'm not going to take no for an answer!"

As they leave, some of the staff glance at them, because they're laughing. They are glancing, because to stare would be obvious, and they are curious about this man. Where did this guy come from, they're whispering when away from the bosses.

The next week flies by for Nico. At the post office, people he works with are asking about the opening, getting more details, because Nico has invited almost everyone that works there. He has invited them, partly out of guilt and partly because he has gotten to know some of them and wants some support. They have all accepted, without one person declining, and if nothing else, he'll have friendly faces there, regardless of how the show is received.

The Friday night before the show, he's restless and just wants it to be Sunday and over with. Then he'll know for sure how people react to his work, and if this has all been worth it.

He finally gets to sleep, after a couple of glasses of wine and staying up late to watch an old black-and-white movie on TV, "Sabrina" with Audrey Hepburn. He's kind of fuzzy about why he would stay up watching it, but it's interesting, the way Humphrey Bogart and William Holden are trying to play brothers. "Is there any way those two could be related?" He halfway laughs and scratches his head. "If nothing else, it's great to see Audrey Hepburn age through the movie. Cute." He wakes up after it's over and realizes he needs to hit the bed. Tomorrow will be a busy day.

Saturday is finally here, and he's going over his plans for the day and hopes it all happens the way he'd like. He will go by his mom's for breakfast and then take Sera with him to the gallery, around one, to check on everything. He'll take Sera home and drive to San Diego to see if he can find his letter writer.

He just hopes that traffic is not too bad, so he can get home to change and get to the opening before anyone notices he's late. Luckily, Maxwell knows what he's doing and will cover his tardiness. Maybe being late will be a good thing. He can only hope.

Breakfast at his mama's is uneventful. In fact, it's purposely calm because has Annamaria decided it would be that way. She wants him to be able to relax and take a few easy breaths before this important day gets into high gear.

She has everything ready when he gets there, so all the time is spent just talking and enjoying being together. She has total faith that tonight will be as great as he's hoping, but she's trying not to bring it up, because she knows it's weighing heavily on his mind. Tonight will be a make-it-or-break-it situation, and she's a little nervous for him.

It seems like a lifetime ago since his first show, so Annamaria will definitely be going to her church, this afternoon, to light a candle for her only son and his dreams.

Towards the end of breakfast, Sera and Roger arrive and sit down and start nibbling on the food on the table. Roger gives Sera a look and says, "You just ate a big breakfast, my dear. Are you still hungry?"

"Not really, it just looked like it would taste good. OK, Roger, I see the look, and I will stop." She puts down a piece of bacon, placing it back on the serving plate. She licks her fingers and then wipes them off on Nico's napkin. Nico softly laughs

Mama asks what his schedule is for the day, and what time she should be there tonight. Nico says, "Sera and I are going down to check the final set up, and then I'll be taking her home to get ready. I have something I have to do, and then I'll be at the museum around eight tonight. So you all can come whenever you want—and make sure to tell me your thoughts. Sound like a plan?"

They all nod their heads, and Sera gets up and grabs her purse and looks at Nico like, "OK I'm ready!" The rest of them get up from their chairs, sliding them back toward the table. Nico and Sera head for the door, while Roger helps Mama clear the breakfast table. On one trip to the kitchen, Roger leans over and says, "Mama what do you really think about the show?"

She stops for a half second, gives Roger a look of surprise, and says, "Roger dear, I have not seen any of the work yet. He has kept it all a secret from me. As far as I know, only Maxwell has seen the work, other than Nico. And before you say anything else, yes, I'm a little nervous for him. Quite frankly, I don't know what to expect. But I do think that it will be great."

"What? I can't believe you haven't seen any of it! Doesn't that make you wonder what the collection looks like?" Roger follows Annamaria into the kitchen.

"You know I did wonder, but I saw that the more Nico painted, and the more paintings he finished, the more he seemed to get comfortable in his own skin. It was like he was finding himself, and seeing those changes made me feel like I didn't need to see the paintings, because I saw the change for the better in him."

Roger is rinsing off the dishes while listening to Annamaria. He stops for a minute and looks at her. He can only smile because her face is glowing, and he understands that she's content, because her family is getting to a really good place, individually and together.

He doesn't say anything for a while and just helps his mother-in-law clear the breakfast table and clean the kitchen. Once that's done, he tells her he's going to run a couple of errands before he meets Sera later, at home. They'll pick her up for the opening around seven, so they have plenty of time to get to the museum. She walks him to the door and watches as he walks to his car and drives away.

As Sera and Nico walk to the museum door arm in arm, Nico confides in Sera. "I cannot tell you how nervous I am right now."

Sera smiles and says, "It's going to be great because you have worked so hard, and I think I have noticed some changes in you lately. It seems like you're more comfortable with everything. So just remember to smile, because, my hunky brother, you look better when you do!"

He laughs and opens one of the big brass-and-glass doors to the museum, and they walk in. In the wing where the opening is being prepped, with lots of staff running around, they suddenly see Maxwell. They walk over to him while glancing around at the paintings, all hanging in the right places, interspersed with trees and flowering planters. There are three bars, including an espresso bar on the open patio.

He hadn't realized there was a kitchen hidden at the back of the museum, which is being using to warm up and fix all the food. He's seeing all the prep work that's going into this event—his event! Maxwell asks, "Is it looking like you imagined?"

Nico smiles really big and says, "No, it's better." Then he strides over to stand in front of the first of the pictures, then slowly walks along, pausing in front of each one, remembering the letters that led him here.

He looks back at Maxwell and Sera standing by the doorway, chatting about the way things have turned out, and how great the space looks and how amazing the paintings look, especially in the order that Nico wanted them arranged.

"I remember my reaction when he first showed them to me, I was just floored. He had all these "jewels," and I was so happy that he was able to finally breakthrough and create these..." Maxwell's voice trails off as he looks around the room, almost speechless. He glances back at Sera, who's distracted looking around the room as well.

Nico walks back towards them, noticing the museum staff, the caterer, and the planner's staff all busy doing different things, all making sure they tend to the smallest details. Audrey is conferring with Courtney and a couple of other ladies, and they motion to him as he walks by.

Nico walks over to them. "Good afternoon, ladies. I want to thank you for all your hard work. I'm very pleased with the way it's turning out. So, thank you very much. Did you have a question for me?"

Audrey says, "Thanks, Nico. Yes, we have worked really hard on making this the right setting for this wonderful collection."

Courtney adds, "Yes it's quite an emotion-evoking collection."

Courtney's assistant adds, "May I ask where your inspiration comes from?"

"Well, inspiration comes from many places. Ah...I haven't met you yet, have I? My name is Nico Moratelli, and yours is?"

"My name is Tess. I'm Courtney's assistant. That really didn't answer my question though, Mr. Mortatelli. They are just so compelling, and I was just curious."

"Well, Tess, the most recent one was inspired by an afternoon at the beach. I was watching this couple watch their son play in the sand and with the waves, and he couldn't have been more than three or four. It was just the way their umbrellas cast shadows and the spirit of simple joy. I hope that's a more complete answer for you."

Tess, Courtney, and Audrey just stand there listening to this handsome man speak with kindness and perception. It's intoxicating, and they all three just stand there, for half a minute more than they had intended to, because they got caught up in his eyes and his smile.

He smiles and says, "Unless you have any anything else, I would like to excuse myself." He pauses for a moment. All three just nod and smile, and he returns to Maxwell and Sera.

They are talking about when Sera and Roger's baby is due, and Sera is rubbing her belly, smiling. Nico walks up and rubs her belly too, smiling at Maxwell. "Isn't she a beautiful pregnant lady? And I can hardly wait!"

Maxwell watches Sera and Nico as they go to another area to check on the rest of the collection and the setup. This is the first time Sera has seen this part of the collection, and she brings up different points on each one, remarking on the planters and trees that look so great. They turn a corner and see a fountain placed in the middle of the room. The painted ceiling above it is accented by lights reflecting on the water in the fountain.

Nico turns to Sera, "I'll tell you a secret. This is only half of the collection, Sis. We have at least this many more at my place. And the very best part is that I still have ideas. I'm having no trouble now. So if this is well receive, it will make it so nice. I feel like I'm finally across that bridge or whatever you want to call it."

They walk back toward Maxwell, and Nico extends his hand for a handshake. Maxwell extends his hand to Nico, as well, and puts his left hand on his shoulder. "Well done, you!"

Nico says, "Well, I'm going to take Sera home to change, run my errand, and then meet you here later."

Maxwell has a mild look of alarm on his face, "I'd be nervous if I didn't know you better. Be careful, and see you later. I'll be changing here, so I'm not leaving until it's over. Let me know if you need anything."

Nico yells over his shoulder as he and Sera are walking out, "You know I will! See you in a while."

As they stride out of the museum and into Nico's car, Sera starts talking. "I knew you had it in you, but I never thought it was *that!* I'm amazed at what you have created. Each one made me feel something different. And every one was a complete story. Oh, I'm amazed..." Her voice trails off as she looks out the window, remembering the feelings he was able to evoke. The rest of the way home, she just sits there smiling wryly.

Nico is so preoccupied with how he's going to get to San Diego quickly that he doesn't notice that Sera has quit talking. They pull up in front Sera and Roger's house, and Sera opens her door and grabs her purse, looking at Nico. "OK," she says, "We'll pick up Mama and be there, probably around eight. Is that OK?"

"That's great. I should be there around then, so save me a place." Nico laughs, and Sera just smiles and shakes her head at him. She shuts her door and walks up the sidewalk and into her house.

Nico drives by his place, picks up his clothes, and hustles to get to the freeway to San Diego, knowing traffic might be bad. He's going to make this happen.

He daydreams off and on while driving, finally gets close to the exit that he needs, and pulls off. He finds a public parking spot close to the docks and parks. He walks down to the piers, where all the boats rented out to "Neptune" burials are docked. It was not four o'clock yet, so he's doing well with time. They probably wouldn't leave the dock until four or four-thirty, at the latest, to get out far enough from shore to be able to scatter the ashes.

He walks to the bait houses where they do the paperwork to pay for the boats, looking for someone he thinks could be this woman. This is the one person who has changed his life forever. He wants to find a face that he can put with all those letters. He starts searching, glancing around, trying to not look like a stalker.

There are five different "bait houses" that he wants to check out. He almost feels desperate. It would make tonight so meaningful if he knew what she looks like.

Twenty minutes go by, and there is no one yet who seems to fit the bill. But he keeps looking, and more and more time is going by, with no one yet a candidate in his mind. He keeps walking from one pier to the next. Close to four thirty, he looks two piers down and, for a moment, thinks he sees a girl that was just at the museum—and then shakes his head. He mutters to himself, "I probably need glasses. Oh well, I need to go, because this is not working."

He walks back to his car and changes his clothes in his car, right before he backs out and drives away. He heads down the highway trying not speed too much to get back to the museum. He figures it's only a little past five o'clock on Saturday, so traffic is better than on a weekday. Small favor, he thinks, and if he's lucky, he'll get there not too much past eight. He knows Maxwell will be glad that he's not too late.

He's only slightly disappointed he didn't see anyone who might be his letter writer. He's thinking about the gallery and all his work waiting to be seen, and his butterflies are starting up again.

Walking into the museum, he is immediately greeted by people, left and right. Maxwell sees him and, grinning really big, rushes over to Nico's side and starts the introductions. Each person that Nico meets is smiling largely and is effusive about how much they are enjoying his work. Everyone wants more time with him, and he's finding it hard to speak because no one will let him.

People are coming fast and furious, and he's almost overwhelmed with the passion everyone is saying they are picking up from the paintings. He's only able to smile and nod.

Maxwell is trying to guide Nico through the maze of people who are stopped in groups in front of each painting. They were smart to not place them too close to each other. Being so large, they use the space so well. Nico is trying to keep up with Maxwell, and it's over two hours later when he finally gets a chance to nibble on something and get something to drink.

He sneaks out to the espresso bar for a little caffeine jolt, so he can then dive back into the "meet and greet." He gets a cappuccino and stands there for a few minutes by himself, just looking out at the night. He tries to see the stars, but most of them are not visible because of the city lights. He takes a long, slow deep breath, and he thinks, "Is this really happening? Could all this really be happening...and I don't even know her name."

"There you are!" Maxwell interrupts his thoughts, walks up, and takes the cup and saucer out of his hand, putting it down on a table nearby. He guides Nico back into the thick of admirers inside the museum.

Hours later, Nico is finally given a chance to sit for a minute. He looks around for a place and then remembers he hasn't had much chance to talk to his family all evening. So he decides to find them instead.

They are talking to a few people that Nico remembers meeting earlier in the evening. He walks up and asks how everyone is doing. And the general response is "Yes, oh yes."

Sera grabs Nico's arm and says, "You won't be mad at me if we leave soon will you? My feet are starting to kill me. You know a pregnant lady and her swollen feet really need their rest."

"Oh definitely, I understand. I really appreciate your support. Now Roger, get this woman home, will you?"

Roger smiles, grabs Nico's hand, shaking it warmly, then does that shoulder bump that guys do when they don't want to hug but don't want to leave it at a handshake. He says, "No problem, and I have to tell you, I'm so impressed! I think you have quite a success on your hands. Let's talk tomorrow, OK?"

Annamaria adds, "Yes! Breakfast at my house. I will do something special for my wonderful family. I'm so proud of you. So we talk tomorrow, yes?"

"Yes Mama, I'll be there." Maxwell comes back then and retrieves Nico to introduce him to some more people. And the rest of the evening flies by.

When things finally wind down, Nico and Maxwell stand at the champagne bar, toasting their work. Maxwell finally mutters, "My cheeks hurt from smiling so much."

"Mine too! Now that's something I did not expect." Nico finds a place to sit and watches as Maxwell joins him. They both let out a sigh of relief and then laugh at their timing. They watch as the last of the guests leave, and the cleaning crew starts picking up and packing up everything.

Nico turns to Maxwell after a long pause and asks, "So this will move in two weeks to the Basil Grey gallery, right?"

"That's right. She says she might want another opening then, for a different group of people."

All Nico can add, at this point, is "Wow." He stands up slowly and says to Maxwell, "Well since the party is over, I'm going home to bed, because I'm beat!"

"No problem. It was an unbelievable success, and I have no doubts that all reviews are going to be great. Have a great night. Be careful, and I'll call you in the next couple of days."

"Goodnight, Maxwell." Nico practically floats out of the museum and into his car. When he gets home, he barely gets his clothes off before falling on the bed to sleep. His dreams are disjointed. In them, he keeps walking up to women, reaching toward their shoulders to turn them around, and they disappear.

The next morning, he can hardly believe that, the night before, he shared his visions with the world—and it turned out well. He hadn't needed an alarm clock, because as soon as the sun started coming up, he was awake. He isn't moving quickly. This morning needs a slow and steady pace. He doesn't have to go to work, though he will continue working for a little while longer. He wants to make sure he finds all the letters he possibly can before he leaves there. The letters have provided a kind of journey not just for her but for him as well.

He feels lucky that no one knows his inspiration, because it makes it all the more special. Besides, if she ever knows what he has done, she might be embarrassed—or even furious with him for the invasion of privacy. The odds of ever finding her are getting slimmer and slimmer, and he's fine with that. It's probably all for the best.

"Besides," he starts mumbling out loud, "I've never even known her name." He's shuffling into the kitchen in his boxer shorts and a T-shirt to make coffee. Even though he's meeting his family at his mama's house for breakfast, he still needs his coffee. He wants to jump for joy that the challenge has been met, and he's still on his feet. He's so relieved.

While the coffee is brewing, he goes over to turn on the radio, and a song by Bob Schneider is on, "Let the Light In," He goes to his easel, where another blank canvas is propped up, ready to go. He just walks through the room and looks around at the other paintings that won't be shown until the end of the year.

He passes the credenza holding the carved wooden box that houses all the letters he has taken. Pausing for a moment, he puts his hand on the locked box and pats the top a couple of times. The buzzer goes off, marking the end of the brewing cycle on his coffee pot, and he proceeds on to the kitchen to get a cup. Just as he adds a little milk, his cell phone rings. It's Maxwell.

"Good morning Max, how are you doing today?"

"Good morning yourself genius! I'll have you know that last night was a complete success in every way, and you're my new hero. How are you feeling this morning?"

"Max, I'm fine, really fine. Happy too. I just got my first cup of coffee, so your timing couldn't have been better."

"I've gotten some of the early reviews, and it's a resounding success. When we move the collection to the Basil Grey Gallery, it will probably sell out in no time. So I want you to start thinking about the second half of the collection and what we need to do for that. I think we were right in only putting half of them out there for now. I'm just so pleased that the event went well, and that it all went according to plan. Even I could not have planned a better reception. So what are your plans now that we have round one of the collection being viewed?"

"Well, first of all, I'm not quitting my job at the post office just yet. I really like the routine and seeing everyone every day, so I think I'll stay just a little while longer. Other than that, I plan on being an involved uncle soon and just appreciating everything that's going on around me—and of course to keep painting. So Max, why don't you keep me posted on when the collection will be moved and what you need from me."

"Nico, it sounds like you'll be busy, and I like that. I'll let you know the timetable as soon as it's decided—and if and when they decide to have the gallery opening. Just stay in touch, so I can keep you updated. I'm sure when they get to Basil Grey, it will be exciting. Did I tell you that they could all be sold in just a few days?"

"No. That's cool! Can't tell you how relieved it makes me. Thanks for not giving me a hard time about wanting to stay on at the post office. And thanks again for always supporting me and my work, no matter what's going on. You're the best, and I really do appreciate all your hard work. I know I haven't been easy to work with at times, and I'm sorry for that. So I just want you to know that I don't take all you do for granted."

"Nico, I don't know what happened, but you've changed. You seem different from when you were first starting to create again, and it's all very positive. I hope you don't mind me mentioning it, but I didn't know if it was a conscious thing or if it just happened. All I know is that you seem to be more comfortable in your own skin."

"Funny you should mention that. Yeah, it kinda feels that way too. It's like the pieces are falling into place. Sure is nice."

Chapter Nine

Daylight is starting to trickle in the windows of her apartment, and it wakes Bear up. It's not quite seven thirty on Saturday morning, but it's an excellent time, as far as he's concerned, to wake Tess up. He stands up slowly, stretching as he rises up, shaking his head vigorously, rattling the tags on his collar. He turns around in place because he sleeps by her bed, and stands facing the head of the bed. He drops his head and rests his chin on the mattress, right by her face, and just stares at her. He stays in this position until he sees her eyes.

Then his tail starts going and, when she speaks, his whole body wiggles. She sits up and stretches her arms out to the ceiling and says, "Good morning, Sweet Face! You're just the best alarm clock anyone could ever want." With that, he's practically in convulsions, he's so excited. She gets up and has to calm him down, because it's going to take her a few minutes to get it together, so she can take him for a walk. She hurries, because you never know how badly a dog has to go, sometimes until it's too late.

Before too long, they are halfway down the block, and Bear is relieved and ready for a stroll. Tess remembers how he used to pull on the leash because he was so excited to go out. Now his pace has slowed down, because he's getting up there in years. She reaches over to pat his head as they walk along. She likes the fact that his head is high enough for her to drop her hand down—and just touch the top of his head. A perfect fit.

The rest of the walk, she smiles knowing what a blessing he is in her life, her constant companion who never judges or wavers in his affection. "My perfect partner," she thinks, "is it wrong to love you this much?"

By the time they get back to the apartment it's overcast and cool, and she decides to put an old movie on. She puts on "Sabrina," with Audrey Hepburn, Humphrey Bogart, and William Holden. While the previews are playing, she makes a pot of coffee, then sits down on the couch with Bear lying nearby. She has to step over him to get a cup once it's brewed, then settles back down with her coffee. Anticipating the plot of her movie escape, she says the lines out loud along with the characters.

Her thoughts drift to all that has happened, and she sighs, trying to let it go. By the time the movie is over, the sun has come back out a bit, and Bear is ready to go back outside. She decides to take him to the off-leash park. As old as Bear is, he still tries his best to run with different packs in the park, and when he finally lies down at her feet, she knows he's ready to go home. She lets him rest a little. Then when she gets up, he gets up automatically, and they stroll back to the Jeep.

Just before she drives off, Courtney calls and checks in. "Hey there! What time are you going to come over so we can get to the museum and start to set up?"

Tess looks at the clock on the dashboard. "Well, it's ten thirty, so I'll go home for a minute and then head your way, if that's OK. Should I bring Bear?"

"That sounds great, and yeah, go ahead and bring Bear. I know Maya would love his company."

"Sounds great. I'll be there within the hour."

"See you then." When Courtney hangs up, Tess gets on her way.

On their drive to Santa Monica, Tess and Courtney chat about little things and just enjoy the pretty day. At the museum, they get immediately involved in the production that's going on. They check in with Audrey and Maxwell and learn that Nico is on his way in a large van with the first half of the collection. Audrey is visibly anxious about everything going as planned. She's flitting around the gallery wing, checking and double-checking everything against her notebook, and anxiously watching the loading dock through a first-floor window.

Finally, she sees a large white van back up, and Nico and a very pregnant woman get out. Maxwell is there to meet them. He gives the woman a warm hug and excitedly shakes Nico's hand, doing the shoulder bump thing that guys do.

They walk around to the back of the van and start unloading the large paintings. Museum staff help move them off the van and carry them to an odd dolly used to roll the paintings onto the elevator and to their temporary home in the wing upstairs.

The loading dock is in the museum basement, with access from the back. All public areas are on the first floor, with the offices mostly upstairs. The museum looks like two floors from the front and three from the back.

Most of the staff have heard about Nico and have seen his previous work. They're excited to work on this exhibit—and be able to see the work firsthand, before anyone else. As they bring the large canvases up from the basement loading dock, they are still covered from shipping in the rented van. Maxwell instructs everyone where to place them for mounting on the walls, in the grouping that Nico and Maxwell have already decided. They look like ants, with everybody doing something different, all at the same time, a controlled chaos. You could recognize the museum staff, because they all had on white cotton gloves, ready to gingerly handle these precious pieces.

As the groupings are being placed, the covers are coming off the paintings, one by one. The staff placing the groupings lean them against the wall, roughly where they will be hung. Once they place them and take a step back to look at the work, they suddenly forget to breathe. They are so startled that they just stand there entranced until something jars them out of their momentary trance. It's difficult for anyone to say anything because words do not easily come to mind. So there's an awkward silence when each group sees the set of paintings that they are prepping to hang.

The staff notices Nico leave with the pregnant woman to get the rest of the paintings. Just after they leave people take a few minutes to gawk at the paintings and try and wrap their heads around what they're seeing. They are all mesmerized.

They listen to Maxwell explain which pictures are grouped together and in what part of the wing. Audrey follows right behind him, making notes and pointing to her museum staff, giving them verbal directions that follow Maxwell's lead. Everyone is buzzing because all the covers are coming off the paintings.

Courtney and Tess are busy double-checking how many tables they have, where they are going to be, and all the other details that go into a large-scale event. They make decisions on uniforms and instruct the waitstaff with guidelines for this exhibit. Tess is following Courtney, making notes to double-check later in the day. Suddenly she sees a painting for the first time, just after they take the cover off, and she completely stops, forgetting what she's doing, and just stares. It's like someone grabbed ahold of her guts and yanked them out, only to drop them onto the floor. She even feels like she stopped breathing and is not sure if her jaw dropped.

Before Courtney realizes Tess is no longer following her, she gets about ten steps ahead. She looks behind her, only to see Tess stopped in her tracks in a completely different world. Courtney walks back to Tess, nudges her, and says, "Hey, are you OK? You look like you've seen a ghost!"

"What? Oh, yeah, I guess I got lost for a minute. You need to look at that. I don't know why, but I feel so connected to it—and in such a strong way that it doesn't make sense." Tess shakes suddenly, like she got a cold shiver and says, "Courtney, do you know anything about this guy? Where did he come from? What does his other work look like, do you know?" She was pausing only slightly between questions, not really giving Courtney any time to answer.

Courtney's head pops back, in shock, when she turns her head to see what has mesmerized Tess. She's thrown for a loop for a moment. Then she grabs Tess's arm, pulling her out of shock and back to work.

Courtney leans over and quietly says, "Tess, these are really good, which is going to make this show a big hit. So we really need to make sure our part of this is perfect. So I need you to be present and not get distracted."

Nodding her head in agreement, Tess is now following Courtney, while listening intently. She's still a little shook up about the connection to the painting. She's trying very hard to concentrate on the task at hand and keep listening to Courtney. So she avoids looking at any of the paintings as they walk, looking only straight ahead.

The workers suddenly get quieter when Nico and his companion arrive again with the other half of the exhibit. They are trying to get a good look at this guy, to see if they can figure him out—and the very pregnant woman he's with. He's absolutely doting on her. Are they married? Somebody notices Sera's wedding ring and jumps to the conclusion that, indeed, they are married.

This obviously talented and good looking man is being given the cold shoulder in a very subtle way by women that normally would be fawning all over him. And if he wasn't so preoccupied with the showing, he would probably take it all to heart. But right now he has more important matters on his mind. Since there's still so much to be done, he ignores it and focuses on more important—and more immediate—things.

Tess is checking on a few items for Courtney and has to walk past Nico a few times. She wants to check him out and see if she can better understand the gut-wrenching pictures that she's seeing. It seems every time she walks by him, he's in deep consultation with his manager or walking arm in arm with "her." It flashes through her mind, "The good ones are always taken."

Courtney is checking things in the kitchen, which is located downstairs from where they are setting up. She wants to make sure the catering staff has the right setup available. She calls Tess on her cell, "How's it going upstairs?"

"We have all the tables for the setup that you requested, along with linens, and some of the food stations are starting to take shape. Oh, they haven't started working on the espresso station yet…wait a minute… I'm looking out there. Never mind! It looks like the artist and his manager are having a quick meeting there. When are they supposed to start setting up the coffee bar?"

"They might start today, but we still have a week. We are right on track so far. But if we check on it towards the end of next week and nothing is done, we might have a problem. So far, so good, though."

The afternoon flies by, and they notice Nico and his companion hugging a few people on their way out the door, with Maxwell walking with them. By the time Maxwell comes back, voices are getting louder and people are more animated. The energy level has just jumped a few levels because everyone is no longer holding back their enthusiasm.

Tess is trying to stay busy, going over the details that Courtney has brought up, but she keeps getting distracted by the paintings. She's feeling connected to a lot of these paintings, not every one of them, but a lot more than she's comfortable with. It's like he knows what she's feeling and going through, almost like he understands. But the trouble is that it's just a feeling and nothing definite.

Things are get wrapped up for the afternoon, and everyone is making notes of where they want to start when they come back and what might be missing from their part.

Tess is glad to be leaving, because the more she's around some of the pictures, the more uncomfortable she feels. She hopes it's just because she's tired. It really has been a long day. She's just being sensitive, she tells herself. After all, she's never seen this guy before, so she must be making more out of it than she needs to. He's just a good artist. That's all.

She and Courtney are fairly quiet on the ride to Courtney's house. They are going over last-minute notes for what they need to do next week—Saturday in particular—the day of the show.

When they drive up Courtney's driveway, Tess says she needs to get Bear and just drive home. She can't believe how appealing a hot bubble bath sounds and maybe a glass of wine and some music...yeah, that's what she wants right now, more than anything.

She and Bear get to their apartment and go straight up. After all, Bear was outside all day in Courtney's backyard. Bear goes directly from the front door to his big floor pillow, curls up, and lies down.

Tess drops her things on the table, puts some music on in the background, and starts her bath. The paintings are still haunting her, and she tries to forget the feeling they gave her. Instead, she thinks, "I'm just going to enjoy this bath, forget how tough today was, and concentrate on how much we got done."

She lies back in the lavender-scented bubbles and breathes a sigh of relief, closing her eyes. She startles herself back awake after dozing off. From the tepid temperature of the bath, she's been in too long. She gets up, towel dries, turns off the music, and goes to bed.

Sometimes it is hard to believe that she is close to the day she has arranged to scatter not just her mother's ashes, but her little brother's as well. She remembers talking to Courtney about it, saying that you can never be ready to lose your parents or siblings. She runs down the checklist she remembers in her head, and remembers that the representative will handle most of the details for her. The most important thing is to be there. They received copies of the death certificates and they have the needed permits for the boat. It looks like it's all taken care of. They are also providing baskets and rose petals for the "release." Tess decides she wants to take some champagne to toast them, and it would be the correct thing to do to write something for the occasion.

She stays busy all week, helping Courtney with details of the show and trying to forget what's haunting her. She thinks it will be interesting to see the art again—to see if her reaction is the same or if it was just because she was really tired.

Early Friday evening, Courtney calls to make sure they are on track for Saturday. Tess appreciates Courtney's attention to detail, and seeing the final effect of everything at these events is really amazing to her. She does not envy the pressure that Courtney is under, and she wants to help make sure that her friend's vision of the evening happens just as she wants it to. They go over all the details that they need to handle, starting Saturday morning, and then confirm that Tess is bringing Bear to her house and that they are taking both cars to the museum.

Tess also feels the need to apologize again for having to leave early to go to San Diego. Courtney says that the way things have worked out is better than she had imagined. It looks like the event will be memorable.

Saturday comes too quickly, and Tess has to make sure to pack her car with her mom and brother's ashes, and everything else she needs, before she leaves to go to Courtney's. She's already arranged for Bear to go with her, so he can stay there while they take care of the opening and Tess goes to San Diego. Tess will pick him up on Sunday.

When she gets to Courtney's house, she's ready to go, so Tess follows her in her car to the museum. They get there before ten in the morning, and the guards are waiting inside at the locked front door to let them in. Tess is a little apprehensive about seeing the collection again, hoping it doesn't unnerve her like it did last Saturday.

Tess and Courtney walk to the wing where the collection is being shown and start pulling out their notes to get to work. The museum staff is already at work, and there is a really nice feeling, with everyone enjoying what they are doing and feeling privileged to be working on this exhibit.

Every department is busy trying to get the setup finished. The pictures have all gone up, as of Thursday, and Maxwell had a walk-through on Friday. He approved it for Nico, and now the plants are all being brought in, along with all the finishing touches to give just the right atmosphere.

Courtney has already checked on the kitchen, and the food prep is going well. They don't anticipate any issues. Tess is going over notes with Courtney, when they look toward the front doors and see Nico and his wife walking up to the doors. After the guards unlock the door, they walk in laughing, arm in arm.

Tess and Courtney are going through her punch list, and they are dividing the detail work for them to follow up. Audrey walks over to see if she can assist. All three get distracted as they look up to see the artist walking toward them. They all stop talking in reaction the handsome distraction.

"Good afternoon ladies. I want to thank you for all your hard work. I'm very pleased with the way it's turning out. So, thank you very much. Did you have a question for me?"

Audrey is the first to speak and says, "Thanks, Nico. We have worked really hard on making this the right setting for this wonderful collection."

Courtney adds, "Yes, it's quite an emotion-evoking collection."

Tess adds, "May I ask where your inspiration comes from?"

"Well, inspiration comes from many places. Ah...I haven't met you yet, have I? My name is Nico Mortatelli, and yours is?"

"My name is Tess. I'm Courtney's assistant. That really didn't answer my question though, Mr. Mortatelli. They are just so compelling, and I'm just curious."

"Well Tess, the most recent one was inspired by an afternoon at the beach. I was watching this couple watch their son play in the sand and with the waves, and he couldn't have been more than three or four. It was just the way their umbrellas cast their shadows and the spirit of simple joy. I hope that's a more complete answer for you. There are times, that if you are observant, you will see things that may have been hidden from you before. Have you ever felt that way?"

Tess, Courtney, and Audrey just stand there, nodding their heads, listening to this handsome man speak with kindness and perception. It's intoxicating, and they all three stand there, speechless, for half a minute more than they had intended to.

Nico smiles and says, "If there isn't anything else, I would like to excuse myself." He pauses for a moment, and all three just nod and smile, and he turns and walks back to Maxwell and Sera.

They are talking about when Sera and Roger's baby is due, and Sera is rubbing her belly, smiling. Nico walks up and rubs her belly too, smiling at Maxwell. "Isn't she a beautiful pregnant lady? And I can hardly wait!"

Roger smiles at both Sera and Nico, as all three walk to another part of the wing to check on the rest of the collection.

Tess, Courtney, and Audrey try not to watch him walk all the way down the wing, but do anyway. Then Courtney takes a quick breath and says, "OK, Tess what's left on the list that needs to be done? We need to go over it before you need to leave?"

Audrey says, "I need to go to my office for a minute, but I'll only be about fifteen minutes or so. See you in a bit."

Tess and Courtney go over the last-minute details and the status of her list of items. They get it all organized, and Courtney says, "I really appreciate your help and hope that the boat trip is not too much to handle by yourself. Call me if you need to talk when it's over, OK?"

"I'll remember that. I just want to make sure that I get to the dock in enough time. I'll talk to you later, I'm sure." Tess turns and walks out the front door. It's just past four, and she knows she can't waste any time getting to San Diego. For once, she thinks, traffic is not too bad. She arrives at the dock a little past four thirty, and finds the bait house for the dock she needs. She goes in and meets the Sidney the representative from the company that arranged everything and walks up to the counter to check in for the boat.

Once that's done, they walk down the pier, find the slip they are looking for, and ask for Captain Tim. He smiles and walks over to help them on the boat along with all they are carrying—two boxes of cremation ashes, two wicker baskets, a big bag of red rose petals, and two bottles of champagne.

They get everything situated and pull away from the dock. Sidney, is getting the baskets ready, pouring the ashes into them once the boat gets close to the coordinates listed on the documents.

They stop pretty far from the shore and can no longer see the dock, but they can still see the big arch bridge that's a good landmark. Sidney asks Tess if she's ready. She says yes. Two of the crew help get them to the back platform where they will do the send-off. They hang on to Tess and Sidney, while they drop the baskets in the ocean, one at a time. Once they let the ashes go into the water, Sidney hands Tess the rose petals to throw into the wind to symbolize letting their spirits go.

Tess reads what she has written for the two of them, with a glass of champagne in her hand. She manages to get through almost the entire eulogy, if that's what you want to call it, without crying. Her voice does crack a couple of times, but she manages to get it read. After that, she raises her glass, and so does everyone else on the boat. She says, "To Mom and David. I will love you always." Everyone says, "Cheers!" and they all take a sip. They stay until the sun sets and see the "green boom" when it "hits" the water.

Once the sun has set, they pull anchor and head back to the dock. Once they arrive, Sidney walks Tess out to the parking lot. Tess thanks her for everything, and Sidney tells her the paperwork with the coordinates of where they were will be listed on the documents. Tess keeps the champagne bottles. She doesn't know why, but she does.

Driving back home, Tess realizes that the event should be in full swing right about now. She decides to text Courtney, asking her to call on her way home and let her know how it went. Since she doesn't have Bear tonight, she goes home and gets into some comfortable clothes. She fixes a bowl of cereal, plops down on the couch, grabs the remote, and checks to see if there's anything good on TV. She doesn't really care what she watches. She just wants to decompress from this eventful day. Staring at the TV, she's not seeing anything, because her mind is on that beautiful sunset and the events that happened earlier.

Her cell phone rings, startling her out of her thoughts. Courtney is checking in on her way home.

"Well, how did it go, Tess?"

"It was fine. My voice cracked reading what I planned, but it was a beautiful sunset, and it went really smoothly. Tell me, how did the event go?"

"Wow! It was amazing. Everything went according to plan except that the response to his paintings was through the roof, it was so positive. The art was better than anyone thought it would be. It seemed to energize everyone, and there was not one person who was not affected. You should have seen the faces. The critics, the big art house people, the private collectors, and everyone else were just floored. And it seemed like no one wanted to leave. Audrey and I were over in a corner, just watching everyone, and they kept going back and looking at each painting over and over. It was like they were trying to pick a favorite. Just amazing!"

"Wonderful! That's terrific. Did anyone notice the food and drink by chance?"

"Tess, you know that if they did, it was all positive. The show was some kind of record or something...I overheard a couple of private collectors talking about it, and it was going to make him a lot of money it looks like."

"That's great. The paintings really made me uneasy for some reason, and I found them haunting."

"Well, they will be at the museum for two weeks, and then they are being transferred to Audrey's Basil Grey Gallery. And you should have seen how excited she is to get them there. That's when they will start selling them. Did I tell you that since the museum event went so well she definitely wants me to do a second party there, once they are moved?"

"I think that's great Courtney! Have you been there yet? When do you meet with her for details?"

"Well, since this will be a smaller venue and a lower-scale event, we're going to meet next week and put it together. I'll call you tomorrow morning when we get up, and you can come over and get Bear then. He's lying on the floor next to my chair right now, and Maya is lying right beside him. They are two tired but happy campers."

Courtney thanks her again for all her help, and Tess says she will tell her all about the scattering tomorrow, when she sees her. Right now, she's still taking it all in and is not sure exactly how she feels.

Once they hang up, Tess walks to the patio door, slides it open, and steps out. There is only room for two chairs, and one is folded up and leaning against the wall. She sits down and looks up at the sky. She leans back, takes a deep breath, and thinks of her family—her mom and her brother.

Looking at the sky in L.A. is like looking at an ink pool. It's all dark with no stars, because you can't really see anything above all the lights in this major city. She sits in the quiet for a while, then realizes that something is missing, her constant companion, Bear. She says a silent prayer with thanks for him and everything he has brought to her life. He's the constant friend and the only constant presence she can count on.

The fact that Bear is now fourteen years old is a little scary, because she doesn't want to think of what her life would be like without him. She tries to shake off that feeling.

Her thoughts turn to what we all need, a chance to be validated, a chance to know that we count, that we matter in this vast sea of humanity. We all deal with the insecurities of wondering what we are here for, after all. Unless you have found a calling that you're able to pursue, you wonder what your life is supposed to mean. You just want to know that you count…that you matter. There are so many people who are just struggling from day to day, who are just happy to make it to the next day.

She starts talking to herself. "Why do I feel like I need to tone down who I am? Why do I think, when relationships don't work out, it was because I was too much or not enough? Why can't I accept that it might be them, and they can't accept me because they don't accept themselves? And maybe I really am better off when it doesn't work out? Well, all I really know is that I feel better talking out loud to myself when Bear is here to act like he's listening!" She laughs, walks back inside, and glances at the clock.

She turns off the TV and the lights, and goes to bed. Since she doesn't have Bear, her built-in alarm clock, to wake her up at six thirty, no matter what, she sleeps in a bit.

There's no need for a walk this morning. She lazily gets up thinking: it's much later than a little past eight. She makes coffee and checks the news on her laptop. By the time she's on her second cup, she has read most of the news outlets on the web and caught up on the world. After a few minutes, she sits down with a pen and paper and writes her mother another letter.

> Dear Mom,
>
> I have decided that I must now be brave, to imagine what my life can be. I have no anchor, with you, Dad, and David gone, so that means I must fly. I must spread my wings and try to fly on my own.

But if truth be known, I'm scared. I don't know what I'm exactly scared of, which makes it irrational. Maybe I'm afraid of success of some sort—that if I'm brave, and I face my all-too-uncertain future with straightened shoulders and chin up, even if I fail, it's better than not doing anything about it.

Sometimes, I just wish this was a nightmare that I could wake up from, and things would be different.

What's important to me today is Bear, my friends, and being creative. And I think I'm going to try and make something with my photography. It's important to me to take those little slices out of life and keep them frozen in time. You always did say that you liked the pictures I take, so I'm going to try and do something with them. I don't know what just yet. But I need to find a beginning.

I miss you guys so much. I hope you are all together. I love you.

Me

She folds the paper, slides it into an envelope, addresses it to Mom in Heaven, and puts a stamp on it, while placing it by the front door. Looking at the clock, she decides to take a shower and be ready to go when Courtney calls. She's missing Bear more than usual and hoping Courtney is going to invite her to have lunch, because it's always fun to be with all of them.

She's drying her hair when Courtney calls and says that they are up and wanting to have a cookout. So come on over when she's ready, and they will hang out. As Tess hangs up the phone, she smiles, thinking this is gonna be fun. And I need some fun for a change.

Tess is anxious to get Courtney's feedback on trying to do something with her photography, since it seems to be the one thing that might get her through this.

She finishes getting ready, and when she passes by the front door, she picks up the letter she wrote to her mom—and slides it inside the book she's reading, so she knows where it is. She wants to mail it later this evening, when she takes Bear for a walk. Then she absentmindedly sticks the book in her shoulder bag. She slings is over her shoulder and heads out the door for Courtney's house.

When she gets there, the outside grill is going, and Brad is tending to it and talking on the phone. Natalie answers the door and gives Tess a big hug and tells her Courtney is in the kitchen. Then she goes back to her room, and Tess walks in the kitchen.

"Hey there! Glad you could make it," says Courtney as Tess puts her shoulder bag on the back of the bar chair. As she does so, several things fall out onto the floor. She bends down and grabs them, stuffing them back inside her bag.

Before she knows it, Bear comes running in from outside, from hearing her voice. She loves on him a minute, then turns to Courtney and says, "I got this bag a couple of weeks ago, and I swear every time I turn around quickly, things fall out. Guess I need to either take less stuff in it or get a new one."

"Yeah, I know what you mean. It seems like the larger the bag I have, the more things I suddenly *have* to take with me, when I really don't need it all." Courtney opens her refrigerator and looks over her shoulder at Tess. "Want a glass of wine or a beer or Diet Coke?"

"A beer would be great. Thanks. What is Brad doing?"

"He has his friend Jack, who is a professional tennis player, on the phone. Jack is trying to get a job as a club professional in Pacific Palisades. He and Brad are talking strategy, so he's tending the grill while talking on his cell. He's going to be a while."

Tess takes the beer from Courtney and sets it on the counter. "Yeah, I got this bag on sale, of course, and I thought it was really nice. But my things keep falling out of it, unless I zip it up all the way. Fortunately, it has only spilled at home, mostly. But there's something I really want to talk to you about, and since Brad's outside, now is my chance."

Courtney leans on the counter opposite Tess, props her head up in her hands, and smiles. "I'm all ears. What's up?"

Tess takes a sip of beer and sets it back down. "Well, I have decided to try and do something with photography. I have been doing some thinking about what makes me happy. So I took my camera on a couple of drives that Bear and I did, and I really liked it. Once, I took pictures for fun, and when I got some good responses to my prints and wanted to continue but I got distracted. I really enjoy taking pictures of trees for example. And in getting back into this, little by little, I'm not feeling that heavy blanket of sorrow I was feeling as much. I think it's helping."

Courtney stands up straight and says, "I was hoping something was happening. It just takes time to adjust to all the changes. You were getting slammed by major changes every time you turned around. This is really good news. Why haven't you shown me any of the pictures yet?"

Tess sighs and says, "I wanted to, but I just wasn't ready to share them yet. But I will, very soon. I'm really finding that it makes me smile. It's been really good for me to be creative."

Courtney is fixing a salad for the meal and is in the process of chopping and slicing up veggies to go in it. She pauses a minute, looking at Tess, and smiles. "I can tell it's good for you because your face looks, I don't know—brighter? You don't look like you have so much weight on your shoulders, so that's a good thing."

Tess picks up a piece of carrot and takes a bite, "So when is your next event, Miss World-Class Bash-Thrower, you? Do you have something I can help with? I'm in need of the money for more photo paper for my printer!"

"Oh, we don't have anything happening until Thursday, so I have a couple of days to prep. The plans are all made, and I just need to check the venue. It's a very special birthday party at a mansion. I could use your on-site help on Thursday. Sound good? I'll have to look at my calendar in the office, but I think it starts at seven thirty. So we need to be there about four for set up."

"Sounds good to me. Since I have a few days off, I think I'll try and go to the beach and walk around Venice—and take some pictures."

Brad is talking as he walks through the door, saying good-bye, when he looks over at Tess. "Hey, Tess, how long have you been here?"

"I got here about fifteen minutes or so ago. Got the grill going?"

"Yes, ma'am. Court, is the stuff ready for the grill? I thought I would go ahead and start the grillin' if that sounds good to you."

"Brad, it's in the fridge, under the saran wrap. The other stuff is ready when you are. Do you want something else to drink?"

"Thanks, baby, but I'll get something in a minute. Tess, are you going to stay long enough to enjoy the fire in the fire pit tonight?"

"That would be great. I guess I could consider that an invitation. Thanks Brad. I appreciate it. Your fires are fun to watch. Do you have more of that Campfire Blue that makes the colors?"

Brad grabs the chicken and skewered veggies out of the fridge and answers. "Yeah, I think I have some left, and I think it would be a great idea for tonight. Glad you're staying."

Tess takes another sip of her beer and says, "Thanks Brad. Believe me, it's my pleasure." Tess turns to Courtney and says, "Did I tell you that I was talking to the Burbank Parks Department? They have a program called Art in Public Places. They are always looking for artists who want to display their work and get more visibility. And I have an appointment in a week to see them. If they want me to show my photos in their program, there are lots of city buildings and offices that do really creative things, like make cartoons."

"Wow!" says Courtney. "That sounds like a great opportunity. I'm so happy to hear about it."

Tess starts getting excited, "Yeah, I'm going to put together a portfolio with a sampling of what I have so far to see what they think. I've mostly been taking pictures of trees and weird buildings that have some character. You know, there are so many cool-looking buildings in Venice. You know that section that has all the art galleries, where they used to have the head shops in the seventies? They are all so old and have so much detail. They don't make them like that anymore.'

"Yeah, I know. There are some that are really beautiful." Courtney is still busying herself in the kitchen while she listens to Tess. She's smiling broadly. "You know, for the first time in a long while you're getting back to being the Tess that I know and love. You show a passion when you talk about photography, and it's great to see again. You've gone through a lot, and it's hard to keep your balance."

"Thanks. I hadn't really thought about it. It just seems to be happening. For a while, it seemed like a whirlwind was all around me, and I was standing in the center, not feeling any breeze. I was just watching everything swirl around me. But now I'm feeling better every day, so that really helps."

They both get a little quiet just listening to the music in the background and hanging out. Then, abruptly, Natalie comes bounding in with a neighbor friend about the same age. "Mom! Hey, Mom. Cynthia wants to know if I can go swimming at her house. Can I? Can I?"

"Natalie, go ask Brad when lunch will be ready. If you can be back when the food is ready, I think it will be OK."

"OK. Thanks, Mom!"

And then Natalie and her friend run outside to Brad who's at the grill, and you can see them in animated conversation. Then Natalie turns to walk quickly back in the house grinning. "Mom, Brad said that we are going to eat in about thirty minutes and that I should go after lunch. So is that OK with you?"

"Yes, that's fine. Does Abby want to stay for lunch with us?"

"No, she said she wants to go home and go swimming. But I'm so hungry and can hardly wait!"

Tess and Courtney start laughing at the exuberance of Natalie talking about food.

Before long, they're all sitting in the shade, around the table outside, passing around plates and bowls of great food. When the meal is over, it's only a little after four. Natalie leaves as soon as she's finished, while Tess, Courtney, and Brad linger at the table. The afternoon is really warm, and with the wonderful breeze, Brad decides it's a great time to take a nap in their hammock.

Tess and Courtney sit at the table for a little while longer, before getting up and taking all the leftover food back to the kitchen. Once the kitchen is squared away, they go back outside and sit down at the table.

They watch the dogs play together and run in and out of the flower beds. Tess tries to keep Bear out of the beds, but he's just following Maya, and Maya's favorite thing is to run through the flowers. So they give up, after chasing them around the yard for a while, and just watch them and laugh.

Courtney says, "Those flower beds needed to be redone anyway. I think the flowers must be soft, because sometimes I find Pumpkin our cat lying on the flowers too. That is, until she sees Maya running towards her. They served their purpose in the spring with the bluebonnets, and they'll come up again next spring if we get enough rain."

Sitting back at the table, they just quietly enjoy the late afternoon breeze. Picking up her phone to check the time, Tess sighs a little. "Wow, I didn't know it was that late," she says to Courtney.

"Hey look, Brad is awake. I guess that means he'll start getting the fire pit ready for tonight. That also means we need to do poop patrol—to get any land mines before it gets dark. I just hate it when we wind up bringing poop in the house on the bottom of our shoes!"

"No problem. I'm used to doing that with Bear. One time, I waited about three weeks before cleaning it up, and it seemed to take forever. I agree; doing it every day is so much easier." They both get up and start surveying the yard for dog poop to throw away.

Once they give the yard the once-over, they sit back down with fresh drinks and start watching the sun set. Brad has cleaned all the old ashes out of the pit and is now putting fresh wood in and making a short stack by a nearby tree.

It's starting to get cooler, so Tess goes inside and grabs her sweatshirt. Then she goes out to meet everyone by the pit. It's starting to get dark, and Brad has started the fire. He uses a long carved walking stick that Courtney gave him as a poker, and it's a good thing the stick is five feet long, because the fire pit is pretty big.

He gets the fire going well, and everyone settles in a chair placed around it. The wood is crackling and everyone is smiling. It has been a great day. Brad throws some of the blue powder on the fire, and it turns colors. He says, "Tess, I heard you telling Courtney that you're going to try and do something with photography. I think that's great. If you get where you want to design a website to sell it, I know someone who is starting a new company and needs clients. He could probably set you up for a good price, because he would want to show yours as an example of what he can do."

"That's a great idea, Brad. Thanks so much for the offer. I may have to take you up on that one. It's funny that since I started playing with my camera again, I've felt more centered. Guess there is a lot to be said for being creative. It sure has helped me." Tess takes another sip of her beer and turns to Courtney. "Did I tell you a couple of small cafés on the coast might want to put a couple of framed pictures up for sale?"

Courtney nods her head, "Yeah, and I think a couple of the stagers that my real estate agents use might want to get a couple of them. That could be good visibility too. I'm sure there are quite a few ways that we can get your work visible. And I'm glad you have found this outlet. I just have one question though, are you still going to work for me when I need you?"

Tess laughs, "Of course I'll work for you...whenever you need me to." After that, they're quiet again, except for the crackling of the fire now roaring in front of them"

After a couple hours of relaxing and watching the flames dance around, Tess glances at her phone for the time. "Wow, I can't believe it's almost ten. I better get Bear and head home. Sorry, the time got away from me."

Courtney stands up. "It got away from me too. We need to get Natalie in bed. After all it's a school night!"

Brad starts poking the fire to get it to die down and says goodnight to Tess. Tess goes over and rubs on Bear and says, "Come on, Big Guy, we need to go home." Bear slowly gets up and walks to the back door of the house. Tess is right behind him. Courtney and Natalie are already inside, and they say good night, and Tess walks to the front door.

"Why don't you call me when you get up, Tess? I'll be up early with Natalie, getting her off to school."

"Sounds like a plan. Sweet dreams, you guys."

Tess and Bear walk out to the Jeep and climb in. Tess starts driving home and turns on the radio. It's in the middle of a song called "Best Year," by Callaghan.

Tess is singing along. "This could be the best year of our lives, if we tear up the rule book and leave it all behind...and I feel good times comin' and I see a new sun risin'...this could be the best year of our lives."

And she's smiling all the way home.

"Hey Bear. I'm starting to believe it. Aren't you thinking that way too?" She looks over the seat to see Bear stretched out on the back seat fast asleep.

Chapter Ten

A couple of weeks have passed, and Tess has decided to just observe everything around her today and not take any pictures. She had the meeting with the Burbank Parks department, and that went really well. They are definitely interested, but they want to see a few more photos. She only had about twelve good shots to show them, and she thought she would have more. So today she's just going to take it all in, and see where the inspiration comes from.

They have already scheduled another meeting with her in two weeks to see if she has a larger portfolio by then. She's not feeling the pressure, yet, to build her collection rapidly without much thought behind it. So her plan is to observe and see where her observations take her. Another good thing is that she can spend the morning at the beach with Bear and read, all within the concept of observation.

It's another beautiful day at the beach, and Bear is lying in the shade of her beach chair and umbrella. He's already napping, and Tess has settled down and started reading her book. She has placed the umbrella so that it's mostly over Bear, and she's getting a little sun. But her hat blocks her face. After a while, the constant breeze from the ocean and the sound of the waves are making her sleepy, too. Before she realizes it, she wants to take a nap and just let everything go for a while.

She falls asleep with her book in her lap, and she dreams of being in her mom's kitchen. She can hear the birds in the backyard singing, and can almost smell the fresh coffee. It's early in the morning, and she's looking out the back door. She hears other people in the house and tries to turn around to see them—but wakes up. So startled by the visions and the feeling of being there, she pulls out a pen and a piece of paper and uses her book to write on top of. She puts down her feelings in another letter to her mom.

Dear Mom,

I guess when you're faced with life by yourself, with no one to answer to or to count on, you learn a few things. That would seem undeniable.

Things that are basic truths—like everyone wants to be "seen" and "heard" and accepted for who they are, without being molded or changed by anyone else, no matter their intentions. At times, it's an aching to be recognized as a good person or someone who did something special. But we don't always get that chance, and most of the time what we do goes unnoticed.

Losing you as the one anchor in my life—even though we didn't agree a lot—made me feel adrift for a while, until I started thinking that I need to sail this boat myself. I cannot rely on anyone but myself. And as alone as I feel at times, I know there are other people that feel that alone too. It's a very small consolation, I know. But it made me go to those places in my head that I have never wanted to go to much, so that I could see why I'm me, because of fear of what I might find. But it has turned out OK, and I know I'll be alright.

I know you're still with me in spirit, and when I talk to you I know you are listening.

But it's at the odd times—when I need your feedback or you telling me your straight-laced, small-town opinion, which I usually scoffed at, thinking it was too unenlightened—that I miss.

You're now the little angel on my shoulder that says, "If it doesn't seem right, then it isn't." In other words, I need to trust my gut instinct.

Well, my gut instinct is telling me to try living—completely and without boundaries or any preconceived notions—to be bold and put myself out there. And I'm scared, but I think you would be telling me to do it. I think that you would say, "Take a chance."

I know that you took a chance when you were a young woman. You didn't want to stay in that really small town where you grew up, in the house on the farm that had a no indoor plumbing.

You took a chance in moving to Chicago. And in your day, that was really bold. You moved by yourself, starting working, and lived boldly. So I thank you for your example, and I hope you will be cheering me on as I try this too. It's unfortunate that my greatest teachers won't be there to see what I accomplish, but I'm going to try my hardest.

I miss you so much, and wish, oh God, do I wish, I could just have one more conversation at your kitchen table over a cup of coffee. I love you mom. Wish me luck!

Me

Tears are falling down her cheeks, but she's not sad. It's a release, a letting go. She smiles and reaches over to stroke Bear a few times, folds up the letter, and puts it in the envelope with another letter she's already written and intended to mail later to her mom. She slides them in the front of the book she's been reading and puts them in her bag.

Bear is starting to get restless and is now sitting up. She glances at her phone for the time and realizes she's been at the beach far longer than she expected to be. As she gathers up her things, Bear is getting anxious to start moving around. Once everything is packed, she grabs it all, and Bear leads the way back to the Jeep.

On the way home, Tess calls her favorite veggie-Thai place with an order, so she can pick it up on the way home. She has no desire to cook now and is starting to get really hungry. So takeout is the way to go.

Once she gets home, Bear has to go on a walk before they even get upstairs. When he's content to go home, they head upstairs, and she feeds him and then warms her food. While it's in the microwave, she turns on the TV and checks to see what's on. There is really nothing she wants to watch, so she puts on music instead. "Bing!" Her dinner is ready, so she fixes her plate and takes it out on the small balcony. Bear follows, thinking there might be something for him on that plate, and leaves his half-full dish, hoping for a handout. She laughs at how obvious he is, and sits down in one of the two chairs that are there. The sun is already starting to wane, and traffic is starting to pick up on the streets below.

By the time Tess finishes her dinner, Bear is asleep at her feet and making jerking motions in dreamland. She watches him for a minute before she gets up, then winds up waking him when she stands. She takes her dish back to the kitchen and cleans up her mess. Bear follows her back to the couch, jumps up, and lies down beside her. She has one hand on Bear and the other one on the remote control. She finally finds something to watch and, within five minutes, is asleep on the couch.

The TV wakes her up with the news. She gets up, turns everything off, and stumbles into bed.

She sleeps in, a little, the next morning and is slow in getting Bear out for his morning walk. By the time they get outside, Bear is marking every bush and tree in sight. She's listening to her iPod and feels like she's just shuffling down the street. Her energy is lacking and she feels totally uninspired.

They make it around the neighborhood and back to the apartment. Tess did not start coffee before she walked Bear, so she's doing it now. She feels out-of-sync with her world today, and she can't quite put her finger on why. The apartment is quiet, no music, no TV. Bear lies down on his oversize pillow and drops his head down for his mid-morning nap. Tess wanders around the room, moving small objects on the entertainment unit, straightening magazines, and is just restless. The coffee buzzer goes off, so she walks back in the kitchen to get a cup. She stands in the kitchen, leaning against the cabinet, sipping a fresh cup of French roast coffee.

Standing there, her thoughts start rolling around, and she tries to pull together a plan of action for the day. The first thing is to call Courtney and find out what she has coming up—and see when that second show is for that painter. Then her thoughts skip to that show, all those paintings, all those images that made people not want to look away, and the connection she felt with some of them.

That was really kinda weird. Was he that good as an artist? He certainly was interesting enough, but then it was probably the day or her mood or something that made her too sensitive that day…must have been something.

She takes another sip and calls Courtney. "Good morning, my friend," Courtney says. "What's going on in your world?"

"Well, Bear and I just got back from our morning walk, and I just made some coffee. What are you doing? Do you have any work coming up for me?"

"I'm on my second cup of coffee and have been on the phone since early this morning. Yes, I do have some work coming up for you. Things are really good, but you don't sound quite like your yourself today. Anything you want to talk about?" says Courtney.

"You know, I'm a little off, but I can't quite put my finger on why. Maybe by my second cup, I'll be as bright as you seem to be today. What have you got?"

"Well, Tess, I have at least three jobs I would love your help with, and one of them is the second party for that artist at the Basil Grey Gallery. And that one I'm told is bringing the m-o-n-e-y. Since the showing at the museum, the talk in the art world is that this collection is not going to last long, because they will probably sell quickly for him. It's kind of exciting when I talk to Audrey. She's so full of information about this gallery exhibit and how it was a very well received collection at the museum. According to her, the museum event was *the* event. So thanks again."

"That's great. I'm really happy for you." Tess's voice trails off because she's distracted by people making noise in the street below her apartment.

"Tess? Are you listening?" Courtney speaks a little bit louder.

"What? Yeah, I'm sorry. I was distracted by some shouting on the street. What were you saying?"

"I thought I lost you there. Anyway, we have a banquet on Thursday, a fancy birthday party on Saturday night, and then, next Saturday is the second party for that artist. So I'll definitely need you for these three if that's good with you, Tess?"

"Thanks so much. Yes I need the work. Still nothing on the full-time job front, so I guess what I might do is try and get another part-time job, and things might work out fine. So this Thursday, Saturday, and next Saturday…Do you need me for any pre-event planning, or do you have that all under control?"

"Well, the banquet is pretty straightforward, so I'll need you to help me on the evening of the event. The fancy birthday party, I'll need you to go with me Friday to do a little early set up, and then for the gallery party, I hope you'll go with me on that Friday to finalize the arrangements for Saturday."

"No problem, Court. Just tell me what time, and I'll be wherever you need me."

They chat for a while longer, and Courtney tells her to put some up music on when they hang up, and she'll feel better. Tess promises that she will, and they talk about their dogs, Natalie, and Brad. They decide to go to lunch the next day, so they can go shopping for some things for the banquet.

After they hang up, Tess puts some music on and starts singing along with the song—and dances a little in her living room. She's never been the most graceful person, but with no one looking, she feels like she can dance. When the song is over, she gets another cup of coffee and sits down with her laptop and tries finding a part-time job. Maybe she will have better luck with part-time, since she can't seem to find a full-time job.

When the searches she usually uses are done, she takes a shower and decides to take Bear to the park and read a book she got about Beach Town Architecture. She'd thought the book might give her some inspiration for photos.

She gets to the dog park, and there are all kinds of dogs and owners hanging out. She finds a shady place with a chair and sits down and watches Bear make new friends for a while. Remembering the book she brought along, she starts looking through it.

The smaller coastal towns in southern California all have a history, and some of it's really entertaining. Not to mention some of the older buildings and landscape. She thinks that's where she needs to go—Venice and Manhattan Beach. Now she's getting re-energized, because she has a purpose, a direction to take.

The next day she's up as soon as it's getting light, even before Bear comes over to wake her up. She wants to take Bear and go to Venice and maybe Manhattan Beach. She's planning on walking around to get some new shots to add to her small portfolio. Hopefully, she will be lucky today.

She drives around the area to check out some of the older buildings and finds one street that has some small businesses. She parks the jeep and gets everything she needs—her bag, camera, Bear, and her water bottle. When she throws her bag over her shoulder, she tries to jam her water bottle in too, but the bag is overflowing, almost spilling everything out.

"Why do I like this bag? Arrgh!" She's a little frustrated. Though she means to, she keeps forgetting to take things out of the increasingly heavy bag. After reshuffling everything, she finally gets her water bottle in. Bear is sitting on the sidewalk right next to the jeep, waiting for Tess to pick up the leash so they can go. She finally gets everything squared away, and they start walking down the street. She has her camera out and is taking pictures of some of the old storefronts, not really noticing what businesses they are. She's really having fun, and Bear is not pulling on her.

She walks further down the street and can't help but notice the name of one business, Basil Grey. She tries to remember why that sounds familiar while still taking pictures. She's so lost in thought, and in looking through her camera, that she spins around and abruptly bumps into someone—hard.

"I'm so sorry!" she says, as her purse falls off her shoulder and spills everything out on the sidewalk. Her water bottle is rolling down the sidewalk. Her wallet and her book fall out loosely. The letter to her mom even falls out of the book. She looks at it all, "What a complete mess! I'm so sorry!"

"No, I'm to blame," the guy says. "I should have been looking. Let me help you pick this up."

He squats down and picks up the book and then the letter, and he reads "Mom in Heaven" on the front of the envelope. He stops dead in his tracks. Everything suddenly stops, and the world is turning backwards. The air is suddenly sucked out of the universe. "Oh, my God," he thinks, "This is her! What do I do?"

He hands the book back to Tess and hangs on to the letter a couple of moments longer than he realizes knowing he has to say something, anything. He doesn't want to let go until he tries to talk to her.

"Are you getting some good shots?" he asks.

"I hope so. I need some more good ones. You look familiar to me, and that's not a line. Have I met you before?" Tess asks.

"I remember meeting you at the Santa Monica Museum. What was your name again? Mine is Nico."

"Yeah, I remember now. Hi Nico, my name is Tess."

Nico is struggling to find some way to hang on to the moment. This is her! This is the woman he has been trying to find! He has to do something. What does he do? What does he do? Think!

"Well, ah...are you busy? Do you want to get a cup of coffee? I'd like to hear more about your photos." Nico finally gets the words out and hopes she will just say yes.

"Nico, I would like to, but aren't you married?" Tess asks.

"No, I'm not married, and I'm not seeing anyone either. Why do you ask?"

"That very pregnant lady that was with you at the museum, wasn't she with you—I mean married to you or something?" said Tess.

Nico laughs. "That's my sister, and we are close but not like that."

Tess smiles broadly and says, "Well then, yes, I think I would like to get a cup of coffee with you."

Nico helps her gather up the rest of the items spilled from her bag, and they head down the street toward a coffee shop. He takes Bear's leash from her hands, so she can square everything away while they walk together down the block.

His mind is racing, and he's grinning from ear to ear. He found her!

Tess is amazed that he doesn't look like the same guy who was at the museum. But he's smiling at her in such a way that she wants to find out who this guy really is—because her first impression was not at all what she thinks now.

They sit outside so that Bear can be with them, and she is curious about this guy.

Made in the USA
Charleston, SC
02 June 2015